A Chrysalis Withou[t]

Copyright © Jeffrey Brett 2020

The right of Jeffrey Brett to be identified as the author of this work has been asserted by him in accordance with the Copyright, Designs and Patents Act 1988.

All rights reserved. No part of this publication may be reproduced, stored in a data base or introduced into a retrieval system, or transmitted, in any form, or by any means (electronic, mechanical, photocopying, recording or otherwise) without the prior written permission of the author. Any person who commits any breach of these rights in relation to this publication may be liable to criminal prosecution and civil claims for damages.

This book is a work of fiction, references to names and characters, places and incidents are products of the author's imagination. Any resemblance to actual events, places or persons, living or dead is purely coincidental.

For more information, please contact: **magic79.jb@outlook.com**

Cover design by Kathleen Harryman

First published 2020

A Chrysalis without Wings

Introduction

Without warning a falling kernel nut hit the ground hard landing with a thud from the tall branches overhead, rolling through the autumn leaves before coming to a halt. Jakub Hesseltolph stopped walking to listen, crouching low his eyes scanned behind, left and right, but the only movement came from a grey squirrel high up amongst the branches, its body held spellbound by the presence of the man below. Ordinarily the squirrel had the wood all to itself and residents from the village never ventured this far out between the trees.

A moment later another squirrel appeared, a rival grey and instantly a frantic chase ensued their tiny bodies twisting, running and leaping between branches with the agility of an acrobat in flight. Jakub watched, in a way he was just like the tree rats and he liked their solitary existence, attacking anybody who would dare to invade his private space. Kill them if necessary, yes definitely he would do that, protecting at all costs what belonged to him and not others.

His thoughts had him think about his sister Julianna, only it had been some time since he'd had any word from her. Observing the two squirrels squabbling he wondered if anybody had found the body of the dead psychiatrist.

When the squirrels suddenly disappeared from sight Jakub resumed walking happy to have the sunshine bathe his face in warmth and light. It had been a long time, indeed a considerably long time since he had been able to walk alone in the sunshine unaccompanied and everywhere up in the trees the birds were singing, chirping to one another. It felt good to be out. Free to do whatever he liked, free to have his thoughts to himself and not explain them to others, doctors mainly. For some time now he had been making plans.

Stepping beyond the fringe of the trees he noticed a solitary farmer ploughing the field from the cab of his tractor, but the man was too far away on the other side of the field to pay Jakub any real interest. If he had, he would most probably assume that the stranger emerging from the wood was just a local taking morning exercise with his dog.

Selecting even ground he upped the pace resisting the urge to run, giving the impression that everything was normal even picking up and broken branch and moving it to one side, anything to show that he had no concerns. But Jakub was no fool, keeping the trees close by he was forever alert, his ears listening intently for an unfamiliar noise, the sound of an approaching vehicle or voices. Constantly watching he breathed in the air, it was fresh at last and plentiful.

Heading for Kurlor he felt no remorse for the death of Alexander Koskovsky. For too long the psychiatrist had been allowed to do exactly what he liked with the lives of the inmates, controlling their routines, their daily exercise, meal times, but more importantly their minds, delving into their thoughts, using his drugs programme to help. Forceful and domineering he constantly over-ruled the opinions of junior medical staff, doctors and nurses alike. Koskovsky's death had been long overdue and it had surprised Jakub that other inmates had not tried to kill the doctor before he did.

Smiling to himself he knew that the psychiatrist's absence would spark a flurry of panic throughout and a frantic headcount would show that Jakub was missing as well. It had been part of the plan to take Koskovsky deep into the wood, to torture and leave him dying, but once found the hunt for his executioner would mean Jakub having to work fast if he was to succeed. Time was never a luxury that was on his side.

And whoever found Koskovsky would themselves need help, witness to the horrific manner in which the egotistical eccentric psychiatrist had been left dying, they would have seen the many injuries inflicted upon his body, stretched between the trees, the deep lacerations and cavities having invited a variety of woodland insects to the dying body. Unable to resist the temptation they would crawl inside and begin gnawing through soft tissue, anxiously searching and stuffing themselves greedily as they marched on before making their way up to the brain where the good stuff was. Walking away without looking back Jakub had fisted triumphantly his escape wondering what thoughts had gone through the doctor's mind as the army of centipedes, spiders and black shelled beetles had consumed his grey matter.

And it was unimportant that forensic examiners would prove that they were his fingerprints found on the murder weapon which killed the doctor and that later when interviewed the medical staff would tell the police, maybe exaggerate perhaps about Jakub's psychotic, delusional tendencies. Anything that would detract from the truth that lie hidden behind the walls of the sanatorium at Ebenstatt, saving both their reputations and jobs.

Detectives would spend hours reading though Jakub's medical file and the notes made by Koskovsky, separating then piecing them together again, but eventually they would call upon the help of a criminal expert, a psychological profiler who would build a bigger picture of the missing murderer. And soon after a detailed analysis would foretell how he worked, how he planned, how he sought out his victims, everything down to the enth detail that would assist the investigation. Catching Jakub Hesseltolph however would be the most difficult task.

An hour maybe more had passed since he had left the woods and soon the trail would already be going cold. Overnight it had rained hard making the ground wet the fallen leaves oily, making it difficult for the tracker dogs to pick up a decent scent. The police searching would have four choices in which to take, although north meant backtracking through the grounds of the sanatorium which was highly unlikely, leaving the mountains to the east, open farmland to the west and to the south Kurlor. Victor Boucher, second most senior of the medical staff believed that even Jakub wasn't that mad that he would return to his home village.

The official line released publically later that day would state that the doctor had died from natural causes, having suffered a sudden unexpected heartache whilst out walking alone in the woods taking the opportunity to gather his thoughts for the day ahead. And other eminent medical professionals who knew him, some friends would extoll praise on their friend and colleague, detailing to the media his medical achievements, praising his unwavering dedication to his life's work in an effort to help the less unfortunate whose terrors had plagued and tortured their souls for so many years. None would ever know the real truth. Buried in the grounds of Ebenstatt along with the graves of dead inmates Alexander Koskovsky would be deemed forever a medical visionary.

The lasting image however that Jakub saw was the lifeless body of the psychiatrist, his arms splayed supporting his naked body stretched tight between the trunks of two tall trees where he was unable to resist.

Detectives and forensic examiners would conclude that the doctor had been horrifically tortured before relenting and that when the end had come, it would have been a happy release, his death having been slow and terrifying. Jakub had wanted it that way, so that Koskovsky finally acknowledged and understood exactly how fragile the mind could be under such extreme conditions and pain.

Missing also were the doctor's clothes. Similar in height and build they were a good fit and it had been a long time since Jakub had worn a decent suit, clean shirt only he left behind the patterned bow tie.

It was much later that day that Trevor Baines received the call from Detective Anders Wilmer in Austria to inform the English investigator of Jakub Hesseltolph's escape and Alexander Koskovsky's gruesome death. The news neither surprised nor shocked Baines. Having spent time interviewing Jakub, Trevor Baines had seen the look in the killers eyes, a look that he had seen before in madmen, a look that said it wasn't over yet. Neither did it surprise him that Koskovsky was dead.

He went to his study and checked the lunar cycles on a trusted astrological website. Beginning Sunday night it had been a full moon. Picking up his cell phone he called Ashworth High Security Hospital to check that they still had Julianna Hesseltolph in their possession.

The charge nurse who took the call informed Baines that Jakub's sister was still with them although she had been unusually agitated during the past few days and that medical staff on the wing had noticed a peculiar change in Julianna's mood.

Keeping herself to herself she had refused to talk to anybody, taking instead to pacing the floor as though expecting something to happen and at night she would keep the other inmates awake making the sound of a wolf howling, like that of an alpha female pining for the soul of a lost cub.

Arriving at the fenced edge of the village Jakub crouched low using bushes for cover as his eyes keenly scoured the main street up and down, looking and listening, but everywhere was quiet and deserted.

The walk from Ebenstatt had been long and uneventful and he had stopped only once to feed on berries and mushrooms, drinking the cool water from the mountain stream. In the half-light the darkness would arrive soon.

Just over three years previously another inmate had escaped the grip of Ebenstatt, a woman, but it was a further six weeks later that they had found her half eaten body.

Wild speculation and rumours had quickly circulated throughout the sanatorium suggesting a black bear had been responsible for the attack and killing the escapee, although many were of the opinion that it had been the grey timber wolves who had attacked the poor woman because of the manner in which she had been found. Nobody could really be that certain as her decaying remains had been cruelly weathered beyond recognition.

Jakub watched the interior lights go on and off in the houses in the street wondering if they were still occupied by the same people, neighbours that he had once known.

He was still looking when something behind him the undergrowth suddenly moved. He turned sharply to investigate, finding a large stone he threw it at where he thought the rustling had originated. Whatever the creature it was small, a hedgehog perhaps or domestic cat, but the animal scurried away without retaliating. Man or beast nothing, would prevent him in his quest.

Under the light of the nearest street lamp he emptied the contents of the doctor's wallet, throwing aside anything that was of no use, but which the middle-aged couple who occupied the house would find come the next day.

They would of course inform the police who would know in which direction Jakub had left the sanatorium, although piecing together his time spent in the village he would be long gone that same night.

Jakub kept the cash and several credit cards. He found a creased photograph of the psychiatrist's wife and son which he held up to the light to study their faces. The wife was pretty, much younger than Koskovsky. He replaced the photograph, keeping it in case it would prove handy for a later time.

Breathing in deep he filled his lungs with the scents of the evening air, picking up aromas of nearby flowers as their petals closed in readiness of the coming night, his senses also detecting the odd whiff of burnt ash emanating from the chimney tops. Everything was exactly as he remembered before being taken away and imprisoned in Ebenstatt.

Soon, very soon, the initial stages of his plan would become a reality. Part one had already been accomplished, leaving Alexander Koskovsky dead and escaping the sanatorium.

Moving away from the security of the bushes it was time to go to work.

Chapter One

Looking at the reflection in the window which stared back at him Jakub was not overly surprised to see how Ebenstatt and Koskovsky's cocktail of drugs had taken their toll on his appearance. Running his fingers through his hair it wasn't as thick as it used to be when he was younger, gone were the shoulder length locks of dark strong brown hair, replaced by wispy strands of luck-lustre grey. He stood back where in the half-light he looked like a timber wolf.

His eyes were dark had always been dark, a feature that Jakub particularly liked. Just staring could make others wary, perhaps uneasy and almost certainly indecisive not knowing if he was friend or a foe.

Scratching his chin he was also overdue a shave plus a haircut, but both would have to wait as other pressing intentions needed to be dealt with in addition to taking back some of the time that had been stolen from him, years of his youth and his early twenties, years of resentment.

Running along the backs of the houses he heard the nearby water lapping against the grass banks where the source had originated high in the snow-topped mountain.

He remembered the evening when he and Julianna had stripped naked, jumped in the stream where they had kissed, touched and made discoveries about one another in the cool running water and evening breeze. Special moments that he had entrusted to Trevor Baines, the

English detective, trusting the policeman to be true to his word and make sure that his sister was well cared for at the hospital, giving her the protection that he said she deserved.

Trudging through the long grass that separated the bank and the rear gardens he made his way stealthily towards the house, a place that he had waited so long to visit. His approach swift and unseen meant keeping to the shadows, movements that he practiced as a young boy tracking his sister when they had played in the woods. Like a lone wolf his feet padded silently across the stone patio and the closer that he got to the house the more intense the feeling in his gut knotted like hands around his throat. He swallowed, the years of hate quickening the pace of his heart, he was so close that he only had to reach out and touch the man walking towards him in his mind

'Do it,' urged the insistent voices,' *do it now...!'* they demanded.

Way up in the mountain the howl of a lone wolf cut abruptly through the evening calm where rising above the peaks was the moon, a white ball tinged with a lunar blue halo. Not the halo of an ethereal being, but the blue ring of surprise and Halloween wasn't that far away. He stood still and raised his arms high, absorbing the lunar power that streaked to earth unseen except in the pull of the tides. It felt good, he felt good. Jakub had always liked the moon. Magically captivating things happened when the moon was full.

With the moon covering the mountain in a blanket of white light the wolf ceased it's baying, a sure sign that it had started to hunt for its prey. Jakub smiled liking the silence, it was time that he joined the wolf in the hunt.

He was about to move forward again when the voices inside is head started talking all at once and he had to tell them to stop. If they wanted to argue amongst themselves then they should do so on their time and not his, only right now he was busy. Reluctantly they heard him and ceased. He thanked them knowing that there were times when he had needed them as much as they had needed him, but now that he was free, it was time to show them all how right he had been to kill Koskovsky and go on the run.

A year ago Alexander Koskovsky had surprised Jakub during a one on one session in admitting that there was actually very little difference between the world of make believe and that of reality. *'One journey,'* he had said, *'ended as another adventure begun, the time in between was generally unimportant.'* Jakub wondered if the good doctor had considered the bit in between as insignificant as when they had walked together in the woods, or had it simply been a bad dream.

Rather irritatingly, frustratingly he could not recall much of the discussion with Koskovsky because the voices in his head had been insistent upon asking so many questions wanting answers, answers that Jakub needed to know not them, but it had been Jakub who had run the edge of the knife across the doctor's throat leaving him to the mercy of the woodland insects and creatures. Had he killed the doctor later at night instead of mid-morning, maybe the wolf wouldn't have had to hunt so far up the mountain.

Looking up at the first floor bedroom at the back of the house he saw a teenage girl pass across the open window, the fleeting vision reminding him of Julianna, when she had been that age. The policeman's house had not changed much since he had seen it last. It was still badly in need of maintenance and was now showing signs of being weather beaten too, why even the brick chimney appeared to be leaning to one side having been constantly battered by the wind blowing down from the mountain.

Sinking deeper into the recess where the shadow was darkest he watched the girl move about the bedroom as he flexed the muscles in his arms and fingers. She was young, very pretty and it was obvious that she was unaware of his presence as she paraded back and forth.

Standing there watching Jakub remembered the night that the constable had come to his house to investigate the torture that he had inflicted upon his classmates. Unable to comprehend why the boys had been punished so horribly even his parents had found it unacceptable, siding with the constable and then later the magistrate. Julianna was Jakub's love, his sister and his responsibility, and there was no way that he was going to standby and have her defiled by such trash.

He sensed the anger in their voices returning arguing amongst themselves once again, some saying that Thomas and Gabriele Hesseltolph had a duty to their son, that they were his parents and they should have protected him, whereas others were insistent and like the constable they said punishment was justified. The day, that night had changed everything and he could accept any punishment, but what had sent him over the edge was when his mother and father had threatened to send Julianna away, somewhere where he would never see her again. That is what had sealed their fate.

He remembered Albrecht Hartmann standing in front of the fire grinning as his parents argued knowing that he had them both right where he wanted them. Whoever was right or wrong, Jakub blamed all three for what happened later that night. The memory haunted him, made the bile rise in his throat, he didn't hate his parents, but he did Albrecht Hartmann, equalled only by that of the magistrate. Coming to the police station Matthias Baumgartner had used his public position and influence to twist the interview.

Mentally abused by so many questions the voices had shut down and hidden themselves away where they could not be found. Physically abused, coerced into accepting that he was wrong Jakub didn't know which way to turn for help. Shouted at, threatened and slapped hard several times by Baumgartner, he had refused to cry or be intimidated by the two men in the room. Instead he had glared at them and promised that one day he would find them.

Baumgartner, who proclaimed to be a Baron and considered himself unanswerable to anybody had gladly signed the order and had Jakub committed to Ebenstatt without a proper trial. Together the constable and the magistrate had conspired to destroy the life of a young boy, Jakub's life. He swallowed again the hatred burning deep inside.

In the bedroom the young girl had started to undress and in the background her music was heavy with too much bass and the man singing sounded drunk. When the dark clouds moved across the moon Jakub stepped out from the shadows where he could follow the girl around the room. In just her underwear she danced to the music, her hips and arms moving to the beat. Jakub watched until the music died and the room was plunged into darkness.

Passing across the night sky the moon cast down a luminous beam of earthshine over the village. Standing at the bedroom window the girl who was now naked, caressed herself dreamily looking up at the stars. She was still a young teenage girl, but soon she would develop into a woman. Julianna had been like the girl the last time Jakub had seen her.

When she moved away and back into the darkness again Jakub moved from under the shadow of the apple tree making his way around to the front of the house where the constable had his office and one cell to the side which was only ever occupied by the odd drunk on a Saturday night. At the far end of the village a church bell chimed, Jakub counted nine chimes. Several moments later Albrecht Hartmann opened the door of his station office. The policeman had put on a little weight since Jakub had seen him last.

Patting his stout chest approvingly he pulled up the breeches of his trousers adding the cap to his head. With one last look back inside Albrecht considered going back in and upstairs to apologise to his eldest daughter for arguing with her earlier, but the night was young and it was likely that she would still be awake when he returned after his rounds.

Grinning, he shook his head. Once again it had been a trivial argument and didn't all daughters argue with their fathers from time to time. Pulling the door shut he would kiss her goodnight later with a promise to make it up to her the following day.

He tested the beam of his torch illuminating the gate, happy that the recharged batteries would last until he at least finished his rounds. Albrecht was about to step down from the covered porch when he was consciously aware of a movement in the garden, something or somebody was watching him maybe a cat, a dog or fox, at worst a wolf. He flashed the torch back and forth, but he saw nothing despite narrowly missing Jakub standing under the apple tree. Had the beam landed on the missing inmate, Jakub would have acted on instinct killing Hartmann there and then, but he had no intention of involving the constable's family. A sudden attack would almost certainly have the constable challenge him or call out. Inside his head the voices agreed telling him that the family were innocent like Julianna and that he should follow the policeman instead. Taking one last look up at the bedroom window where the room was still and dark Jakub moved away from the tree.

Pulling the gate shut Albrecht Hartmann breathed in deep striding confidently towards the other houses and properties at the far end of the street. Jakub waited a good minute before he followed.

Between the houses the air was moderately warm, despite the month and had not been affected by the cool current coming down from the mountain. The moon was bright, lighting the front gardens and shop fronts so Albrecht kept the torch switched off instead of wasting power as he continued on his patrol and there was also the street lights to help adding an amber glow.

He checked the door handles of the butchers, bakery and grocers store satisfied that all was quiet and as it should be. And furthest along the long narrow high street was the old coach inn which was unusually quiet. Albrecht licked his lips, he would pop in before going home to say hello, talk with a few of the regulars and sample a pint of the landlord's finest lager.

Walking down the high street he had heard the baying of the lone wolf high up in the mountain which was not out of place, not in Kurlor. But all that he had to defend himself was the torch. It was not unusual for the wolves to walk the village late at night looking for food and he had already had an encounter a month back with a stand-off in the middle of the high street when everybody else was asleep. It was an encounter that he didn't want to repeat using the torch and a dustbin lid that night to frighten away the beast.

Having had the silly argument with his daughter earlier the only other significant call that afternoon had been from the deputy medical officer at Ebenstatt to inform him that the boy, Jakub Hesseltolph had escaped from the sanatorium. Told also of the gruesome demise of Alexander Koskovsky, Albrecht had felt it necessary to check his ammunition drawer where he kept his gun and bullets. Replacing the receiver of the phone down confidentially on the cradle he had dealt with Hesseltolph once before and he could do the same again. Checking the handle of another door Albrecht sucked in air through his teeth, thinking that the boy would now be a man.

The policeman was still walking his beat, taking the same route that he did every evening peering in occasionally through a darkened window when a marked police unit came around the bend in the high street. Jakub ducked himself away in a service alleyway hiding between the shops, where he was out of sight, but within range to hear what they were saying.

'Any sightings yet Albrecht?' asked the passenger.

'Huh, he would be foolish to come back to Kurlor.' Hartmann scoffed. 'Hesseltolph knows that I would check all his old haunts first and then the house where he had once lived with his parents and sister. It's not been touched. Pretty soon the old place will fall down.' He sounded happy that it would.

'I'm surprised it's still unoccupied?' remarked the driver leaning towards the open window.

'Would you want to live in the house after what took place there, I certainly wouldn't.' The village constable scoffed loudly. 'Rumour has it amongst the children in the village that the place is haunted. No, I tell you Jakub Hesseltolph will be long gone by now and probably heading for the other side of the mountain. That would be my guess.' Albrecht puffed up his chest. 'Besides which he'd be a bloody fool to contemplate coming back here.'

The passenger and driver nodded at the village policeman hoping that he was right.

'Did you hear what he did to Alexander Koskovsky, the principal psychiatrist at the sanatorium?'

Albrecht coughed and cleared his throat.

'Yes, I heard. That was similarly what he had done to the boys in the woods. His actions that day had him committed to Ebenstatt. In my opinion he should rot in hell. Jakub Hesseltolph was never right in the head.' The policeman tapped his finger to his left temple, indicating the madness. 'Did you know that he raped and cut his sister that night as well.'

Standing in the alleyway where he heard them talking Jakub angrily clenched his fists tight. The constable would pay dearly for bringing his sister into the conversation and for making such wild unsubstantiated accusations. What he and Julianna had done together was between them and made them happy. It was also private and certainly not to bandied about with strangers like an unsavoury bad joke.

The driver leaned back, righted himself in the seat before switching on the ignition.

'Well whatever you think Albrecht, you would do well to be on your guard this night only I certainly wouldn't want to cross swords with Jakub Hesseltolph.'

Albrecht Hartmann stood up straight adjusting the thick leather belt slung around his waist. 'You need not worry about me Lukas Lorenz. If that crazy madman does show up here, he will still find me a force to be reckoned with and the pair of you can pick up whatever's left in the morning.' He laughed, although neither occupant in the car joined in.

'Be careful Albrecht. What he did to the psychiatrist wasn't pretty. I've seen the photographs!'

Hartmann slapped the end of the torch into his open palm.

'Once a madman, always a madman. Maybe the wolf I heard earlier on the mountain side had himself an early meal, who knows. Much like he did to the last inmate that escaped Ebenstatt. It's my guess that either a shepherd or a walker will come across Hesseltolph's skeletal bones sometime in the future, it would be a fitting end for a monster to be killed and then devoured by wolves.'

The conversation ended there as the patrol car pulled away and passed the darkened alley heading towards the outlying woods. Jakub was left seething and for once all the voices were in agreement.

Albrecht continued rattling doors for a good five minutes longer before turning down a grassy cut between the houses where the dirt track served as the entrance to a solitary farm around back of the residential properties. The farm house together with several other outbuildings lay back from the road by a good quarter of a mile.

Traipsing up to the farm was in Albrecht's opinion totally unnecessary and keeping him from enjoying a refreshing drink at the coach inn, but if he didn't check the farm he would find himself in hot water with the senior officers at division. The farm belonged to an old school friend Fredric Leeson. Walking dead centre of the track Albrecht was unaware of the shadow following behind.

Keeping to the shadows Jakub's plan had suddenly gained an advantage as he knew the farm layout much better than Hartmann.

Most weekends, every summer evening and always in the school holidays he had helped out at the farm and had especially liked harvest time and the lambing season. Had Ebenstatt not featured so early in his teenage life becoming a farming assistant would have been his ideal choice of career, happy to be out in the fresh air every day and amongst the animals. Jakub liked the animals, the cows, pigs, horses and sheep, and they never talked back, never chided or made fun of his unusual habits. Occasionally he would have to exert his authority and slap a cow on the rump to make her move, but more often than not a gentle coaxing saw them move away of their own accord. Jakub didn't object to mucking out in the pig pen and would watch the pigs go about their business. Ferocious eaters, forever hungry their jaws were powerful enough to crush a man's leg. Different to that of a dog gnawing a bone, pig's incisors were razor sharp and strong.

Since his arrest and incarceration at Ebenstatt, Jakub had not seen Frederic or his wife. He had missed them both. They had always been so kind to him and he wondered if Anna was still alive as she had suffered from ulcerative colitis.

Pushing aside the gate leading down the dirt track to the nearest outbuilding Hartmann shone his torch about checking the machinery that lay idle and silent. A hundred metres away sat the farm house the kitchen illuminated by a single light. Albrecht knew that Frederic and Anna were early risers, no doubt they were enjoying a late supper before bed.

He had on several occasions approached Frederic about taking on his eldest daughter Liselle, encouraging her to work part-time on the farm during the school breaks, but she had emphatically refused stating that she wanted to be with her friends instead, boys being the main influence.

The subject of boys in the village had caused the argument between Albrecht and Liselle and fast approaching sixteen she was now sneaking off to meet a boy in the nearby woods or going to parties at the weekends without her father knowing. Father and daughter clashed frequently because like him she was headstrong and unwavering, where her younger sister was much like their mother calm and easy going. When eventually boys did land on the interest scale Erica would be more subtle and choosy.

Checking under a dirty tarpaulin he let it drop back down quickly the air trapped beneath overpoweringly pungent, it made him cough. Disinterested to know what was under the tarpaulin, he assumed that not even Jakub Hesseltolph could stomach hiding underneath. Albrecht continued searching heading past the chicken coup, the pig pen, hay barn and cow byre. Next to where Frederic was drying rolled grass for the sheep come the winter was the stable where the farmer kept his only two horses, pushing aside the huge wooden door Albrecht stepped inside.

At the far end there was a single bulb offering just enough illumination to keep the horses happy during the night. Muttering to himself he considered his time at the farm a complete waste, there was no way that Jakub Hesseltolph would come anywhere near Kurlor and his mouth was dry, he was badly in need of a lager. Oscillating the torch beam he went to calm the agitated horses, stroking their large heads. Wishing the horses a goodnight he pulled the stable door shut. When the metal shovel hit the back of Albrecht's cranium the light inside his head went immediately out.

He regained consciousness to find that he was naked and on his knees, and his hands were tied behind his back. Coarse metal strands bound his ankles together. Albrecht winced as the dull thudding pain inside his skull felt like he had run headlong into an express train. It took him several more seconds to clear his vision, but luckily the bulky pink creatures shuffling past were as yet not showing any interest in him.

'Daft bastards,' he mumbled, his eyelids fluttering until he was fully conscious. When he did look he recognised the figure standing beside the wall. Even with the moon overshadowed by a solitary cloud Albrecht could make out the familiar features, the dark eyes black like unburnt coal and anxiously penetrating. Standing before him was Jakub Hesseltolph. The only word that came forth from Albrecht Hartmann's lips was *'fuck.'*

Jakub stepped forward raising the spade head high once again.

'If you dare cry out or attract Frederic's attention I'll leave the spade embedded in your skull. Do you understand?'

Albrecht nodded. 'I thought you would be long gone, at least on the way to Stardrecht.' He said, his voice carrying a slight tremor.

Jakub came close, bending low over the prone man.

'You've always had this bad habit of jumping to the wrong conclusions. It's a mistake to also think of me as a fool Hartmann. Talking with your colleagues in the high street you referred to me as an imbecile without a brain. I could forgive you that, but you should not have insulted my sister. She is the angel that walks through my dreams every night.'

Jakub walked around the back of Albrecht checking the bonds.

'And what was that you said…' he gave the metal strands a twist cutting into the constable's flesh, 'about handing over what was left of me come the morning!'

Jakub kicked the policeman forcibly in the back making him fall forward hearing the cheek bone smack hard against the concrete, having the pigs nearest take interest, the sound of crunching bone getting their jaws rolling. Next Jakub pulled the pitch fork over from the other side of the wall, much to the horror in Albrecht's eyes as they opened wide.

'We can work this out Jakub, come to an amicable agreement you and I. There's no reason why you need go back to Ebenstatt, perhaps somewhere much nicer, less secure. There's an open unit at Walsdtrad where you can virtually come and go as you please. Where Julianna came come visit you. Surely you'd like that?' It would have sounded sincere had Albrecht's voice not trembled.

Jakub responded with a short chuckle. It fascinated him that his victims always went straight to the option that might save their life, offering an alternative. He knew that grinning was all the more menacing than giving a verbal response. Coming close again he let the fork prongs drag over the coarse concrete making the tips abrasive. He placed the prongs against Albrecht's omohyoid muscle denting the soft pliable skin of the neck. Adding the minimum of pressure it made the constable gulp.

'You should know from previous experience that I always make a point of catching up with old adversaries, friends. Ask my classmates. I would have come to Kurlor long before now, but certain forces, restrictive factors prevented that from happening.'

Jakub grinned.

'As for your interesting offer...' he stroked his fingers tantalisingly down the metal prongs of the fork stopping at the point where they were pressing against Hartmann's flesh, 'on this occasion I must however decline, only you see I've no intention of ever seeing Ebenstatt again. I have other plans after I deal with you. Alexander Koskovsky also begged, cried and pleaded for his life even when he knew it was futile. Tell me constable will you also beg or will you show your true mettle and be the man that you've always professed to be?'

Albrecht Hartmann looked at the sinewy muscles in Jakub's arms recognising that one swift jerk and the prongs would easily puncture his neck. He sensed it was better to remain silent and let his captor have his say.

'I will see Julianna, but I will go visit her rather than have her come back to Kurlor. Do you honestly believe that I would want my sister to come back here where there is nothing except bad memories?'

With his free hand Jakub rubbed the stubble thoughtfully on his chin.

'Of course telling you about my next destination doesn't bode well for your chances of survival.'

The constable who had been fighting hard to control his bladder, realised that his pleas had fallen on stony ground. He let the urine flow ignoring the puddle that he was creating.

'Please Jakub, I'm just a village policeman. It was my duty to investigate the incident in the woods. I had to arrest and interrogate you. It was not my decision to place you in Ebenstatt indefinitely. I beg you, I have a wife and two daughter's at home who need me!'

Jakub grinned, he'd hoped that Albrecht would oblige. The smell of fear was so strong, everywhere.

'I know. I watched your daughter undress and touch herself earlier before you commenced your patrol. She's maturing quite nicely. One day she'll make somebody a fine wife. It wouldn't surprise me if every young buck in the village isn't fighting for the privilege of deflowering her.

'You never did understand why I punished my classmates that day in the woods. Like the devil they wanted to do the same to Julianna, but she was faithful to only me. Maybe when we're done here Albrecht, I'll pay your wife and daughters a visit. If you recall, I have techniques that can save them from sin.'

Albrecht Hartmann eyes bulged with a mix of fear and hopelessness. He wanted more than anything to retaliate and tell Jakub Hesseltolph that he was insane, a deranged psychopath, that he would spend the rest of his days in Ebenstatt so heavily drugged that his only cognitive thoughts would help him lift the cup rim to his lips or feed himself with a soft plastic spoon. He would have, but the fork prongs, damaged and torn at the edges were like barbs of wire snagging at his skin. The thought of the madman abusing his family brought stinging tears to his eyes.

'Please, let me live and I'll help you escape Jakub, it'll be as though you were never here, a ghost!'

Jakub laughed. 'You have a selective memory constable that suit your needs. The description of me to the magistrate was as I recall, *'a twisted, evil, perverted beast that had no place in a decent society.'* Your words hurt Albrecht, they were without compassion. See now how you grovel for your life and that of your family.'

He paused momentarily.

'I've been a long time at Ebenstatt in isolation. The women at the sanatorium were undesirable, walking skeletons, ghosts of their former shells, whereas your wife as I recall is pretty, attractive and your daughters as yet are unsullied. Together, I could change all their lives in just one night.'

Through his tears he looked into the eyes of the madman standing before him. The dark pupils were without light, harnessing only years of hatred. Albrecht wished that he had the courage to end it there and then by thrusting himself down onto the prongs, but he had never been that brave. Jakub moved the pitch fork down to the constable's chest where it came to rest over the heart.

'They say that names can never hurt you, only sticks and stones, but believe me words hurt deep. The same that can be said for the pen being mightier than the sword. To my detriment that was also true when the magistrate signed the order sending me to Ebenstatt.'

Jakub studied the naked, paled figure kneeling before him. A pitiful man when stripped of his uniform he resembled a beached whale that had become stranded on the sand, which had two alternatives, gasp for air and stay alive or wait for the tide to return.

'I will never forget that look of surprise and the warped delight on your face the next morning when you found my sister and me naked in bed together, something that is engrained in my memory forever. You wrongly believed that I had raped Julianna, tied her to the bed and cut her after murdering our parents. My sister asked me to do that to her, Julianna wanted it as much as I did. The problem with you Albrecht Hartmann is that your nanoscopic intellect is incapable of thinking outside of the box.

'Tell me constable, how would feel if you found your daughter's in bed together and naked, repulsed or excited. I'd say turned on. You're as twisted as you described me and parents rarely see the bigger picture. Instead they are blind to the truth. I have not seen my beautiful sister in years, but our spiritual bond is stronger than it ever was before. She knows that I am free and coming for her.

'The cuts you witnessed, saw on Julianna's body were to protect her, to save her from other men defiling her beauty. That is why I punished the boys in the woods. They had planned to take her by force. Nobody is going to hurt my sister, ever!'

Jakub toyed the prongs of the pitch fork down to Albrecht's groin.

'You are fortunate to have a wife with good looks and that the seeds of her beauty has been passed onto your daughters. Maybe I will see how beautiful later, as yet however I am undecided, but I will guided.'

Before Albrecht Hartmann could scream Jakub stuffed an oily rag into the policeman's mouth. His eyes grew wide with abject horror. Spinning the pitch fork around Jakub stabbed the handle into the policeman's stomach extracting the wind from his lungs. Jakub yanked the rag roughly from Albrecht's mouth. 'I don't want you dying feeling that you are so important that my revenge was solely centred upon you, also on my list of visits this night is the magistrate. Tell me, would I find Matthias Baumgartner at home?'

Jakub had the fork prongs resting back over the policeman's heart once again. Scratching down the coarse metal ends tore the flesh like a knife through butter. The blood began to run freely from each wound and inside his chest Albrecht's heart was pumping fast, it only made him bleed all the more.

'No, Baumgartner lives in America... he went to America!'

Using his free hand Jakub grabbed Albrecht by the throat. 'America is a big place, where exactly would I find that bastard magistrate?'

'Somewhere in the Florida area, that's all I know, I swear that's the truth.' The policeman broken and hurting looked up at his captor, knowing that the end was in sight. 'End it Jakub, do what you must, but I beg you, please don't hurt my family!'

Replacing the rag Jakub honoured the village constable's last request plunging the pitchfork deep into the chest he made sure it hurt by kicking hard the crossover bar bringing the tips of the fork through Albrecht's back, but the constable had already closed his eyes accepting the veil of death. Nearby the pigs sniffed the air the smell of fresh blood pumping from the dead man an unexpected feast.

A long way off a lone wolf howled, his cry the acknowledgment of death. Removing the pitchfork Jakub cast it over the wall where it would not injure the pigs. Sensing that there was a meal in the offering the wolf started to descend the mountain side.

Gnashing their front teeth together the pigs began tearing haphazardly at the soft flesh, ripping chunks away and exposing bone. Soon the sty floor would be awash with blood, mud and discarded bone. If the wolf reached the farm in time it would have a wasted journey because the ever hungry pigs never left anything behind and their greed was legendry.

At the farmhouse Jakub saw a figure standing in the doorway, that of a man. Another appeared at his side and Jakub was pleased to see that Anna was still alive. After a minute, perhaps less the door closed and the kitchen lights went out. Soon all trace of Albrecht Hartmann would be nothing, but a memory.

Come the morning when Frederic checked he would notice the blood in the mud, but believe that an injured rogue fox had been savaged by the pigs. Traipsing about the sty after their feast the pigs would also crush what was left of bone and teeth. It would be days before the search party would find the policeman's uniform under the tarpaulin.

Walking back down the dirt track towards the houses the only other clue that Jakub had left behind purposely besides the uniform was Albrecht Hartmann's handcuffs, which he had left clamped to the steering wheel of the tractor. It was not the season yet to be using the tractor so coming across them would be a chance find.

In the high street he stopped and looked in the direction of the policeman's house.

He stood there just looking, but the voices of reason won over the argument inside his head, instead they told him to go elsewhere, somewhere where he had intended visiting after dealing with the magistrate. Turning left instead of right he began walking, eager to arrive.

Jakub was both happy and incensed.

He could tick off Ebenstatt, Koskovsky and Hartmann from his list, but for now Matthias Baumgartner had slipped through the net. With Julianna's help they would find him, redress the balance and turn back the clock to when they had nobody else, but each other.

Standing before the broken gate Jakub carefully lifted it aside so that he could pass beyond. Held in place by a single hinge it looked as though the children of the village had been playing, using it to swing back and forth until punished too many times it had at last relented.

Moments later he stood on the small veranda, where he ran his fingers sympathetically over the peeling paintwork of the window frames. Small fragmented shavings came away, crumbling in his hand. He was sad to see how the old house, once his home had become so neglected, so unloved and cold.

Moving around back he looked up at the window which had been his bedroom, a room he had always liked because it overlooked the mountain and the stream. He was still looking up when he thought he saw a face appear at the glass. It was Julianna and she was standing there naked. She was gesturing that he come inside. Jakub waved back as the image disappeared. Had it just been wishful thinking, he wasn't sure, but it was time to go inside. The only obstacle was to remove the wooden planks that had been nailed across the door.

Chapter Two

He searched around in the tall grass, finding and picking up a discarded piece of old metal which was rigid enough that he could use to jemmy away the wooden planks guarding the rear door. With the strips removed Jakub kicked open what was left of the door having to cover his mouth quickly to repel the cloud of grey powdery dust that had violently belched itself clear of the property, but hacking badly, some of the tiny particles had successfully attacked the back of his throat making him spit out what he could.

He stood momentarily before the open void looking in although having the moon reappear from behind the cloud the room looked unusually very dark. Kicking aside the planks he went in.

He moved about tripping over things, objects that he didn't recognise, bumping into an old wooden box which crashed to the floor where from within fell a number of different spools wound tight with coloured darning cotton. Jakub vaguely remembered his mother making and repairing dresses for Julianna when they had lived at home, rather than live with their grandparents.

Looking around Jakub was dismayed to see that much of the furniture had also been upturned, intentionally damaged some pieces beyond recognition probably by neighbours and children who had entered illegally either ransacking the property after it had been vacated or the children using the haunted house as a play area, daring one another to go inside until the constable had ordered the carpenter to secure the doors and windows. In every nook and cranny thick encrusted cobwebs stretched between wooden beams and light fittings, remnants of an arachnid Christmas party. In the fireplace the spent ash of the last fire lay beneath the cast iron grate like the unwanted remains of a cremation.

Jakub looked towards the stairs that ascended to the first floor expecting to see Julianna standing there waiting for him, but the staircase was empty almost uninviting and he wondered why. If she was upstairs he would join her in a moment.

He took a framed photograph from the mantel piece blowing away a thin layer of dust so that he could study the image. Wiping the glass clean with the cuff of his jacket the image had been taken when Jakub and Julianna had been just seven and five. Standing in front of their parents holding each other's hand, neither had smiled at the camera. It was a rare moment that had been captured and included their parents although he didn't remember when or where it had been taken. Unclasping the back plate from the frame he removed the image and put it inside his jacket pocket.

A sudden cool draught of mountain air blew down the chimney and had the ash in the hearth dance about before settling back down again the same time that Jakub felt a cold embrace sweep through his body leaving his arms pricked with goose bumps, a second later his attention was interrupted, when he thought he heard a movement from the floor above. He uttered his sisters name *'Julianna'* although he wasn't sure that it wasn't just rats under the floorboards.

The scurrying rodents didn't worry him none, but the presence of a uniform holding a gun might, although as far as he could tell the boards and planks on the lower floor covering the windows and doors had been intact when he had arrived at the house. Replacing the empty frame on the mantelpiece he moved about the room checking shelves and cupboards listening out for any other signs of movement from above, but none came, agreeing with the voices that the initial sound could only have been a rat.

He found a wooden cross nailed to the newel post having been put there decades ago by his father, Jakub ripped it away and threw it into the ash where it belonged. God had been absent when he had been in Ebenstatt and it had been the devil who had kept him company throughout the many lonely days and nights. He laughed looking down at the cross which was now half buried in the ash.

'If you want to prove your worth, make sure that Matthias Baumgartner remains in America at least until I arrive, only it would be a shame to miss him again!'

Catching sight of the mirror on the far wall he went across to investigate having seen an inscription written in the dust, words that he couldn't quite make out until close. The inscription was insulting and read 'Julianna, the whore of Kurlor, Jakub's little slut' angrily he picked up his mother's darning stool throwing it at the mirror shattering both glass and inscription. Now nobody would ever read it. If he had known who was responsible he would have left them for dead. Whoever, it didn't matter.

Jakub was half way up the stairs when he stopped climbing and listened, convinced that the shuffling wasn't rats. Adding impetus to the last few stair treads he ran at the door of the bedroom wanting the element of surprise on his side.

Inside it was gloomy, albeit for a large dark mark which had stained the wooden floor where he had cut his mother's throat, left there as a ghastly reminder and when minutes later again the same spot where he had fatally stabbed his father to death. Surprisingly the room was empty, devoid of any soul although strangely his bed had been made. He went to his parent's bedroom next finding the same, leaving only left Julianna's bedroom where they had spent nearly every evening and the night together without their parents knowing.

Turning the handle sharply Jakub stepped inside and was immediately confronted by an icy chill as though he had stepped into an industrial freezer at a cold storage plant. Oddly there was nobody there. Unlike the rooms downstairs those upstairs had been untouched, the furniture, bedding and effects left in place. Standing in the centre of the room he was in awe of the moon outside and it was much brighter than when had been at the farm. He felt drawn to the luminosity which made the ridge of the snow tipped mountain top look like the uneven edge of a damaged knife, sharp although still able to inflict a terrible injury. He turned suddenly sensing that he was not alone.

'I can feel you, why don't you show yourself,' he demanded his hands fisting in readiness.

Beside the wardrobe standing in the corner two figures emerged from the shadows that of a man and a woman. He instantly recognised their faces.

'Yes Jakub, it is us,' his father announced. They turned away from the window where the glare hurt their eyes.

Ghosts didn't frighten Jakub, he had seen enough day or night in Ebenstatt.

'What do you want?' he asked disappointed that it had not been Julianna who had appeared his displeasure obvious. Gabriele, his mother had hoped for a much friendlier greeting.

'Are you not pleased to see us Jakub, we are after all your mother and father?' She had hoped that her approach would change her son's attitude.

'Ghosts are mere hallucinations mother who appear only when they are troubled. I should know, only I've had enough conversations with dead men and women who came to my cell at night. At least they came to visit me, you never did.'

He walked to window where the moon was full.

'Why was that I ask myself was it the shame that kept you away or did my being at Ebenstatt embarrass you.' They didn't reply. 'Did it worry you I wonder, that once inside although ghosts, you too wouldn't be able to get out?' Jakub mocked them both by laughing.

Gabriele and Thomas Hesseltolph looked anxiously back at their son realising that the years spent in the sanatorium had done nothing to quell his frustrations, his anger and if anything Jakub appeared to harbour more hatred than ever.

'Contrary to popular belief Jakub the spirit of the dead cannot just appear when we feel like it. There has to be a very good reason. We sensed your presence coming the moment that you broke down the back door. We also recognise that your coming here tonight will be your last.' Gabriele Hesseltolph took a step forward to be closer to her son, but Jakub immediately took a step back.

'Do you despise us so much that you cannot bear to look at me my son, and yet you took the photograph from the picture frame downstairs?' She touched the fabric of his jacket pocket before he had time to repel her outstretched arm.

'I only took it because it has the image of my sister in the photograph.'

Gabriele smiled at Jakub sensing a spark of humanity, a hope that she had thought lost.

'Is your heart so embittered that you have not one ounce of love for us too?' She looped her arm through that of her husband.

Jakub looked up at the moon searching for an episodic memory, anything that would show him a happy occasion that would make him smile, other than the times spent with his sister. He didn't find any.

'So this visitation, is it to pry into my plans or mock me?' he asked. 'Only I warn you, that imbecile at Ebenstatt, Alexander Koskovsky was annoyingly persistent with his methods using powerful drugs to draw out my demons, but I proved myself to be more powerful than his inadequate methods. When I left him to the mercy of the creatures and insects his dread was no different to that which he had inflicted upon the many poor souls within that terrible establishment.'

Jakub turned to face them.

'Did you know about the good doctor and his unethical methods, practicing the art of black magic, desperate to draw out the truth from a patient. Hallucinogenics were one of his favourite toys. He used to call himself the locksmith telling me that he could unlock my mind, only he never ever found the right key.

'There's no denying that Koskovsky was a clever man although in many ways he was as insane as the ones in the locked wards, many my friends, my neighbours. In the darkness we would spend hours talking under the cracks in the doors discussing the intricacies of the mind, the subconscious and how the complex conundrum had managed to baffle both scientists and doctors for years, centuries possibly. Many of the junior doctors believed that Koskovsky had himself became part of the nightmare that he had worked so hard to unravel.'

Inside Jakub's head the voices were applauding his performance.

'Jakub, my dear son we came here tonight to help,' his mother implored, 'to help you.'

The laughter was much louder than before.

'Help me mother, how on earth could you do that.' He reached forward and touched the dark scar beneath her jaw. 'Visit the pig sty at Frederic and Anna's farm and say hello to Albrecht Hartmann. You should just be in time to see his soul depart this life, or what's left of it. He'll tell you that instead of a boy, a man lives inside my body.

'I plan my executions now rather than pick my victims at random. Did you help me when I needed your help the most? No, of course not and now you show up here tonight expecting to put right the wrong. Is life in the aftermath so powerful and yet your powers cannot stretch so far across the water that you cannot see the plight of Julianna, your only daughter, my beloved sister?'

'We see Julianna and we both feel her pain, as we do yours.' Replied his father, but Jakub wasn't the least moved by what they could see and feel.

'We were the products of your love and yet you didn't share any love with your children. Instead you were happy to let me languish in a mental facility. You wanted to send my sister away. Do you not think that would have made her terribly unhappy, make her feel abandoned.

'Do you not understand why I had to take decisive action to kill in order to break free, to redress the balance of justice. My destiny will take me wherever I need go to free my sister by whatever means necessary, and I'll kill anybody who stands between me and Julianna if needs be.'

Thomas Hesseltolph sighed, his reaction long and drawn.

'Do you not see that the love that you had for your sister was wrong Jakub, had you loved only as siblings and done no wrong, none of this would have happened. You would not have tortured the boys in the woods that day and Julianna might have stayed here in Austria. Things would have been so different.'

At some point in the discussion Jakub knew that they would raise the issue of his love for Julianna. He was ready coming back angrily.

'If we'd had your love, the love of our parents we might have been different, although I doubt it. Whereas Julianna and I do have something special, the love which we possess comes from the devil himself, not your god. You both damned our souls to hell. We did however manage to make a deal with Satan and he has promised to keep us safe.'

Jakub was wary of how far reaching were their powers, he watched them both waiting for any sudden movement, but he had not reckoned upon the love that his mother had in her heart for her wayward son. Gabriele Hesseltolph took up where her husband had become agitated and frustrated.

'The killer that Julianna manipulated and used is dead. His reign of terror lies deep underground where nobody will ever find his body and his soul is destined to live out an eternal existence of terrible penitence. Julianna deserved to be locked away for the part she played in the death of the lawyer and his fiancé, and the many others, but your sister will be given another chance although at present I cannot tell you how or why, when or where.'

Jakub was relieved to hear that Jason Chancery had been dealt with, wondering if Trevor Baines had helped in the final moments of the madman's life, not that it mattered. What was significant to Jakub was that Julianna was safe. He nodded his approval of the English policeman.

His mother wasn't finished and this time she did come close almost nose to nose. This time he didn't back away.

'We did not deserve to die and not by your hands Jakub. I carried you inside of me for nine months. I brought you into this world. We raised you and cared for you. Love and life comes in many forms and not always how you expect it to unravel before you. Mistakes are made, but there is always time to repent and change.'

Eye to eye he responded.

'Before that day, that night you had already arranged to have Julianna sent away.'

'We were only doing what we thought was best. It wasn't right the two of you being together like that, becoming lovers.'

The words seemed to stick in her throat and she could only describe them as lovers, nothing else or more sinister.

'Love is a scared thing Jakub and not to be abused.' The level of her voice softened. 'I was as much to blame only I had known for some time what was going on, but I had kept the secret hidden from your father until it was too late. Sitting in the constable's office that evening while you were locked in the cell I told the policeman and magistrate everything. My honesty brought shame upon our family and I thought the dishonour would kill your father, not you my son. My part in this sorry affair haunts me still.'

Gabriele felt her husband's hand slide into hers. It was the first time ever that Jakub had seen them hold hands.

'Your father is a proud man Jakub. He promised anything that night to the constable and magistrate to have you released, but the law is the law and Matthias Baumgartner wanted justice for the boy's torture in the woods.'

'The magistrate's days are already numbered.'

Thomas Hesseltolph stood alongside his wife.

'But why kill Albrecht Hartmann, he was just doing his duty as a policeman?'

'Because he hurt me. He tried to break my youthful spirit by physically abusing me. He wanted to show Baumgartner that he knew how to break a prisoner. I was a boy, not a full grown man. Worse still was when he came the next morning and found Julianna and myself together, he leered, licking his lips. I saw the desire in the constable's eyes for my sister. I made a vow there and then that one day he would die.'

Surprisingly Thomas Hesseltolph agreed with his son's actions.

'We carry the shame my son and realise that as your parents, we had a duty to protect you and your sister. It is a guilt we will carry into eternity forever.'

Gabriele Hesseltolph smiled, raised her free hand and gently stroked her sons face, Jakub let her do it. 'We loved you both Jakub. You and your sister, but we needed help too. As parents we didn't know how to deal with what you had done.'

'Did you never hear Julianna cry?' he asked.

'We thought her tears were the normal anxieties that teenage girls experience when they are changing, becoming a woman.' She left her hand resting on his cheek. 'We didn't know that she lived in fear of the boys in your class and what they had planned for her.'

Jakub scoffed.

'At last we agree.' He looked directly at his father. 'I did what you could not. Nobody hurts Julianna, nobody!' The room fell silent for several moments.

Thomas and Gabriele Hesseltolph didn't have an answer by which to absolve themselves from the shame and indeed the blame that they felt. Julianna and Jakub had their blood coursing through their veins and as parents they should have protected their children. Maybe the torture and deaths were justified. Jakub sensed a victory.

'I cut them, disfigured them to protect other girls in the village. Who would want to be with a monster who repulsed them.'

'But Julianna, you cut her too!' It was his mother who asked the question.

Jakub nodded.

'To protect her mother. She asked me to do it. If a man really loved her, truly loved her then his stomach would not churn at the sight of my sisters scars. Julianna knew that I loved her.'

He sensed an acceptance in their silence, so he continued.

'Had you survived, you would have known that two of the boys I punished could not live with the shame. Several days later they returned to the woods where they hung themselves. A third went mad and ended up on an adjacent wing at Ebenstatt. I made sure that his existence was a living hell every time our paths crossed. Of all the inmates in the sanatorium I would say he was the only one glad of the daily drug cocktail. I doubt the others never looked in a mirror again. They would be lepers in their own skin.'

'But, I thought Hanno Werner had once been your friend Jakub?'

He brushed the stubble on his chin.

'Once, but he abused my trust to get to Julianna. His torment of her was worse than the others. One day he will lie close to where they bury Alexander Koskovsky.' Jakub laughed. 'He will spend his eternity amongst the trees, a reminder of his folly.'

Hanno Werner had never been mentioned in any of the one on one sessions with Alexander Koskovsky. In fact no names had ever been spoken about. The psychiatrist had only ever referred to the victims and events in the woods as an unfortunate incident. A good artist Jakub had drawn portraits of the other boys - Aldo, Otto, Gregor, Stefan and Kurt. He had put the sketches under Hanno's pillow when his one-time friend had been exercising in the garden. They would become the faces that Hanno would always see in his nightmares. Often he would be heard calling out their names when the moon was full, when a lone wolf howled long and into the night.

'You said that you came to help, how exactly?' Jakub asked, the aggression in his tone diminishing.

'You need to leave Austria and very soon. Go far away and be with Julianna if you must, but be as far away from this place as possible. Kurlor is haunted by many bad memories and not only yours Jakub. We can only advise, not physically help.'

'And what about you,' he asked, 'do you not want to go on?'

For the first time he smiled as a single voice inside his head prompted the question wanting to know. 'Only I have heard about the *gateway* and how going through you pass into a different dimension where you are reborn. Is this not your fate?'

The glance between his parents wasn't missed by Jakub.

'There's more, isn't there. You didn't come here tonight just to advise me to leave Austria or hitch up with Julianna, there's something else, something you're afraid to mention. What is it?'

His mother's hand rested once again softly, affectionately on his cheek as Thomas placed his hand on his son's shoulder.

'To pass beyond and through the gateway you have to be without sin my son. Your soul is as black as the darkest night and your immorality is as bad as the blood that stains your hands. We came because we wanted the chance to be with you perhaps one more time, but our time here is almost done. We want you to know however, that we will always love you Jakub.'

'And Julianna, what about my sister?'

'Julianna has a chance, but it is a slim chance.'

He looked at them both, smiled and nodded then turned and walked over to the door and out onto the landing beyond pulling the door shut behind him. He went back down and out through the rear door where he had entered the property retracing his steps through the long grass to the gate without looking back once. Standing in the shadow of the bedroom window Thomas and Gabriele Hesseltolph watched their son leave knowing they might never see him again. Somewhere in the village and not that far away, maybe the farm a lone wolf howled and kept howling, its long journey down into the village wasted.

He would heed the advice of his parents and leave Kurlor for good, and as planned he would find Julianna and together they would travel to America, where he was committed to executing the last part of his plan.

Jakub had wanted to tell his mother that despite her faults and her betrayal of him in the police station that he still loved her, but as she had clearly pointed out to him, love was never to be abused.

Walking in the opposite direction to which he had arrived he would somehow find a way to get to the port and across to England. Soon Kurlor and Austria would be nothing, but a distant memory.

Chapter Three

The chattering and singing of the sparrows in the corridor beyond the ward entrance was abruptly interrupted by the sudden echo of metal doors being opened, it was early just after seven, long after sunrise and the birds had been up hours.

October had started wet and windy, the expectation of gales an ever present threat. In the exercise yard the large wood barrels that had once been filled with fine wine or beer stored at a local brewery had now a different variety of seasonal flowers embedded in a rich mix of grit, bone meal and compost, although recently battered by the autumn weather they had started to resemble the withering plants found around an unattended grave.

Pulling open the door to the cell a female warder, young in service and smartly dressed with her hair tied back greeted the inmate with a happy smile, the same smile that she saved for every door that she opened each morning.

'Time to rise and shine Julianna.'

The clinical psychologist stared back her dark eyes as penetrating as her brother's. She had been awake for several hours not that time was of any real relevance, but the moon had been bright much brighter than previous lunar cycles and something quite powerful, an unseen force had woken her from her sleep. Whatever, wherever it had originated it had latched onto her subconscious and shook her from her dream.

In the dream she had heard her mother calling out her name, but that was all. In her dream Julianna had tried to reach out, but time she got close her mother took a step back. She saw her father standing behind and behind him was another figure although she could not see the man's face. In the dream she had called to Jakub, wondering if he had heard her calling for him. Withdrawing the key from the lock the warder was in a good mood.

'Did you sleep well?' she asked.

Julianna shook her head slowly.

'More nightmares?'

Julianna nodded. 'A different one… one that I've not had for a very long time. Soon I'll be going on a trip, a long journey.'

Andrea Watkins smiled once again before moving to the next cell calling out generally to the landing, 'Come on ladies, away to the breakfast room otherwise the birds will eat what you don't want.'

Julianna moved away from the bed, she was already dressed having done so when the first light of the new day had flooded in through the cell window set high in the wall. For once the rain had stopped. Feeling a sudden flutter in her chest she whispered *'Jakub'*. It was then that she realised the figure without a face in the dream had been her brother. She remembered the darkened shadow running, but soon after something had woken her from her sleep. Fisting the air triumphantly she knew her brother had escaped Ebenstatt. Julianna placed both hands over her heart and repeated his name *'Oh Jakub'*. She closed her eyes smiling to herself, glad that he was free at last.

Keeping her eyes closed she needed Jakub both physically and mentally. She longed to have him kiss her, caress her and hold her down as they were intimate. Jason Chancery had served only a purpose in her existence, but the deranged killer had meant nothing to her. Instinct told her that he was dead, the dark cloud of death overshadowing her cell as he roamed the streets of London looking Richard Quinn. Chancery had invaded her dreams as well, his screams full of terror as a strange black mass had come tumbling down upon him. She had felt no sorrow for his passing, her carnal desire kept secret for Jakub only. Julianna still had her hands over her heart when she sensed somebody standing in the doorway of the cell door.

'Are you coming Hesseltolph or are you waiting for a royal invitation?' The question asked, was meant only to mock.

Julianna opened her eyes slowly, angry that her private thoughts had been disturbed. Without looking she knew that the sarcasm belonged to the senior warder, her over-weight bulk like that of the barrels in the exercise yard only with arms, legs and a head. It was no secret on the landing that each had a mutual hatred for the other.

'And what was you doing looking up at the cell window, are you planning to escape soon, perhaps become a sparrow and fly away to be with the other birdbrain of the family, your fruitcake brother!'

Julianna held her tongue knowing that the moment would present itself soon when she could make the grotesque woman eat her words.

'You stand more chance of having a secret hook-up with that black tart lover you lust after on the west wing, than ever do of walking out of here a free woman!'

Julianna wanted nothing more than to walk up to the senior warder put her hands around her neck and throttle the life from her body watching her wriggle and writhe in agony as the air was exhausted from her lungs. In the past week she'd been told through a reliable source that the lesbian warder had shacked up with the latest female recruit from the medical block, information that could be useful. She scornfully looked back at the contemptuous fat bastard knowing that things were about to change.

Catching sight of Andrea Watkins way down the landing Gillian Dennerholm felt brave. Reading into the silence from Julianna she wasn't ready to give up just yet with her insults.

'Of course... old west wing Annie, doesn't have a dick does she like your previous lover. I heard that he's so smashed out most of the time that he doesn't have the energy to think about you, let alone pull on his manhood.' She laughed making Watkins turn and smile. 'By the time you two loons get your release paper's you'll both be so old that the effort of just removing your clothes will almost kill you!'

Julianna felt her hands bunching into fists, another week in solitary was nothing to the pain she could inflict upon Dennerholm, but stretching her fingers once again and letting the senior warder have her moment of glory would she knew be short lived.

'Brave aren't you Dennerholm when you know you only have to whistle and help will come running to your rescue.'

Gillian Dennerholm's expression changed.

'Is that a threat Hesseltolph because you know what we do with unruly inmates!'

In no time at all Julianna had moved from under the window to the doorway. Almost nose to nose with the senior warder Dennerholm could see her flection in the pupils of the dark eyes that stared back at her.

'I might not stick around long enough to wait for my release papers Dennerholm, but I promise you this, that before I do leave, you and I will have one last little chat.' Julianna dared to go even closer. *'Just so that we can decide upon which words to inscribe upon your epitaph. Now fuck off and go annoy somebody else before I make it happen today!'*

Expectation was that a warder should never back away or show any weakness before an inmate, however agitated or vulnerable they were, but Gillian Dennerholm could feel the icy hand of the grim reaper squeezing at her heart as it beat fast inside her chest. Julianna Hesseltolph was unlike any other prisoner at Ashworth. Cold and completely merciless a good many people had been killed because of her influence and her words, a promise were full of malevolence. Edging away slowly Dennerholm thought it best to let Hesseltolph think she had won the battle that morning. Instead she raised a warning finger at the inmate.

'You'll pay for your insolence Hesseltolph, I make you eat your words.'

But Julianna was unaffected by the threat, she walked forward again closing the gap once more.

'If that goes any higher Dennerholm I'll bite it off and stick it somewhere, where that lover from the medical block puts her tongue night after night. There's only you and me here now on the landing and Warder Watkins and the rest have gone to breakfast!'

Gillian Dennerholm let her hand fall slowly back down to her side. She wondered how somebody like Julianna Hesseltolph could possibly know about her relationship with Sammie Saunders. After breakfast was over she would pay the medical centre a visit and ask. It might be worth seeing the doctor too and suggesting that Hesseltolph's medication be increased. In her professional opinion the Austrian was becoming very agitated and dangerous.

Walking confidently in the opposite direction to Dennerholm, Julianna made her way to the breakfast room where there was always something left over that would keep her going through until lunchtime. In her mind a plan was already beginning to unfold, it just needed fine tuning before she could put it into practice. She had won a small victory over the senior warder, but the greater prize was when she walked out of Ashworth a free woman, leaving Dennerholm behind, wishing that she had never been born.

Chapter Four

Jakub re-checked the brief message and address on the postcard:

'Climate's changed - going to see Aunt at the winter haven in Melbourne.'

Satisfied that the details were correct he dropped the card in the post-box hearing it drop to the bottom before walking away.

It was first time that he had been allowed to send any kind of communication to Julianna, Alexander Koskovsky imposing strict rules at Ebenstatt that there should be no communication with the outside world and in all the time that Jakub had been a guest at the sanatorium he had only ever seen inmates arrive, never any leave.

He knew that he was taking a risk posting it in Amsterdam, but it was quite possible that the postcard could have been sent via another source and Holland was after all a long way from Kurlor. Jakub had extra been careful not to place any traceable fingerprints on the card or licking the stamp and disguising his writing. All would be checked when it arrived at Ashworth High Security Hospital, but although they would not understand or be able to decipher the message, Jakub was banking on the governor allowing Julianna to have the postcard to help improve her mood. By the time it had been franked, handled and sorted there would be so many different fingerprints that they would baffle the most advanced forensic scanners.

Hitching a lift with a Turkish lorry heading for Frankfurt, Jakub passed through road blocks and border patrols hidden in the back amongst the assorted boxes. The driver also anti-establishment, ignoring rules was happy to help his passenger. He even bought Jakub breakfast when they stopped at a small transport café where the police never visited.

'I do not want to know of your story my friend and what I do not know, I cannot be accused of lying.' The driver chose their seats and called across the waitress, they down next to the rear fire exit. 'And... whatever it is that you are running away from, maybe a woman perhaps, Allah looks after his own!' Jakub knew only two words in Arabic, *shukraan jazilaan*. He put his hands together to say thank you. The driver did most of the talking and Jakub smiled and nodded at the appropriate moments. Haluk proudly showed Jakub a picture of his wife and family, and when nobody was looking pulled up the sleeve of his overalls to show a tattoo with a number inked into his arm.

'It was the number of days that I was in prison for stealing a motorbike when I was still a teenager. I just wanted to prove to my friends that I could do it.'

Jakub was impressed, he liked his new friend, trusted him. Pulling up the sleeve of Alexander Koskovsky's shirt he showed Haluk the scars where he had cut Julianna's name down his left bicep. 'She is the reason I am making this long journey.'

Haluk ran his fingertip down over the tiny mounds that had formed in the healing process. 'She is worthy of your love?' he asked.

'More than anything else in the world.' Jakub replied.

Haluk grinned.

'Then it is good my friend, that you go to her. A man needs a good woman, and a man needs Allah.'

The Turk dropped Jakub near the River Rhine close by the Heidelberg Cement Works where few police patrols ever visited. Walking along the tow path to where the boats were moored he found a long boat travelling up river heading for Amsterdam.

Haluk had swapped an old jumper and pair of trousers for the mohair lined suit, stating that boat crews rarely wore suits.

The barge with its Dutch crew were carrying chemicals although none were marked. Jakub volunteered to work a free passage providing the captain took him to the port. He told the crew that his wallet and cash had been stolen the night before in a bar. Later with the stars appearing overhead he sat alone on the deck of the boat, something told him going to England would be futile as Julianna had already made plans to escape her internment. Picking up his mug he sipped the coffee which was hot and good. His smile was seen by another crewman.

'Good news my friend?' he asked.

'I think so...' Jakub replied, he didn't elaborate.

'We'll soon be at the port, this is always a long run up and down the river, but it pays well and compensates for the risk.' The man who was probably Jakub's age, produced a pack of cards.

'Do the river authorities ever stop the barge to check your cargo?'

The boatman grinned, dealing two sets.

'Not this barge they don't.' With a backward flick of his head he hinted at the flags flying from the boathouse mast. 'The one with the small triangular tells everyone who knows that our cargo is dangerous, highly volatile with a potential to explode, it keeps the officials away!'

Jakub didn't want to know what was in the drums, he was happy just knowing that he didn't have to slip over the side if and when a launch pulled alongside. Having come up from the galley after making the coffee he had secreted a small boning knife inside his trouser belt.

When they reached the port at Amsterdam he said his farewells to the crew thanking them all for their generosity. Walking the container dockside he came across an Indonesian container ship that was sailing to America. And like Haluk the charge hand responsible for the ships labour and stowage wasn't interested in passports or legal documentation only a good crew for the passage across. Men who could stomach the rough seas and ride the waves.

When Jakub had asked how rough the charge hand had laughed and replied *'high'*.

He was still laughing when he told another deck hand to show Jakub where the crew had their quarters, where they slept, washed and took their meals, and where he would find working weatherproofs.

During the next two weeks Jakub found the challenges of the sea as unpredictable as the weather, battling huge, tall waves as the sea tried to claim him several, but Jakub was determined to reach America at all cost. Tossed around like a cork in a whirlpool the container ship survived and surprisingly he had only suffered from mal de mar the once. Given a motion sickness pill by the charge hand his stomach had settled and that evening he was back on deck fighting the elements.

Jakub like the freedom that the seas offered, the excitement and how men were determined to overcome the worst of a storm to show that nothing could dampen their spirit.

After Matthias Baumgartner he considered a life sailing the world might be ideal and easy to avoid the interest of the police forces around the world.

Only once had he seen his image appear on a TV screen in Amsterdam, but the only photo they had of him was as a teenager. So much in-between had changed and time was nobody's friend as the magistrate would soon find out.

After almost three weeks of travelling and being on the run his trail had gone cold, been trampled firmly into the dust. Jakub was on the international top ten list of wanted criminals, but the image on computer was an artist's impression of what he thought would look like years on.

Jakub only saw the captain twice throughout the voyage and each encounter was when they passed in the long empty corridors and when the captain was making his way down to the engine room. The tall Indonesian, a giant by normal standards would nod and look, but not say anything. Jakub would find out that his only interest was getting his cargo safely to the other side of the Atlantic without loss or damage. If a man went overboard he would not turn about, but pick up another when they arrived in America.

Surprisingly Jakub struck up an unusual, but friendly rapport with Bahari Lokman, the charge hand best. A quiet man with a calm disposition despite his ever growing list of responsibilities. Smaller in stature to that of his captain Lokman was a deep thinker and when the men engaged in a boisterous game of poker Bahari would have his head buried in a book at the other end of the room. When he resigned from the game Jakub would sit with Bahari and ask what he was reading, getting the same reply every time.

'About the world my friend, where there is always something new to learn, something I did not know yesterday!'

Jakub would ask about Indonesia, Malaysia and Southeast Asia, sitting quietly as Bahari became excited as he told him about the wondrous places that he had experienced on his many travels, places that Jakub had only ever seen in the pages of a geography book at school. Knowledge fascinated Jakub and having struggled badly at school he was keen to make up for lost time.

Working on deck together when the sea was calm and sunny Jakub would tell Bahari about Austria, the snow-capped mountains, the beautiful green scenery and the clouds which you could touch almost with your fingertips from the top of the highest peak. Intrigued by what he heard Bahari Lokman never once asked Jakub why he had left Austria. Unlike Koskovsky, the Indonesian was tactful and respectful of another man's privacy.

Coming close dark clouds overhead had threatened to delay their arrival at New York, but the captain was never daunted, a veteran sea salt he knew how to navigate the waters and with the help of a skilled pilot brought the container ship alongside the dock where with a shake of a hand Jakub promised Bahari that he would be back for the return journey soon.

The charge hand was sorry to see his friend Jakub walk away from the dockside, still young and raw to the sea, his travelling companion had shown more pluck and promise than any other deckhand that he had taken on down the years and if Jakub did come back there would always be a place for him aboard the ship

Quickly disappearing into the shadows between the dockside cranes Jakub made it a habit never to look back. In his pocket he had a three hundred dollars that Bahari had given him as a goodwill gesture of their friendship and his wages for his work on board the ship. It wasn't much, but to Jakub it seemed like a small fortune.

Passing between the tall steel gantries he nodded at the men working into the night, loading and unloading. Jakub was tanned and lean, and he felt that he belonged on the high seas. He kept his head down heading for the road ahead feeling the buzz that appeared like electricity all about. America seemed alive and had an energy that he couldn't describe. He wanted Julianna to feel and see it too.

All along the waterfront there were garishly lit fish and meat restaurants, continental diners, all-night bars and nightclubs. Jakub elected to drink in the first bar that he came across and as long as you had the cash to pay the drinks tab you could stay all night drinking.

The bar was crowded and much nosier than he had expected it to be, although the people were friendly and the only police that he saw went speeding past in large black and white cars on their way to another location.

Picking at a bowl of peanuts and nibbles he supped his beer thoughtfully. He had been aware of a man watching him for the past hour.

Sat directly behind in one of the many booths that were a permanent fixture of the bar the man's interest in Jakub had never waned. Jakub watched using the large mirror on the wall of the bar where the glass shelves were lined with every bottle of alcohol listed on the specials board.

Smaller than Jakub, of slight build, the man suffered a badly pock marked face, long wispy hair and pushed a pair of glasses up the bridge of his nose not that he needed them as he'd been watching Jakub drink looking over the top rim. Scratching the calf of his right leg Jakub made sure that the boning knife was still where he had strapped it to his leg. When the male drinker siting next o Jakub thanked the barman and left leaving the stool vacant the man from the booth brought his glass over and sat himself next to Jakub. He turned and smiled, his teeth stained where the nicotine of cigarettes had attacked the enamel coating.

'You've almost finished that one,' the stranger said, 'do you fancy another?'

Jakub nodded. 'Yes, thanks!'

The stranger tapped the bar top catching the attention of the barman. He order two rounds, two for them both. 'That'll save his shoe leather and me having to waste his time.' He held out his hand in greeting. Jakub shook it putting his hand in hard into the man's longitudinal crease between forefinger and thumb having his new friend know that he was strong. The stranger looked over the rim of glasses and smiled.

'You've a strong grip my friend, I like that in a man it demonstrates a certain ownership of his destiny.' He let the hold slip. 'Like he knows where he's heading in life.'

Jakub smiled back. 'Maybe...'

'Are you here on holiday?'

Tanned and weather beaten by the suns and spray it looked like he had been touring the freeways from state to state. 'You could I was...' he didn't offer more.

'Distinctly European,' he took an educated guess at the dialect, 'German, umm yes, definitely Aryan. I like that.'

Jakub wasn't sure quite what he was implying, but for now he was prepared to let it go and see where the meeting was heading.

'My name is Adam Jankowski, second generation Polish descendant although for the New York scene and special friends I use Adam Janko which has that fashion house retro street appeal.'

Jakub studied the man sitting next to him, detecting a certain air of femininity about his personae especially his exaggerated hand flicks. Adam Janko continued having swallowed a mouthful of his beer to refresh his palate.

'My home town was sometime back Ottowark, twenty kilometres east of Warsaw. Oh God how I detested the place, a living embodiment of how to travel back in time and still reach nowhere appealing. The place was holding me back, I felt like I was being strangled day in day out, where here in the big city I can be free, be my own man.' He spread his arms like he had wings to emphasise the point, getting a laugh from a table nearby. 'Don't mind those coarse buggers, they're only jealous.'

'Jealous of what?' Jakub asked.

'Me...!' He replied, shuffling a little closer. 'A teeny weeny word of warning, there are some bigoted bastards in here tonight who despise

60

Europeans and they have a thing about Germans.' He moved back to his own space. Jakub eased his grip on the handle of the knife. Nearby a group leaving scraped their chair making him look their way. He realised that amongst so many people he was jumpy, perhaps tense, he had to relax. His nervousness didn't go unnoticed.

'New York can be a little daunting at first, but you'll soon get used to the people and the way they live. Every day can appear frantic, but there are times when they relax. Are you okay?'

'I've had a long day, I'm just tired that's all.'

Adam Janko put his hand on Jakub's left knee and gave it a reassuring squeeze. 'I thought that was it.' He looked at the empty glasses tapping the bar counter again.

The voices inside Jakub's head were arguing again. Some advising that he gut the eccentric queer and leave him slumped over the bar counter whereas others told him to be more subtle and find a dark alley.

Adam Janko continued talking describing the colourful gay scene in New York and Jakub listened as he enjoyed his beer. His uninvited friend was over familiar at times and especially as they had not long met, but Jakub it wasn't a problem that he couldn't deal with. For the present he was prepared to tolerate Adam Janko and see where the evening would take him. Picking from the peanut bowl he introduced himself.

'My name is Johann Roebers and I'm Dutch, not German. I lived in a small village called Anchervelt which was thirty two kilometres south of Amsterdam.'

Adam smiled. 'Dutch or German, I like both and they do sound alike. Have you been in New York long?'

'Almost three months. I've been touring a lot.'

'You have a nice tan!' Adam remarked.

'It's a warm country, bigger than I imagined and the buildings here are so tall.'

Adam touched his knee again, pulling it back sharply when Jakub gave him a sideways glance. 'Everything here is bigger!'

Jakub watched a girl leave, she was tall, slim and her curves were exactly as he remembered Julianna being like the last time that he had seen her. Adam felt the pang of jealousy seeing Jakub look.

'Have you got a place to stay tonight… only I live in a small, but well equipped comfortable condo over in Chelsea. It overlooks the river and is handy for the museums and art galleries. If you're stuck I could put you up and throw in breakfast. We could take it from there!'

Jakub grinned. Homosexuals were always so friendly and willing to share. His thoughts were working through an opportunity. Inside his head the voices were telling him to accept.

'Thank you, that'd be good. I only came in for a quick drink then to find a men's hostel.'

Adam lightly touched Jakub's arm.

'NO… no, you'd be safer with me. The hostels around the dockside tend to be very basic and some can be somewhat hostile. I've heard it amongst circles that some of the men who stay are never seen again.' He came in very close. My friend Quinton, he works in the police and told me that they're always fishing some body or other from the Hudson.'

'I can pay,' Jakub offered reaching for his wallet, but Adam Janko wasn't having any of it, he replied with a shallow laughed.

'Quick, put your wallet away, the customers here will think I'm renting myself out.' He leaned back on the bar stool and looked to where the end booth was full of men. 'Goodness, you'll have the old queens blow a fuse if they see you hand over money. No, call my offer the beginning of a lovely friendship between us.' It was then that Adam realised Jakub had no hand luggage with him. 'You're travelling awfully light?'

Jakub moaned, 'would you believe that I was robbed this morning at the bus station. I had only just put my rucksack down to pay for my ticket when this young guy came up from behind, rabbit punched my back then ran off with my effects. I reported it to a policeman who I found patrolling the bus station, but he told me to go to the police house. I didn't bother.' It sounded plausible.

Adam sized Jakub up and down.

'You and me, we're about the same build. I've probably got a number of old pieces in the wardrobe that would fit you and if not me, then Carlos three doors down from my apartment is in fashion. He'd get you some stuff from the warehouse.'

Things were looking up and Jakub felt his luck was holding out, there was how one important element that he needed to know before going to Chelsea with Adam Janko.

'Do you live alone?'

Adam replied by slapping his own chest. 'Cheeky, yes I live alone. What kind of man do you think I am?'

Jakub knew only he didn't give a reply.

Adam was suddenly serious. 'The young man who stole your rucksack this morning did he wear a bandana, a scarf tied tight around the top of his head?'

'Yes, why do you know him?'

Adam tutted, the disgust apparent.

'Not personally thank goodness, but you had an unfortunate experience with those vile, dirty grease-balls from Hell's Kitchen. The bandana is their gang identity. I call it a lot worse and it's about time our authorities came down heavy on them. At times they terrorise the city.' He seemed to have a shiver pass through him. 'Awful brutish men, always so hell bent on hurting you, robbing you or cutting you. They all carry knives you know and you were lucky that you didn't end up in Lenox Hill for surgery.'

Jakub smiled, he would like to have seen any of them try. He would leave them for the undertaker. Adam Janko had his dander up rambling on about the atrocities that we taking place in and around some of the city neighbourhood's.

'They're worse than savages, always whooping in the dead of night like deranged monkeys suffering from some horrible jungle disease. I find their presence so intimidating when they hang about on street corners, blocking the subways entrances or stealing from the convenience stores. Each has only one ambition in life and that is to rob, maim and scare. They're scum and they should reopen Alcatraz, not rebuild it, but leave it just as it is and let them live there!'

He stopped realising the black picture that he was painting for somebody who had just arrived. 'Anyway, you and me together, we'll be just fine!'

Jakub wasn't worried in the slightest. 'What do you do for work?' he asked.

Adam proudly puffed up chest. 'I'm a free-lance writer. I research historical or important information for company portfolios, supplying factual evidence to support their market growth. It helps sell products or so I'm told, I don't really care as long as the money goes into my account.' He looked along the bar counter in either direction. 'In my opinion they use far too bimbos. Bikini clad girls to help glamourize an ad. Whereas I think a man has the same appeal sex as a young woman, but of course she has boobs.'

He settled the bar tab for the evening suggesting that it was time to leave as it was unwise to be hanging about the subway's late at night. Thirty five minutes later they were walking through the front door of the apartment.

Jakub went immediately over to balcony and where he could see the outside space below. A short way up the sidewalk the reflection of the Hudson shone back at him. It looked cold and uninviting. Adam clicked the door locks into place securing the condo. Hearing them lock into place reminded Jakub of Ebenstatt.

'It keeps the undesirables away,' Adam justified as he walked over to a small drinks cabinet. 'Would you like a brandy?' Jakub nodded.

With a flick of a switch the wall lights illuminated the darker areas. Jakub looked around, it was a far cry from his cell at Ebenstatt, stylishly decorated with artwork and good furniture it was as Adam had described comfortable. He studied each painting in detail, liking, appreciating the expression of colour used by the artist. In streaks of loud, flamboyant pastels, garishly swept across the canvas they came in red, green, blue and yellow making the painting come alive. Watching from behind Adam was pleased to see that his guest liked his choice of art.

'The artist is Porto Rican, a friend who disappeared overnight and no longer wants to know me anymore, not that it's really of any consequence because I have his best creations adorning my walls and it was his choice to walk away. Do you have a favourite he asked?' bringing over the drinks.

Jakub pointed to an abstract mess that appeared dark and menacing, depicting a naked man with horns and sat beside him ignoring a turbulent sea were mermaids. 'Does it have a name?'

'Tempest of the Caves,' replied Adam. 'When the horned beast rounded up all the virgins from the village and kept them prisoner in the sea caves. Any rescue attempts were met with a violent storm as the tempest watched, laughing. The Porto Rican didn't paint this, but I like the tempest. Just look at his muscles, his body.'

Jakub saw the tempest as himself. Did the boys in the woods see him as that when he had tortured them that day. Lying on top of the bookcase he saw a bunch of keys with a vehicle fob.

'Do you have a car?'

Adam was slightly miffed that Jakub had changed the subject so quickly from art to transport. He thumbed at the balcony going back to drinks cabinet. 'The silver Chrysler automatic parked in the lot downstairs. My favourite bit is the interior, a contrasting shade between pale buff and classic ocean blue. I can make heads turn when I go cruising.' He came back and stood alongside Jakub. 'Perhaps, if you've nothing planned tomorrow or later this week we can take a drive down to the beach. I'm sure that there's a spare cossie in the cupboard.'

Jakub agreed. 'A drive out would be good.' He had only ever driven the tractor on Frederic's farm, but it couldn't be that much different to driving the car with an automatic transmission.

Adam excused himself saying he had to use the bathroom. He wanted wash his face and clean his teeth feeling that his luck was in. Not as muscly as the tempest Jakub was still strong. Thinking about him made Adam shiver with excitement. Splashing aftershave to his cheeks and neck it had been too long since the last time and Jiménez had gone so quickly. Adam held his chest feeling the hurt still.

He looked at himself in the mirror. *'The Dutchman doesn't say a lot,'* he considered. He liked that and it demonstrated that Jakub was perhaps an educated man, thoughtful. As long as he didn't beat him up afterwards like some of the others did, Jakub could abuse him all night long if he liked. He added an extra swig of mouth wash. With a flick of his long curls he was ready.

Coming back out Adam found the room dark, the lights out. It was fun, a little scary although maybe it was part of Jakub's approach. He felt excited. He called out for Johann listening for the sound of his breathing, but everywhere was silent. Maybe he's just shy thought Adam, some were until the next time. He would have to keep the bedroom lights down very low, but not low enough that he couldn't see his partner.

Stepping from behind where the shadows were darkest Jakub thrust the boning knife in deep piercing Adam Janko's right lung. He kept his free hand over his victim's mouth to prevent the scream from alerting neighbours, letting the body slip silently down onto the waiting floor. Looking back up he could see the joy in his attacker's expression *'why'* he whispered as the blood rushed filling his lung cavity.

'Because I couldn't have you tell the police where I was heading!'

Adam Janko died looking up at the framed painting of the tempest and he wasn't sure, but for the first time ever he thought he saw the virgins smiling back down at him. Jakub cleaned the boning knife in the kitchen sink adding a generous amount of bleach to the stainless steel basin and then the blade.

In the storage cupboard beside the bathroom he found fresh linen, taking several bed sheets down from the shelves he especially liked the black satin which was perfect for what came next. Rolling the dead body onto the sheets, he folded over the loose flaps then tied the ends. Stepping back he admired the mummified corpse lying before him thinking that Adam Janko looking like a charred Christmas cracker.

Meticulous about keeping fit and his weight down to impress prospective lovers Adam Janko weighed just under seventy kilograms. Jakub hoisted the mummy onto his shoulder and walked the short distance to the river.

Throwing it over the embankment wall it landed with a single splash, bubbled momentarily then disappeared beneath the dark waters of the Hudson, where it would be tossed about by the various undercurrents until finally emerging weeks later down river near Sandy Hook Bay, two weeks after Jakub had been long gone. Two weeks after the barman wouldn't remember nor be able to tell the police who the homosexual had picked up that fated night.

Bleaching and cleaning the wooden floor where the body had fallen Jakub covered the area with a large Arabian carpet that he found in the spare bedroom. Shutting the door the bed hadn't been used, most of the action he assumed, grinning being reserved for the master bedroom.

An hour later he stood on the balcony, enjoying a glass of red wine letting the tension ebb from his mind as he watched a large barge sail on by going down the river heavily laden with an unknown cargo. Jakub grinned and nodded to himself. The wash from the barge would help sink the body to the muddy depths. Overhead the moon was full and bright. He raised his glass giving thanks for getting him safely to America. He added an apology too.

'To my anguished parents, Thomas and Gabriele Hesseltolph, wherever you are I'm sorry, but tonight the killing was necessary to make sure that Julianna remains safe and for me to fulfil my quest!'

He raided the refrigerator and made himself a cold chicken snack and later after finishing the wine bottle was happy to sleep on the comfy settee rather than use the double bed, and from the settee he could watch the moon cross the night sky.

Come the morning he would begin his search again for Matthias Baumgartner.

Leaving the balcony doors open wide he thought about Julianna as her energy was strong and he could hear her calling. When he did finally succumb closing his eyes it would be the first time in years that he could sleep peacefully without having to watch over his shoulder. Even the voices inside his head accepted that he needed a good sleep so they remained silent.

Chapter Five

Julianna Hesseltolph turned the postcard over several times scrutinising the writing, it wasn't exactly the same, but she did recognise several similarities, well hidden, but they were there all the same. She understood the message. Holding it close to her chest, it meant that Jakub was free... the phrase *'climates changed'* told her that much.

How Jakub had managed to escape Ebenstatt and the manner by which it had been orchestrated was of little importance to Julianna, all that mattered was that he was no longer being held prisoner at the sanatorium. She concealed the postcard between the pillow and casing where she could read it again later when the lights went out, but where the moonlight was bright.

In the governor's office at Ashworth, Gillian Dennerholm stood patiently before the impressive oak desk while Ashton Tierney read through the file. When he was finished he closed the front and added his initials to the audit trail.

'Was there any significant emotion when you gave her the postcard?' he asked. He didn't look up, but instead studied the profile photograph top right hand corner of the medical file. Whatever her part in the crimes of Jason Chancery, there could be no denying Julianna Hesseltolph was a clever, manipulative and still a beautiful woman.

Gillian Dennerholm sighed, there were parts of the file on Hesseltolph that she still had to explore herself and she wondered if anywhere she was mentioned. It had been almost two months since the governor had last asked for a written report on the Julianna and she was suspicious as why he should want an update now.

'No, not really, she was relaxed and her normal self-giving nothing away, whereas I'm suspicious. Instinct, experience tells me that it's from somebody close!'

Tierney looked up. 'And you saw that how exactly?'

'I've worked here long enough and amongst them all to know the signs. The flicker of life in their eyes, a slight smile, even a clenched fist of victory. Hesseltolph can disguise her thoughts well and think herself clever than us, but I saw that look in her eye this morning.'

Tierney remained impartial. 'I take it that a photocopy is on file and it was scanned for prints.'

Dennerholm looked down at his balding patch at the back. 'It went through the normal ninhydrin test. We found several prints, but none were anybody in the system, including that of her brother.'

Ashton Tierney opened the drawer of his desk and pulled out an official looking envelope. He handed it over to Gillian Dennerholm.

'This came yesterday. I think you need to read the contents.' Since her arrival in his office for the first time Tierney offered the seat opposite his desk so she could sit and digest the contents. He saw her expression change reading her thoughts.

'Jesus Christ...' she was clearly shocked. 'The psychotic bastard murdered the psychiatrist, left him the woods dying before he made good his escape. And now the village policeman at Kurlor is missing too, presumed dead. Brother and sister are deranged monsters.'

Ashton Tierney held his hand out to retrieve the communique.

'I would agree that monster certainly fits the bill, although my opinion is that neither sibling is what we would class stupid, insane maybe. I believe they both know what they are doing and why. I would like to see them match their intelligence with that of the cleverest analyst around. For what it's worth I'd have my odds on the Hesseltolph's winning. It would take somebody who thinks, breathes and sleeps like them to fully understand what goes through their minds.' He put the envelope back in the desk drawer. He ran the side of his forefinger along his bottom lip, thinking. 'Let's play a waiting game and see what comes of this postcard. I've a feeling that somehow she knows her brother is free, let's see how her mood changes.'

Dennerholm felt her frustration rising inside of her, Tierney was weak and indecisive, always waiting to see what transpired. It was she and her team who suffered the consequences.

'The card was franked in Amsterdam.'

Tierney nodded. 'I know. Keep a close eye on Julianna and if she talks to any of the other inmates, have it recorded which ones. We can talk with them after and find out what they talked about. Make sure you keep me informed at all times. In the meantime I'll make a phone call.'

Although Gillian Dennerholm had never met Jakub Hesseltolph she disliked him as much as she did his sister. In her book paedophiles and then psychos like Jakub and Julianna Hesseltolph should be taken out back somewhere dark and shot through the temple, telling the press that they had died in their sleep of natural causes. She was aggrieved that inmates like Julianna Hesseltolph should be treated like royalty, given privileges, kept safe, have handed to them free meals, fresh linen and laundered clothing, plus soft beds upon which to lie at night. If she were the governor Dennerholm would have made life very difficult all round. 'The moment that I see or hear anything suspicious, I will let you know.' She closed the door quietly.

She found herself a quiet unseen corner of the yard where she could enjoy a cigarette alone and relieve the frustrations she felt whenever she attended Tierney's office. The man was an utter prick, a totally useless tool. Blowing the smoke out through her pursed lips, one day she'd make the decisions at Ashworth and then things would be different, very different and inmates like Julianna Hesseltolph who took the piss out of the system would suffer. Just because she was educated and with a master's degree, she thought she was better than the senior warder.

It made Dennerholm's blood pressure rise. Sucking and blowing out she thought of ways to make it happen now, anything tangible that would stick and make life difficult for Hesseltolph, something that would make the governor stand up and take notice of, anything to put a black mark on her file. She stubbed out the reminder of the cigarette pushing the end into the brickwork and threw it into the flower pot. Spark or no spark having seen the postcard, Gillian Dennerholm knew that a storm was coming.

Around lunchtime the same morning word went around that Judith Banks from B Wing was absent from the dining room. Last seen twenty minutes before the call for lunch to begin nobody could say why she was missing, not even the warders. Speculation spread quickly amongst the inmates that Banks was dead.

Inmates did die, everybody did when their time was up, but at a secure facility like Ashworth the stigma was much worse and scrutinised by relatives and the press whose voice was mighty and wide. Insane or not, everybody deserved to be treated humanely and the good work which went unseen the other three hundred and sixty four days of the year was soon lost in the tide of public opinion. What made this absence particularly worse was that Judith Banks had not long arrived at Ashworth. The fact that she had poisoned her elderly mother in an alleged moment of diminished responsibility was neither here nor there.

'Well, where the fuck is she?' demanded an agitated Gillian Dennerholm. First Hesseltolph and now Banks, this was turning out to be a testing day. *'Somebody look around, she can't have scaled a five metre solid brick wall unless the voices inside her head told her she was Spiderman's sister!'*

Working the in the library where it was always warm and comfortable, a woman inmate sidled up surreptitiously alongside Julianna. She turned to see the silly grin etched on the woman's face. 'How can I help you Susan?'

Susan Mycroft edged a little closer.

'I've just heard that Banks, that new girl has been found dead in her cell. She tore her bed sheet into strips, tied them together then looped them over the handle on the outside of the cell door and jumped down only her feet didn't quite reach the floor. Word is that it was an open and shut case.'

The inmate laughed at the stupidity of her own joke, but Julianna didn't join in. She saw an opportunity ascending from the vaults of hell.

'And how exactly would this news be of interest to me Susan?' she asked.

Susan Mycroft checked to see that the librarian, a warder, wasn't listening. She pulled Julianna over to the corner shelves. *'Cos when they take her body away from the medical block ward, it's the only time that a switch can be done!'*

The older woman who had spent over twenty years at Ashworth had been thinking along the same lines.

'You mean take the place of the deceased.' Julianna acknowledged.

Mycroft nodded, one eye on Julianna, the other on the warder. They moved along choosing different books.

'How long is it before they take the body to the medical centre?'

Susan Mycroft opened the page of her book. 'Sometimes an hour, maybe more, it all depends, but the governor don't like having a stiff hanging about, he thinks it makes the other inmates jittery. Silly bastard, most of us are in here because we left our victims lying about dead and Banks done her mother which is why she's a guest here. I don't suppose she gives a toss when they stuff her in the fridge.'

Julianna stopped flicking through her book. 'Have you told anybody else about this Susan?'

'No, only you, only it ain't right you being in here Julianna. You're an educated lady and you was manipulated by that serial killer. I know cos' I read all about it in the Sunday papers that one of the warders gives me every Monday. You should still be on the outside helping others!'

Julianna Hesseltolph couldn't agree more. She could still see the joy in the faces of jury as the foreman gave the verdict and her defence team lead by Jeremy Tuft QC were totally ineffective. When she was free, he would get a visit from her one dark night.

'They called you psychologically abnormal. You look alright to me!'

Julianna smiled, a plan was forming in her mind.

'And what about the police, do they ever get involved?' she asked.

'Always. The governor has to call them in. They check for foul play, but are keen to bugger off as soon as possible. Hanging around here ain't healthy, you're likely to catch something nasty, like a touch of the loon's tremors!'

'What's that, the tremors I mean?'

Susan whispered. 'When Dennerholm's about we make it our policy to begin having the shakes. The more loony she thinks you are the more she leaves you alone. The coppers think it's catching so they fuck off quick!'

As part of the plan Julianna suddenly fell to the floor.

Susan Mycroft screamed. *'Julianna whatever's wrong?'* The warder rushed over from the desk to assist.

Rolling about, moaning and jerking her upper and lower limbs she appeared to be having some sort of convulsive fit. The warder ran back to the desk to phone for medical help. Opening her right eye Julianna looked up directly at the concerned face of Susan Mycroft and winked. Despite battling each day with her own demons Susan winked back. Replacing the receiver the warder retuned.

'How is she Mycroft?' she asked.

'I think that she's having some kinda fit Miss Pendlehurst, she should go to the medical ward.'

Monica Pendlehurst also new to Ashworth knelt down and checked Julianna's pulse, which was fast, although strong. At least she had stopped thrashing about which was a relief. The door to the library suddenly burst open as two other warders arrived to help. Minutes later Julianna was put on an Evac stretcher and taken to the medical centre.

Putting her book back Susan Mycroft was smiling to herself. No, it definitely weren't right that her friend was at Ashworth, not when Julianna could be outside helping others less fortunate. Looking at the spine of another title she scoffed at *'The Mystery of Desmond Choyles'*.

'I read that last year,' she said shuffling away, 'in the end he murdered his mistress and disappeared. When an opportunity presents itself, all good loonies can disappear.'

Chapter Six

Gillian Dennerholm had her suspicions about the incident in the library involving Julianna Hesseltolph and there was nothing on her medical record to suggest that she'd had any previous convulsions. Leaving her reports until later she went to the medical centre to check.

She found her midway down the ward, next to the washroom entrance and alongside the curtained cubicle containing the dead body of Judith Banks. The only other occupant on the ward was a regular Margarita Henderson, who was altogether too old to be at Ashworth, but she'd been at the facility too long to have her rejoin the rat race outside. Completely gaga and deaf as a post Margarita's day was spent with the fairies at the bottom of the garden. Pulling back the curtain sharply she found the clinical psychologist massaging her forehead. Dennerholm showed little sympathy.

'So what's caused this then Hesseltolph?' she asked.

'I don't know, one moment I was looking at the books with Susan the next I was crashing to the floor.'

'There must have been something that triggered it?'

'If I knew what caused it Dennerholm, I'd be a bloody physician instead of a psychologist!' she immediately held her forehead as though shouting had hurt her head.

Gillian Dennerholm noticed that the eyes always so very dark had lost their sparkle.

'Did Susan Mycroft attack you?'

'No, of course not. Things went dizzy and the next thing I knew I woke up here lying on an infirmary bed.'

The senior warder wasn't entirely convinced, although until medical tests revealed a cause, medical or otherwise her hands were tied and until such time Hesseltolph had to stay on the ward. Something however didn't feel right and Gillian Dennerholm knew it, she sensed it. Tierney was busy dealing with the police over the circumstances surrounding Judith Banks so she thought it best not to disturb him and mention Julianna. Grinning to herself she might just have found the opportunity to put a black mark on the inmates file, when the doctor confirmed that her seizure had been a sham.

'I'll leave you to rest for now Hesseltolph, but I'll be going through this masquerade today with a fine toothcomb and I promise you that I'll find something out of place, trust me I will.' She pointed her index finger at Julianna, 'and I want you back on the wing as soon as possible where I can see you, smell you and know what you're up too!'

Gillian Dennerholm turned to leave, but she felt something touch her left shoulder, she turned expecting to see a nurse having come in through the curtain, but there was nobody there. Overweight and cumbersome she was too slow to prevent the upward shuto chop that paralysed her vocal cord, causing irreparable damage to the cartilage surrounding the larynx. The senior warder's hands went immediately to her throat as she gasped for air needing to inflate her lungs, but Julianna was moving fast repeatedly punching aggressively both lungs. Within seconds Dennerholm's vision had blurred and her head began spin from the lack of oxygen and it felt like the sides of her head were caving in.

Removing the pillow and doubling the cotton case Julianna threw it over the warder's face, yanking back hard with her knee in the woman's spine she cut off the air flow to both nose and mouth. Without oxygen the muscles in Dennerholm's arms began to fail quickly as she tried desperately to get a hold on her attacker's wrists, but time and luck wasn't on her side. In less than a minute, perhaps less than two the senior warder fell across the end of the bed, dead.

Looking across at Margarita Henderson the old woman was smiling gleefully and clapping her bony hands together. There was nobody else about and Judith Banks wasn't about to talk or tell what just happened.

Dragging the heavy bulk to the washroom door nearest Julianna hauled the dead warder through to the toilet and shower block where she dumped Gillian Dennerholm unceremoniously across the top of an open lavatory pan.

'Quite apt for a piece of shit like you Dennerholm!' she said.

She locked the cubicle door from the inside then climbed over the partition wall taking the warders pass card with her. Waving her arms innocently from side to side in gentle sweeps Margarita Henderson was flying with the birds over the park much to the delight of the children playing nearby. Julianna smiled, Margarita was the perfect witness to the crime and she had succeeded in doing what a lot of others had only ever thought about doing.

Killing the loathsome woman, her bullying days had come to an abrupt end and even her lover would find the death a happy release from the overpowering relationship.

Unzipping the black body bag she dragged the dead Judith Banks across to her bed where she laid her on her side and pulled the bed covers high to indicate that she was sleeping. What was fortunate was that the deceased's hair colour matched that of Julianna's.

Not long after as Susan had said would happen the funeral attendants arrived. She felt them check the name tag on the body bag them pull her onto a metal gurney before closing the lid of the casket watched intently by the keen eyes of Margarita Henderson. As they wheeled the gurney from the side of the bed Margarita waved.

'I hope she enjoys her holiday!' The warder accompanying the gurney gave a shake of head in amusement.

'Don't mind her, Margarita lost what little she had left a long time ago. My guess it that the next time you came back will be to take her away.' All three gave Margarita a wave.

In the lift down the younger of the attendants shivered. 'This place always gives me the creeps. I hate it here.'

The older, more experienced man laughed. 'Consider yourself lucky you're not here permanently. Some that I know, like the old girl back up on the ward have been here for years.'

Inside the metal casket Julianna felt it shudder as it rolled over the casters inside the back of the van. She heard the men clip it into place to stop it moving about on the journey to the funeral home where the body was normally prepared in readiness for a family viewing before the funeral. If there were no relatives or funds available the local authority would pay for the bare minimum, a burial without a headstone, just a small wood plaque and a number.

With a loud bang they shut the rear doors and took their positions up front where the driver drove towards the exit gate. After checking the interior and signing the paperwork the guard raised the barrier and waved goodbye.

Susan Mycroft had been right, it just needed somebody with courage to swap places with the dead and in no time whatsoever you would be back out and free. Julianna clenched her hand together giving herself a victory fist, it had been that easy and into the bargain as she promised she would, she had dealt with the brutal Gillian Dennerholm too.

With the zip pulled through to the inside of the body bag Julianna slowly, but gently pulled it open knowing the inside of the casket would be as black. All around the traffic sounds were muffled although useful to disguise any sudden noise coming from the rear of the van. At one time she had to pinch her nose to stop herself from sneezing as the interior had a peculiar odour not just of death, but disinfectant. Carefully prising the lid of the casket open she checked to see that she wasn't overlooked by either the driver or the passenger, but the front to back was separated by a metal panel. The men up front were talking about women, football and the coming match that weekend.

She carefully replaced the lid and sat on top waiting for the van to arrive at its destination looking out through the rear windows which had been screened to prevent the public from peering in. Julianna grinned to herself, she was probably the only one in the back to have ever to have looked out. When the van slowed and came to a halt the underside noise changed from tarmac to shingle. The driver selected reverse and slowly manoeuvred back towards a set of black painted bay doors. Releasing the catch of the rear door she pushed it open and jumped free landing in a bed of soft bushes. When the passenger opened his door she rolled herself under a larger bush and out of sight.

Walking back to open the bay door the attendant noticed that of the van was open. He looked inside happy to see that they still had their passenger then slammed the door shut until they were inside. Normally they would have a cuppa before unloading.

When the roller shutter closed Julianna stood, brushed herself down and walked towards the end of the drive where across the road was a small parade of commercial offices, factories and workshops. The nearest was a mechanics garage where parked outside was a row of various vehicles either awaiting service or customer collection. She crossed the road and made her approach cautiously keeping an eye out for any mechanics or customers. Going between the vehicles she checked each driver's compartment for a key, knowing that back street garages were notorious for leaving the key in the ignition if the vehicle was due an MOT or service. Inside the garage the sound of a hammer hitting an obstinate brake pad could be heard over the sound of a radio as another mechanic whistled out of tune.

In the MOT bay she found an insecure car with the driver's window down and the key in the ignition. Over the seat had been placed a plastic cover to prevent oil from marring the fabric, Julianna didn't see an inspection sheet to suggest that it had been for its service.

Settling herself in the driver's seat she clipped the seatbelt into place, put the gear change into reverse, released the handbrake and fired up the engine, within seconds she was happily driving up the road and away from the garage. In the rear view mirror she saw two mechanics run out from the service bay, cursing loudly and gesticulating obscenities with their raised fists.

The same time that a young funeral attendant opened and unclipped the hasps keeping the casket in place. Pulling it back it felt extra light to when he'd pushed it in. Pushing aside the lid he swallowed the biscuit that he had been munching feeling the contents of his stomach curdle.

He ran frantically outside and looked around and up the drive, but there was no sign of the dead body that they had collected from Ashworth just an empty body bag, a casket and two angry mechanics swearing at something or somebody in the middle of the road.

'Charlie...' he yelled, '*I think you need to come here!*'

Chapter Seven

The ceaseless slow movement of a mechanical road sweeper outside brushing and washing away the dirt from the sidewalk woke Jakub from his sleep, not that it mattered as he'd slept soundly on the settee, his dreams interspersed with visions of his sister and their playing together as children. Stretching until his sinew could stretch no further he felt good and for once the voices had been absent. He filled the kettle and heaped a spoonful of coffee into a mug. The condo looked so different in the daylight, much more spacious and airy without the shadows. Adam Janko had done a good job adding his own identity style with comfort. Jakub wondered how much had been influenced by his last lover.

When the kettle boiled he made the coffee. Everything was so modern, state of the art with clean lines. It would have been easy to stay in the condo until somebody came calling for Adam, not that Jakub wasn't capable of dealing with the moment, but he had come to America for a reason. After Alexander Koskovsky and Albrecht Hartmann there was no going back to Austria so his future had to be made elsewhere. He could sail the seven seas with Bahari Lokman, but Jakub had a restless nature that could never be tamed.

Adding two cubes of natural sugar to the drink he went to have a shower. Letting the water run it was so different to that of the ship, soft and hot it felt good. At Ebenstatt showers were supervised by the nurses and on board they were taken en-mass with the other deckhands at the end of a gruelling shift. Jakub washed twice, enjoying Adam's choice of body wash. He decided not to shave keeping letting his stubble grow a little thicker would help his disguise.

Towelling himself dry he finished off with an all-over body splash leaving his hair tussled rather than comb it through. Half an hour later Jakub felt like a new man as he stood before the open wardrobe where the choice was plentiful. He chose a pale peach shirt to suit the sunshine and clean blue jeans. Taking a travelling bag from the bottom of the wardrobe he filled it with essentials that he thought he would need for the journey ahead.

He spent breakfast watching CNN which he found repetitive and had almost finished when a female called the apartment phone. Jakub let it ring until the ansa-phone kicked in. Her name was Stephanie and she was surprised that Adam hadn't picked up, but she left a message to say that he was not to forget their dat later that morning at the Cosmopolitan Art Gallery. She told him not to be late. Jakub was tempted to lift the receiver and say that she would have a very long wait, but doing so would have brought the police to the door. Throwing the rest of the coffee down the sink, he knew that the time had come to leave New York. His time spent in the city had been short, but time was always against him.

He methodically wiped down all the surfaces that he had touched, threw the wet towels in the laundry bag which he would take with him and dump elsewhere en-route. An hour later he shut the front door using his foot knowing that the police and forensic examiners would have a hard time establishing that he had ever been inside. If anything that they were more likely to question Carlos several doors down. In his back pocket he had Adams wallet, credit cards and an envelope of cash that he had found in the bedside drawer.

CNN would automatically report the mysterious disappearance of the free-lance writer from Chelsea, but other than his missing car, the police and a few neighbours would say that he was probably on a road trip with a new lover. It was only Stephanie who would keep badgering that they take his disappearance more seriously. And weeks later when his body would eventually be washed up and identified by DNA, the evidence would be so old that the detectives would be hard pressed to know where to begin.

With a pair of ray-burn sunglasses protecting his eyes and a black baseball cap with the insignia of the New York Yankees proudly emblazoned over the front peak Jakub looked like any other New Yorker as he walked to the Chrysler parked in the car lot. Sitting behind he took a few moments to familiarise himself with the automatic controls. Starting the engine, it seemed to purr like that of a contented cat and luckily Adam had faced the car forward when he had parked it last.

Selecting *drive* he released the brake, depressing the pedal lightly with his right foot. Jakub smiled to himself as the car moved forward, it was no different to controlling the dodgem cars at the fair with just a few more gadgets to use and master. After a few minutes he was getting the hang of handling the power and pull of the engine as he added a little more pressure to the accelerator. Picking up speed, slowing, braking, turning and enjoying the sunshine it felt good to be driving and nobody knew that he had never driven a car, only a tractor on a farm. He even acknowledged sun worshippers out walking their dogs as he drove past.

Opting to follow his instincts Jakub joined interstate ninety five heading south west, crossing the blue waters of the Delaware and Susquehanna rivers. He continued driving to the outskirts of Baltimore and Washington. Six hours later around four in the afternoon and a little shy of Richmond he arrived at a diner called the *Buffalo Horn*. It looked ideal with only half a dozen family cars parked out front. Locking the Chrysler he went inside where the air conditioning was a welcome change from the dry heat and constant sunshine. The waitress behind the counter smiled and told him to choose a stall where she would attend to his order in a few minutes. Her accent was friendly, her face untanned, but she had a nice smile. Jakub choose the booth nearest the exit, where he could make a quick exit if it became necessary.

He was reading down the menu when he sensed that he was being watched. Peering over the top of the menu card he spied a woman in her mid-thirties watching him. At first he thought that she looked like a large poodle, her hair was a shaggy mass of blonde ringlets hanging down to her shoulders, sporting a pair of round red framed tinted glasses and small scarf tied around her neck loosely. She saw him looking and smiled, seconds later she left her table and joined him.

'I saw you drive in and noticed that you're travelling by yourself.'

Jakub nodded, he wouldn't have been hard to spot as the Chrysler was the closet to the diner entrance.

'Are you going far?' she asked.

Up close he could see her eyes, they were soft although they seemed to flutter a lot. There was something about her manner that he found convivial.

'I've not decided yet,' he replied, 'I'm cruising down the east coast and heading to wherever the road takes me.' Adding to his already weather beaten tan the long drive in the sunshine had made his skin look much richer, a dark brown. He no longer looked Austrian, but Greek or perhaps Italian.

'That sounds exciting, like a real adventure. I have been doing much the same, only using my feet. It's fun, although it can have its awkward moments.'

He noticed that she kept looking out at the parking lot.

'Are you in some kind of trouble?'

'No, I'm keeping a look out for a particular trucker who thinks I should be paying for the privilege of a lift with my body.'

The waitress came over to take the order not in the least surprised to see that the woman diner had jumped tables and joined Jakub. Tanned and with his long hair he was dishy. She asked if they wanted to keep the tabs separate or keep it as one. Jakub told her that he would pick up the bill. They each ordered a double cheese burger with fries and crème coffee.

'That's really kind of you, but it's not why I came over to sit with you for a free late brunch.'

'Why did you come over?' Jakub asked.

'You have that kind of face which radiates friendliness and I thought you wouldn't mind the company. Plus you look like you could handle a trucker on a mission if he was to pull on to the car lot outside. Alone on the road some men think I'm an easy pick-up or a lesbian, either way they still want sex.'

Jakub laughed. 'So I'm a bodyguard now as well as company?'

'Sorry, I didn't know how else to say it.'

'Where did you start out?' he asked.

'Quebec, I live there. I planned to travel down the east coast before turning west landing at Vegas before Santa Monica and then up the coast to Canada. What about you, only you're not native American?'

'I'm Dutch,' he replied, 'originally from Eindhoven, but I got bored with Europe and the climate, and America is a lot warmer and so are the people.' Jakub was pleased that she wasn't from America. 'So what about you, what do you do when you're not getting picked up by sex crazy truckers?'

She grinned, she liked him and he was easy to talk to and not hung up with any preconceived ideas. 'I'm a criminal profiler, but at present I'm on a much needed gap year.'

If Jakub's eyes or expression showed any emotion she didn't let on. The only profiler that he had met had been Alexander Koskovsky. The psychiatrist had tried hard to uncover Jakub's secrets and catalogue them, but his subconscious thoughts went deeper than Koskovsky had ever come across before. Arriving with the brunch the waitress left the tab under Jakub's coffee mug.

'Shout if you want more coffee, it's free.' She went back to the counter leaving them to their meal.

'That has to be a demanding profession.' This time he was looking for a reaction.

She leant forward to explain. 'It is and fascinating delving into how a person ticks morning, noon and night, digging deep to uncover their innermost secrets, although between you and me I'm not always successful, and quite often the person I'm analysing, analysis's me.' It pleased Jakub to hear it.

'You must come across all sorts of people, mass murderers, serial rapists and child offenders. Doesn't that upset you?'

She picked up her burger and took a healthy bite from the side.

'It's one of the reasons why I took a gap year, call it a sort of purging of the soul, my soul.' She wiped the side of her mouth where the sauce had escaped the bun. 'Some colleagues say that I have an inbuilt radar for trouble, that I can sense a bad person. I failed bigtime with the trucker!'

Having added salad to his bun Jakub was hooked. 'And how does that work, the inbuilt radar?'

'Offenders appear normal to you and me, doing everyday things even holding down a responsible job, but outside of the boundaries, the complexity of their habits sets them apart from the normality levels. They crave the abnormal, setting challenges, a sort of testing ground by which they have to beat an imaginary opponent. Many say that voices in their head demand they push themselves to the limit of their endurance. I think this is what pushes them over the edge and they fight back. A sort of Jekyll and Hyde syndrome.'

Jakub was enjoying his late brunch, it was fascinating and so was she. He particularly liked the bit about the voices.

'And this persona does it have distinctive characteristics?'

She cut the bun half. 'That's the interesting bit. It could so easily be you or me. Ordinary people doing ordinary jobs or having fun, but when darkness falls or the moon is full, they don't howl and grow fangs, but a demon inside takes control. It is that which tells them to become the monster.'

'And the voices, what about them?'

She took another bite from her burger. Jakub wondered when she had last had a decent meal.

'Oh yes, the voices. Yes, they can be so controlling, so demanding of the individual. When I'm profiling, setting out my theory page I often feel an empathy for the offender as they cannot always resist the voices. They tell me that there are so many and always, they have divided opinions or objectives. No wonder so many are considered insane.' She looked at him as he sat watching her and listening to her explanation. 'Yes, I believe the voices are the most challenging factor.'

Jakub smiled. 'Like an express train full of loonies, only some getting off at the next station and others get on, so a person is never free of them. That's enough to drive anybody mad.'

She grinned adding more chips to her mouth and masticating them quickly.

'That's an excellent example. You have a real grasp of the subject, you're not in the profession are you?' she picked up more chips.

He gave a definite shake of his head. 'Who me…no, I am just interested in your theories.'

'A psychologist by any chance?'

'No, but I do know a very good one.'

She took a sip of coffee to help wash down the last mouthful.'

'Well you have a very good concept of what makes the mind tick.'

Jakub laughed. 'The human mind is such a complex anomaly. I have my own theory and that from the moment that we are conceived, the embryo has a brain however miniscule and as we develop so do our thoughts, our expectations of life. We are building, creating our foundation stone, like a bricklayer builds a wall using bricks, from inside the womb we hear sounds, we hear people talking, singing, arguing. All the time we are forming opinions on who we are going to be when we enter the world. Evil only comes later and can be the failings of others, not necessarily of our own doing.'

'Wow, that's an approach that I've never thought about.' She was clearly impressed as the waitress retuned with the coffee pot. Without asking she refilled their mugs.

'And you'd present a good argument for an offender.' She looked, studied and smiled. 'A defence lawyer then. Your theory has conjecture and reasonable doubt rolled together for good measure.'

Again Jakub shook his head.

'I am just an ordinary woodsman. I like trees and open spaces. I can't stand being shut inside where it's stuffy and daylight cannot penetrate. In the woods there are no restrictions. Offices, factories and prisons are much like the mind, confused and cluttered. In big open spaces my thoughts are free.'

Jakub didn't feel threatened sitting opposite as she sipped her coffee thoughtfully.

'I envy your freedom,' she replied, wiping the froth from her lips.

They sat in silence for a minute drinking, collecting their thoughts. She was the first to speak again only this time she held out her hand.

'It's a bit late, I'm sorry... but I am Elise Theroux. My grandparent's parents were originally from Avignon, in the South of France, but grand-pere wanted to expand his horizons, so together with grand-mere they went west by boat landing at Quebec. Both my parents were killed in a car crash when I was twelve so being with grand-pere and grand-mere was the obvious choice. I went to university and the rest as they say is history.'

Wiping his hands free of grease he shook hers.

'I am Johann Roebers and my parents are also dead.' He didn't give an explanation how and she didn't ask, instead he smiled and rank his coffee.

'I couldn't do what you do. You build a picture of somebody's character, you draw a line under a case and then move onto to the next. Do you never feel that one day all that you've been told, learnt and witnessed might come back to haunt you?'

Elise looked slightly perplexed.

'I try not to let them invade my private space that way I keep a safe distance between me and reality.'

'The fine line between reality and fantasy!' He remembered the conversation that he had with
Alexander Koskovsky in the one-on-one session.

Elise stopped sipping. 'Yes, exactly. Like walking through your wood and dreaming that there are fairies living there.'

Jakub didn't know about the fairies, but he knew about the trees. Strong and sturdy they could easily support the weight of a man, or boy.

He enjoyed the rapport giving a little and her coming back with snippets about her life, her work. Somewhere at the back of his head he heard a small voice telling him to ask more.

'After I leave here I'm heading south, is that any good for you?'

'Yes, that'd be great as long as I'm not interfering in any of your plans?'

'No, I'm sort of making them up as I drive and we can talk some more on the way!'

Elise felt the relief ease from the inside of her chest. Being with Johann would mean no further possible confrontations with the truck driver. Finishing her coffee she wasn't nearly as confident as what she made herself out to be whereas Johann appeared very competent and confident.

Jakub was glad of the company and missed the rapport that he had built with Bahari Lokman and having somebody to talk with would make the journey seem that much shorter. It would also work to his advantage travelling with a female as the police would be looking for a single man not a couple and if stopped she could show them her credentials with the Canadian police, that alone should quell any suspicion. He could produce Adam Janko's old driver's licence, issued before a photograph became a necessary addition. Any other documents he could say were stolen in a street robbery, there was always a way around a problem, without using violence.

'Thank you Johann you really are very kind.' She placed the crumpled napkin on the plate then stood up. 'I just need to use the bathroom and then I'm ready whenever you are.'

He watched her walk to the end of the food counter and turn from sight. Opposite sat her rucksack, he was tempted to look through it, find out more, but he resisted the urge. Instead he went to the till and paid the tab for their food and drinks. Becoming Johann Roebers was proving useful and for the meantime he was happy to be somebody else.

Chapter Eight

Julianna kept on driving until she reached the Liverpool ferry terminal where she abandoned the vehicle leaving it parked amongst dozens of others where in all probability it wouldn't be found for a week, maybe longer, time enough for her to be long gone.

Mingling with a group of excitable and vocally loud ladies from Warrington she manged to board the ferry that was bound for Dublin having dipped one of their travel bags, removed the purse from within and used the cash to pay for the fare. Regulations had not changed and a passport still wasn't required.

The missing purse initially caused a furore, but with the help of friends and the ferry company representatives the female passenger was promised a free afternoon tea and return ticket. Keeping close to wherever they went Julianna considered herself safe in a group rather than be alone. She even struck up a conversation with a timid looking member of the party to draw away any attention from herself establishing that they were on a three day excursion to relive old memories of when they had toured as a dance troupe in their younger days.

Living up to its name and reputation the Irish Sea was a formidable challenge with the bow going up and down having many on board scurrying to the washrooms where the crew were having a difficult time trying to keep conditions hygienic. Julianna only went once, but it was to find a long coat that would fit her. When she departed the ferry at number one terminal she also had on a staff uniform that she had found in an empty cabin. It was only slightly on the large size, but if anybody questioned why, she would reply telling them that she'd lost weight recently. Ignoring the whistles of the dock workers she made her way to the nearest hotel.

The Mermaid was not overly large, but ideally tucked down a side street where several shops ran conveniently adjacent to the entrance. Small and friendly was good and would serve the purpose of somewhere to stay where it was less likely that the hotel would attract any real attention unlike the bigger corporate accommodations. Taking a seat at the bar she ordered a sandwich and coffee. Julianna noticed that sat not too many tables away was a business woman of similar age and build. Unaware of anything going on around her the woman was tapping away furiously at a handheld iPad. After working for at least an hour, time enough for Julianna to eat and drink the woman closed the lid of the iPad and rushed across to catch the lift going up. Julianna did the same and just managed to slide her hand in before the door shut. Stepping into the lift car she smiled at the woman.

'That was close,' she said as the doors closed. 'What floor?'

'Fourth please.' She recognised the uniform. 'Do you have a stopover?' she asked.

Julianna gave a shrug of her shoulders.

'Yes, although it hardly seems worth it sometimes. Booking into a hotel I mean, only I have to be back up by four thirty and on the boat going back around seven thirty. Still it's only twice weekly.' Julianna smoothed the side of her hair watching the lower floors disappear. 'What about you?'

Smartly dressed in a business suit the woman held onto the extended handle of her small travel case. 'I have the luxury of a lie-in until seven, grab a quick breakfast then a conference that begins at nine. Three nights and four days here in Dublin. I didn't really want to come, but my new boss was insistent, giving me some old line about it helping promote my career.

'Is he here as well?'

'Yes, he went into town to find an ale house where they do draught Guinness. He's all for the real stuff, none of what comes out of a bottle or can.'

'Sounds boring. And what exactly do you do?'

The lift slowed, the floor number coming up red on the indicator board as they arrived at the fourth floor.

'I market and sell telecommunications space. Nothing glamourous like NASA, more the menial satellite dish coverage on a multi-usage receiver tower. I might get the odd trip out on a boat to see and view an oil-rig or other times a boring old church.'

Julianna feigned interest as the lift came to a halt. 'Sounds exciting, you must get about a lot?'

'Sometimes. I tend to carry my passport around with me in the hope that one day I'll be sent somewhere exotic or warm.' Outside it was raining.

'Somewhere further than Europe then, I hear the States is good!'

The young woman laughed. 'The furthest I've been so far is the Isle of Wight and now Dublin.'

The lift car came to a gentle halt and the instantly the doors opened. Pulling her travel case clear the woman from marketing and sale stepped out and onto the landing. 'Perhaps if you're around in the bar later we could have a drink together?'

Julianna accompanied her onto the landing and instantly the doors closed.

'It seems that we both have a room on the same floor. Yes, a drink would be nice. I normally need something to help me relax after a long day before I hit the sack.'

They walked down the corridor together until the younger woman stopped having arrived at her door. Confirming the time that they would both be downstairs in the bar they said goodbye. Julianna waited until the woman had inserted her entry card into the lock before she chopped the woman's neck from behind. Instantly her hand slipped away from the door handle and the case as she fell forward into the room. Removing the entry card and picking up the case Julianna went inside stepping over the unconscious woman before she grabbed both wrists and hauled her inside. The door closed automatically.

Stuffing a handkerchief into the woman's mouth she opened the case and removed a pair of stocking. She then undressed her removing the blouse and skirt before securing the ankles and wrists together, before lifting and placing her victim on the bed.

When she came too again Melanie Anne Smith could only recall feeling a sharp dull thud then the ground rushing up to meet her a split second before somebody switched off the lights. Her head felt fuzzy and her neck was like a ton weight on her shoulders. Oddly enough she was on the bed and looking across at the wardrobe at the side. When she tried to move her hands which were behind her back and then her legs, she found that both had been tied together and a gag was preventing her from speaking. Fear struck hard in her chest as she realised that she was being held captive. Somewhere inside her head she heard herself scream.

Having turned out the contents of the handbag Julianna went back over to the bed where she sat beside her captive. 'I'm sorry about this, this is a case of wrong place, right time…'

She gently stroked Melanie's face.

'I have a desire to be elsewhere and I need a passport. Mine was taken from me, but yours will do. It just needs a few alterations to the details.'

Melanie had stopped screaming, was listening now and wondering why she had been stripped down to her underwear. She followed her attacker around the room as she went through the rest of her case, checked her suit pockets and spread the contents of her handbag over the desktop.

'I have to go out for a short while, but I promise I'll be back very soon!'

To make sure that Melanie didn't roll off the bed or create a commotion that would attract the attention of other guests Julianna touched a nerve at the side of the neck and instantly Melanie co-operated by going to sleep. Making sure that her bonds were secure Julianna dressed and left the room.

Crossing the concourse at James Street Station she spun the seat of the photo booth to the required height and inserted five coins into the slot. Five minutes later the kiosk produced four images of sufficient quality for a passport. She visited one other shop on her way back to the hotel for some essentials items, before ordering an evening meal charging it to Melanie's room.

When the pressure in the room changed with the closing of the door Melanie opened her eyes once again. Like before her head felt groggy and heavy. She watched as the woman, wearing her clothes worked at the desk carefully making changes to the passport. Unstamped and never been used she would need another after the ordeal was over.

When it was done Julianna made the edges a little abrasive and creased the cover to make it looked well-travelled. It also helped that customs officers around the world couldn't be bothered to stamp an entry or exit. She took it over to show Melanie.

'Not my best creation, but it'll do.' Melanie wriggled on the bed feeling that her dignity had not only been invaded, but her identity too was under threat. After a few moments of struggle and realising that it was futile she stopped. Julianna stroked Melanie's hair. 'Who I am and where I'm heading is not your concern. What I will say is that I escaped Ashworth this morning. My guess is that you've heard of it. I have killed already today so another unfortunate mishap here would merely be an inconvenience in my schedule, however should you co-operate and promise to keep quiet, we can share the bed tonight and come the morning you'll still be alive.'

Melanie nodded and Julianna smiled.

'Look upon this episode in Dublin as a godsend only you won't have to attend that boring seminar in the morning and when the police tell the press how brave you were at the hands of a known killer, that promotion will soon be yours for the taking. Whereas I will be a nonentity and you'll be the celebrity. Who knows maybe the compensation you receive for the stress and torment will go towards buying a house or a new car. Just do as I say and we'll both come through this night happy!'

Again Melanie gave a nod of the head to indicate that she understood. With the passport in her hand Julianna checked her handiwork again.

'Now there's something that you've learnt today. Nitrocellulose dissolved in ethyl acetate, no more than your common clear nail varnish has excellent adhesive qualities. Ideal for those emergency moments where you've nothing else to hand and good for repairing a laddered stocking!'

She went over to the travel case sifting through the contents selecting the clothes that suited her taste, putting aside anything gaudy that might make her stand out. Clipping shut the case, she replaced everything back in the handbag. A cheap imitation leather bag with a fake known brand logo it looked the part, but up close anybody could tell that it wasn't the real deal. When the food arrived they shared it with Julianna threatening again that any unnecessary noise would result in instant death. Julianna allowed her to use her hands, but kept her ankles tied just in case.

When it was time for bed she surprised her captive by untying everything. 'You should use the bathroom before we sleep.'

When she reappeared she went back to the bed knowing that she would never make it in time to door before the woman attacked from behind. She watched as Julianna stripped naked seeing the scars that criss-crossed her body. Slipping in between the sheets Julianna surprised

Melanie by cuddling her, the feel of a soft mattress after Ashworth a luxury.

'I leave the bonds off if you promise not to try and escape. I warn you that I'm an incredibly light sleeper, and if you move I'll know about.'

'I won't run, I promise!'

Julianna switched off the light and undone the clasp keeping Melanie's bra is place. She lay beside the younger woman stroking the contours of her body. It had been a long time since she had felt the soft skin of another human without the threat of violence or injury. Letting her fingers do the walking. Julianna whispered softly to Melanie.

'Do you remember the serial killer that had the whole country in the grip of fear back in nineteen ninety seven before he mysteriously disappeared. He went by the name of Jason Chancery.'

Melanie said that she remembered.

'That's good, only my guess is that you wouldn't have thought that we were lovers. To pass the time together we would devise different games, erotic games to see which of us would surrender first. Some involved using a knife.'

She felt Melanie tense so she put her hand over her captive's breast.

'Relax I didn't bring a knife to bed, I can kill without using one. I saw you looking and wanted you to know how I got some the scars. The rest my brother gave me.'

The more Julianna touched, caressed and explored the more relaxed it made Melanie feel and soon she started to do the same. If that's what it took to stay alive she would do anything, but never again though would she invite a stranger for a drink. Outside the rain had stopped, the moon was full again and the stars were plentiful.

Chapter Nine

The night had been better than either had expected and both experienced a pleasure that neither knew existed. When Julianna had tied Melanie to the bed like Jakub had done on a number of occasions, the young saleswoman had surprised Julianna by responding eagerly. When they did fall asleep it was through exhaustion and together.

Just after seven somebody walking past the room woke Julianna. Several men followed the first on their way down to breakfast. Lying beside her and still resting peacefully Melanie Smith looked almost angelic. If she could Julianna would shower, dress and slip away unnoticed, but she needed time to get away to flee Dublin. An hour, two at the most just wasn't enough time.

Reaching down the side of the bed she retrieved the stockings and it wasn't until she tied the second wrist to the bed post that Melanie stirred from her slumber. She licked her lips and opened her eyes. She was surprised to see her hands had been bound again. Naked and helpless, Julianna came back to the bed kissed Melanie in the lips then her nipples.

'Ummm I'm going to miss you,' she said.

The compliment made Melanie smile. She felt different, not used like when she'd been with men, but like she was an equal. Other than the times at school when she had watched girls shower or change after a games lesson she had not seen another woman naked, let alone be close or touch one intimately. She liked it, liked what they had done. Julianna kissed her again only this time it was a long, lingering kiss.

'I'm going to take a shower. Remember no attracting anybody's attention. We had us a deal.'

'I promise…' Melanie looked at her wrists which were tied secure. 'I won't run!'

Julianna smiled as her hands swept down over Melanie's breasts then down to her navel before reaching the nether regions.

'I know, but this way we end the encounter without any upset.'

Melanie smiled, she understood the alternative.

Fifteen minutes later Julianna came back out from the bathroom her body cleansed and draped in a towel, her hair wet. Melanie's eyes never left her body as she walked from one side of the room to the other. During their love-making she had touched, traced the scars, the abrasions, gently kissing each line showing that she wasn't repulsed. She didn't know it, but her feelings of men had changed too.

'When you leave, please pull the cover up. I promise that I won't scream not until you want me too. At some time after eleven the maid will come to make the bed and clean the room. Then I can scream.'

Julianna sat back down running her fingernail down between Melanie's breasts. 'What are you saying?'

Melanie was more confident. Unafraid.

'Last night I was scared, yesterday terrified, but I liked what we did together. 'I've never done anything like that before. It felt different and made me feel good, kinda like natural. I would give you time to get away.'

Gently caressing the neatly trimmed tuft of pubic hair Julianna saw an image appearing before her, a vision where Gillian Dennerholm was forcibly holding down Sammie Saunders, the younger and less experienced woman trying hard to resist the brutal advances of the senior warder. She saw Saunders smile when she'd heard the news that Gillian Dennerholm had been found murdered.

Looking at Melanie she wondered how long it really would be before she did scream. Five minutes, the time that it took for her to reach the lift or down to reception, ten minutes perhaps as she was walking down the road or an hour waiting at the airport. Julianna was wary of Melanie's growing confidence.

'And you would just let me walk away from the hotel with your passport, your clothes, the designer handbag, all your personal belongings, purporting to be you and all the time you were here tied to the bed you wouldn't bounce on the bed and attract somebody's attention. You do realise that the police will hold you for questioning for hours and that when they establish that it was me holding you captive, you'll be relentlessly grilled until they're satisfied that you were an innocent victim and not complicit in my escape. You would do that for me?' Julianna looked directly into Melanie's eyes, searching for a sign of weakness, but there was none.

'I would be tied to the bed. I could hardly have done that myself.'

'I would have to replace the gag again to make it really convincing.'

Julianna had a thought. She stroked the side of Melanie's face.

'When I was a good, safe distance away, I could ring the hotel. That way they would find you.'

Melanie liked Julianna touching her, it made her feel good.

'Yes, that would work. The hotel wouldn't be able to trace the call, you could be anywhere. By the time the police arrive you'll be long gone.' She suddenly looked pensive. 'Will we ever get the chance to see one another again?'

'Perhaps.' Julianna examined the marks on Melanie's neck where she had chopped her the day before rendering her unconscious. 'The bruise will show the police that I hurt you, that'll add weight to your story. I'm sorry, but it had to be done.'

Melanie smiled. 'I know, it doesn't hurt anymore and the bruising will fade soon. Nobody will notice because of my long hair.'

Stroking the long hair Julianna had also been excited having been touched by Melanie and their time together had unlocked emotions that she didn't know existed. She also found the naked female form exciting too. She was tempted to untie the bonds and spend the morning with Melanie, hoping that there would be a later flight, but come nine, very soon she would have people knocking on the door asking why she wasn't at the conference. Julianna always felt that there was an annoying obstacle in the way of her happiness.

'Okay, that's how we play it then,' she said looked at the clock, 'on one condition.'

'Anything.' Melanie responded.

Julianna dropped the towel and released the bonds tying Melanie's wrists to the bedhead. 'You do what you did to me last night and then we take a quick shower together.'

They stepped out of the shower just shy of eight twenty. Melanie dried herself and lay back on the bed, but not before she had slipped into her underwear. It made Julianna smile. Melanie even opened her mouth to accept the gag, but not before asking for a last kiss and making her request.

'Please, not as tight as before, it hurt.'

They kissed then Julianna did what was necessary. Dressing and checking herself in the mirror. She breathed out long and hard. For the first time throughout the night she hadn't thought about Jakub. Inside she was a knot of emotions, guilt and shame, excitement and joy. All of which was confusing. In the mirror she looked at Melanie Anne Smith.

Compliant with the situation Melanie was staring up at the ceiling. Julianna stood watching as she made a minor adjustment to her skirt wondering about the thoughts that were going through Melanie's mind. Could she be trusted, was she genuine, she wondered and would she do as they had agreed or was it just a ruse to stay alive, Julianna didn't know. For all her expertise, the confidence and all the sessions that she had conducted with paying clients as a clinical psychologist, she was now in two minds as to what to believe.

Going back over to the bed she kissed Melanie's forehead then placed the pillow over her face and leant down. After a minute, maybe longer the thrashing stopped and the chest stopped rising then falling. She left the pillow in place not wanting to see the shocked and terrified expression in her lover's eyes.

Extending the handle of the travel case, she picked up the imitation designer handbag, made sure that she had the passport, before taking one last look back at the bed. She deeply regretted having killed Melanie.

'I am really sorry my darling,' she whispered softly, 'If it had been up to me, I would have left you safe and alive, but Jason once told me never to leave loose ends.'

Chapter Ten

The freeway was much busier than Jakub had expected it to be around tea time with commuters travelling home from offices, shops, warehouses and production lines. The breeze coming in through the open windows was westerly, although very welcome. Taking a quick glance sideways he noticed that it made Elise Theroux's hair fly back. She looked relaxed and for once he felt the same.

Nestled comfortably in the seat beside his Elise felt safe and she was enjoying the ride, soaking up the late afternoon sunshine. There wasn't a cloud in the sky.

'Isn't this amazing,' she remarked breathing in deep making her chest rise. Jakub liked that too.

'America never ceases to amaze me,' he replied.

She pulled her knees up to her chest.

'The land of opportunity and money, pro football and long sandy beaches!'

They all sounded good although he'd only caught a glimpse of the football that morning on the news channel. Jakub concentrated on keeping to his lane letting the faster motorists speed on by. Elise especially liked that he was in no particular rush to be anywhere soon. The last couple of years in the department had been tough and getting the recognition that she deserved much harder. Stepping into a predominantly male orientated field of expertise she accepted was never going to be easy, but more and more females were filling the course seats at university each year so pretty soon the numbers would equate the balance.

Having taken stock of her emotions, professional and private she also accepted that it had been the right time to take back some time owing. Caseloads, the offenders and even friends had become too intense. Liking the breeze blowing through her hair she remembered the lecturers warning the students in the class not to let the intensity get to them.

Still able to visualise her last case in her mind, she had somewhat failed, but there was some evil in the world that you just couldn't shake off. Lying each night awake she had sensed, felt the killer albeit he was behind bars probing deep inside her, seeking out her innermost thoughts, secrets that only she knew. Elise realised that she was one step away from a psychological breakdown or indeed madness. Here now though, beside Johann with the sunshine beating down on her face she felt safe.

Closing her eyes she exhaled long and silent drawing a line under good and evil, determined that she wouldn't be sucked in again.

Of course the recent breakup with Oscar from Internal Affairs had been another emotional drain that she was happy to be leaving behind. Six years ago the affair had started out as exciting with each day different and the evenings magical. She would listen for the sound of his footsteps as they took risks, stolen moments under the scrutiny of colleagues, sending out and receiving text messages until one day they stopped, ceased to happen. As were the knocks late at night on the door, the rose on her pillow and the surprise weekends away. Seasons changed and so had Oscar. What hurt the most wasn't the void created by his absence, but that she had to be told by another colleague that Oscar had been unfaithful to her for the past six months. Johann was the first man that she'd approached in all that time.

Johann wasn't much of a conversationist as he drove, but Elise wasn't complaining, she liked the way that he took things steady, his driving and approach to life. When the traffic had left the freeway at the last junction the countryside had turned a deep green and yellow where crops were ripe and ready for harvesting. Five miles down the road he gently tapped her shoulder bringing her fascination from the window back to him. 'Are you okay?'

'Yes, I'm fine, just admiring the view. There are times when it's so nice, just watching and forgetting your thoughts!'

'And people.'

She turned again to look, his perception was incredible.

'People can be as fickle as autumn leaves when the chlorophyll breaks down and they have no choice, but to fall from grace. There's very little loyalty about these days.'

'You sound disillusioned.'

'Not entirely, but I admit to running away to find myself again.'

She breathed in the warm air filling her lungs, it felt good and helped wash away any bad memories.

'That and run away from the faces of the offenders that haunt my dreams.'

Jakub glanced back in the rear view mirror.

'Sometimes Elise we all need saving from a dark place and if anybody ever claims that they have never been in one, then they're a liar.'

Elise found being with and talking to Johann easy. He was quiet, profound in what he had to say. It made sense.

'Have you any brothers or sisters?'

Jakub checked both door mirrors for signs of a highway patrol, but behind was clear.

'One, a sister. She's currently in England, although we're due to meet up soon.'

'That's nice.' Elise didn't ask when only it might cut short her own plans.

'I've not seen her for a while, but we're close, very close!' How he had said and emphasised close, sounded like they had a sibling love to be unrivalled.

'I would have liked a brother or sister, or both, but my parents were career minded, so I lost out.'

Jakub checked the rear view mirror again. A double wheelbase Winnebago had come over the hill behind and was gaining fast. Elise was watching a horse stand under a tree eating the grass. Jakub had no idea what was going to come of their being together, but it would have to end abruptly when he met up with Julianna. For the present however there was no harm in telling Elise more.

'My sister is a clinical psychologist. I guess a similar field of expertise to you, only she sorts the mental issues where you pick through the jigsaw and make the puzzle fit the crime.'

'That's a good way of looking at it although often or not it's the detectives on the case who build the evidence and present a case, but one or two, mainly the young eager type, keen to impress hold back. They leave out a piece here and there to see how good I am at my job. I think it's because I'm a woman.'

With a toot of the horn the Winnebago went sailing on by. The driver waved and thanked Jakub although he wasn't quite sure why. When Elise touched his forearm he turned quickly.

'Are you alright,' she asked, 'only you looked as though you were miles away as the camper went past?'

'Yeah, I'm fine. I was just thinking about what you said regarding hiding evidence. I knew somebody that did that a long time ago. The accusations against a person I once knew stacked up and all because the authorities didn't review all the evidence.'

'What happened to him, the person you knew?'

'They robbed him of his youth.'

He realised that she might probe a little deeper so he changed the subject.

'What about you. Didn't you ever want to get married, have children?'

She held up her ring finger which had not been bleached by a ring, engagement or other.

'Maybe one day, only not yet.'

'I thought as much. I watched as you went to use the bathroom back at the diner.'

She laughed. 'And how exactly would going to a diner bathroom indicate that I didn't have children?'

'Because women who have had children don't wiggle like you do!'

She laughed again.

'Not all women that give birth, lose control or the power of their hips, thighs or stomach.' She didn't mind that he'd looked.

'Call it a man thing,' he said checking the fuel gauge, 'you have a nice figure!'

Concentrating on the road ahead he saw a vision appear in his mind of when Julianna had walked naked into his room with their parents sleeping along the landing. Tall and slim, her hips wiggled seductively as she walked towards him. Elise had done and looked the same visiting the bathroom.

'Thank you, it does a girl good to get a nice compliment every so often.'

Oscar had said nice things like that once. She felt foolish and should have known that something was wrong, should have noticed the signs when the sex had been less and less, the touching remote and his sleeping over on the couch instead of the bed giving the poor excuse that he had a really early start and didn't want to disturb her. She ran her hands down her bare legs, smooth and tanned they had shape. When the colleague had let the cat out of the bag and amongst the pigeons the news had punched her hard in the stomach. She could still feel the bruising.

'Now who's miles away?'

She smiled. Fuck Oscar she was having a good time with Johann.

'Just letting the breeze blow away the cobwebs. You know I wouldn't want to get in the way when you meet up with your sister. You can drop me anywhere that's convenient Johann, the next town if needs be.'

Looking ahead the Winnebago had disappeared from sight. Jakub pushed his foot down a little and increased the speed.

'That's not a problem.'

He knew it wasn't and whatever the outcome, he would cross that bridge as and when the time arrived. Turning the driver's wheel with the natural flow of the bend they suddenly had the sun on their faces, the sudden burst of energy passing through them like the rays on a scanner machine.

'We should really think about finding somewhere to stay for the night and I don't know about you, but I'm getting hungry and very thirsty.'

It wasn't meant to sound like he was asking Elise to share his bed for the night, but merely that they needed to be on the lookout for a motel and diner nearby. Checking the map that Elise had in her rucksack she found both on the grid ahead.

'We just passed a place called Langley. The next main town is Wilson.'

'That'll do. I could do with a cold beer!'

Nine kilometres shy of ten exited the freeway pulling onto the entrance of Hollyoaks Motel, set down a short way past a small shopping mall. Adjacent to the motel was Hogan's Bar and Steakhouse.

Booking in with reception Elise filled in the registration book and paid for the single room.

'We save money this way Johann and it'll make me feel a heap better for lunch and the fuel that you've put into the car. I am really grateful.'

Jakub didn't put up a fight and watching Elise wiggle to the chalet he was glad that she'd made the decision and not him.

They took a table in the steakhouse where they were close by the flame grill and bar. They started the evening ordering two cool beers. Running his fingers down the steak menu the voices in his head told Jakub that Julianna was already on her way. Elise caught him smiling.

'You look happy.'

Jakub was still smiling when he replied.

'I am thanks, very happy.' He put down his menu. 'It's good here. Have you decided on what size steak you're going to have, I like mine medium rare.'

Chapter Eleven

Ashton Tierney, walked briskly down the centre of the infirmary feeling the weight of responsibility resting firmly on his shoulders. First the death of Judith Banks and now Gillian Dennerholm. He smiled and waved at Margarita Henderson. Ordinarily he would engage her in conversation and talk about the games they could play in the garden, but today he had other things on his mind, more pressing worrying things.

Margarita followed him with her eyes as he passed through the bathroom door and disappeared. Since the men had come to collect that dead woman there had been a flurry of visitors back and forth. Straining hard she just make out people talking in the bathroom, but without her hearing aids in they sounded like birds singing.

A member of the medical team held open the cubicle door so that Tierney could see inside. Slumped ungraciously over the pan Gillian Dennerholm looked positively uninviting, her huge rear like that of a bullock. Tierney didn't feel it necessary to go any further forward to have a close look.

'And where's Judith Banks?' he asked, adding a sigh.

'On the bed opposite Margarita.'

Tierney needed a cigarette to help calm his anxiety. There would be an official enquiry and again the police would be involved, inevitably so would the press. The events kept going around and around in his head, a dead warder, an escaped prisoner and another inmate the result of a suicide, it was turning out to be a bad day, a really bad day.

The enquiry and police investigation he could handle and he'd been in charge long enough to know that a secure establishment such as Ashworth might arouse public suspicion and controversy, especially from the majority who knew or didn't want to know what went on inside, day or night, but the media was a different ball game. Bloodsucking leeches he called the reporters, they were the real enemy. Turning over and over every scrap of gossip, they would hound, follow and speak with staff when they were off duty, giving assurances that anything said would remain anonymous.

He looked at the dead senior warder, the press would have a field day when they flipped over the stone and uncovered the affair between Dennerholm and Sammie Saunders. Worse to come was when somebody within Ashworth let leak that the missing inmate was Julianna Hesseltolph.

Reporters and Editors would instantly link the disappearance of her brother together with that of his sister. Making national headlines the pair would sell papers, be broadcast every hour on TV and radio, and when it went down the wire to press offices around the world, his phone would never stop ringing. Tierney massaged the pressure points of his temples with one hand feeling a headache developing. He was still rubbing his forehead when Andrew Templeton, the head of medical services arrived. He took a look inside the toilet cubicle.

Clearing the bathroom of all unnecessary personnel Tierney and Templeton stood alone.

'This place never gets any easier Ashton,' said the doctor as he held open the cubicle door. 'Although I can't say that I'm surprised. Gillian Dennerholm was a nasty piece of work, worse in some areas than the inmates under your charge!'

Tierney shook his head. 'I know, only it wouldn't be half as bad if it wasn't Julianna Hesseltolph who killed her. Any other inmate and the press would very quickly lose interest overnight, but this... this won't go away for days, weeks. Do we know why the medical staff on the ward?'

Conscious that governor might be looking for a scapegoat Templeton was quick to defend his team.

'I asked before coming to see you. Hesseltolph had been checked ten minutes before Dennerholm arrived on the ward. She was sleeping soundly so they left her to it. It must have been Dennerholm who woke her. I'd be pissed waking up to find that damn woman at the side of my bed!'

Tierney raised his eyebrows. He knew Templeton had been at an inquest at the time. He'd going to another soon.

'At least now Saunders can rest easy at night.'

Templeton nodded agreeing.

'Dennerholm had also told the members of my team that she wanted a quiet word with Hesseltolph alone. They were only complying with her wishes Ashton, my staff aren't to blame in this sorry affair.'

Tierney raised his hands placating the moment and that he understood. 'I know Andrew, I'm sorry it's been a bad day so far.'

Templeton made a cursory check of Gillian Dennerholm, but comprehensively a post mortem would say how she had died. He saw the bruising on her neck and the burst blood vessels in her eyes.

'I'd say she was disabled with a punch or chop to the throat then suffocated.'

Ashton Tierney went to the door of the bathroom where he looked across at Margarita Henderson.

'I don't suppose by the remotest of chances that old Margarita is lucid enough to answer any of my questions or hint at what took place here?'

'Not unless you want to be a garden gnome in her fantasy for the next couple of hours and sit on the toadstool alongside Margarita. She is way beyond any risk level here Ashton. Really she should be seeing out the rest of her day's in a care home not Ashworth.'

'And she still need the nurse to help get her out of bed?'

Templeton was ahead of Tierney's thoughts, consciously knowing where he was going with the question. 'You can't be serious Ashton. Margarita can just about lift a tea cup to her lips let alone kill a woman of Dennerholm's size and then drag her through to the bathroom before dumping her over the pan.'

Tierney shrugged his shoulders.

'I have to review all possibilities Andrew before I'm interviewed by the police. It might be easier too, for us both if we said that Julianna Hesseltolph's escape was a mere coincidence.'

'And Dennerholm, what she drowned committing suicide in my toilet block?'

'No. As you've just said, Margarita isn't dangerous, unpredictable yes. Not noticing that Margarita had spilt her drink on the ward floor Dennerholm approached, she slipped, caught the underside of her neck accidentally on the bed safety bar and struggling for breath she died as a result of starvation of oxygen.'

It was wild though probable, but Andrew Templeton saw a flaw in the explanation.

'And how did Dennerholm get to the bathroom from the bed.'

Tierney had been expecting the question.

'Anybody gasping for breath would stumble about and I'd assume somewhat disorientated as the brain began shutting down starved of oxygen. The cubicle isn't that far away from Margarita's bed.'

Templeton walked over to the doorway to look across at Margarita.

'Make the arrangements for her release to an old people's home where she'd be amongst men and women her age, where she can see out the rest of her day's in comfort and peace, and I'll agree to your proposal. I would also like to protect Sammie Saunders, she's young and has her whole life ahead of head. As for Dennerholm I don't really give a flying fuck about her reputation!'

Sticking his head through the curtain to see the sleeping corpse of Judith Banks, Andrew Templeton went bank to the nurse's office to talk with his team leaving Ashton Tierney to take photographs that would be necessary for the hospital files. Exiting the bathroom his told Margarita to smile as he took her picture.

'Did they play nicely together?' she asked.

'Yes, they did and like the nursery rhyme Humpty Dumpty had a great fall and broke her crown, and all the king's horses and all the King's men couldn't put poor Humpty together again.'

Clapping her hands joyfully together Margarita was happy that it all ended well.

Sitting on her bed Ashton Tierney patted the back of Margarita's hands.

'Would you like to go on a long holiday with lots of ladies your own age?'

'Can Popsie come too?'

Tierney had been told about her imaginary mate which was a rabbit.

'Of course Popsie can go!'

His pager beeped to inform him that the detectives had arrived and that they were waiting in his office. Tierney had already spoken with the Detective Chief Inspector of the division covering the hospital about the escape of Julianna Hesseltolph. It was double embarrassing having to phone again about the unfortunate demise of Gillian Dennerholm.

Ten minutes later Ashton Tierney opened the door of the toilet cubicle once again. The policemen looked in, but touched nothing.

'It was my impression that Julianna Hesseltolph had been ordered by the court to be held indefinitely because of her links with Jason Chancery.'

'Yes that's right.' Replied Tierney.

'Did she befriend anybody in particular at Ashworth?'

'No, not really she kept herself to herself most of the time, unless she attended for meals. Why do you ask?'

'I was looking for an accomplice who might have helped with her escape.'

Tierney gave his answers keeping them brief and with the minimum of information, believing that the police would draw their own conclusions. James Bates, Detective Chief Inspector was an old hand and knew all the angles. He paced back and forth sizing up the distance from the bed occupied by Margarita to the toilet cubicle.

'And the theory is that she slipped onto the bed bars crushing her wind-pipe then staggered about coming to rest in the cubicle collapsing over the toilet pan.' He looked at Tierney his eyes never blinking.

'That is the opinion of Doctor Templeton and myself, yes. As you can tell Gillian Dennerholm didn't keep in good physical shape. A month back we'd had a discussion in my office regarding her health.' It was indisputable although with no witness to say different it made the tragic accident more plausible. Bates was sceptical, but had to admit that the injuries were consistent with a crushed windpipe.

'And the only witness other than Hesseltolph was the old woman?'

'Margarita yes, although she's hardly what I would call a reliable witness.'

Bates wanted to judge that for himself. Standing bedside the bed he smiled at the elderly inmate. He introduced himself, although he might as well have said that he was Peter Pan for the notice that Margarita took of his title.

'Did you see the Senior Warder, Gillian Henderson fall against the bed side?' he asked.

Margarita liked visitors and the nice policeman had brought with him a Detective Sergeant a much younger man, and that nice Doctor Templeton whom she really liked, he was coming up the ward to be at her side.

'It was Humpty Dumpty,' she replied, 'she had a great big fall and bashed her head badly and the horses couldn't help!'

Standing behind Bates, the Sergeant put his hand up to his mouth so that nobody noticed his grin.

'Alright, thank you Margarita.'

He asked to see the body of Judith Banks then suggested to Tierney that they went back to his office. With the assistance of Andrew Templeton, Bates and the Sergeant examined the ligature marks around the deceased's neck which were consistent with a suffocation. When they left the bedside drawing together the curtain again Margarita waved.

'I'm going away on my holidays soon, you can come too if you want. Popsie's coming!'

Bates smiled.

'I'm satisfied for the meantime that Gillian Dennerholm's death was an unfortunate accident and that Hesseltolph used the opportunity to escape by swapping places with the dead Judith Banks. She certainly had some pluck. Did you know that her brother escaped from an Austrian sanatorium several days back, quite a coincidence, I'd say wouldn't you?'

Ashton Tierney told Bates about the postcard that Julianna had received, he lead the way back to the office where they had coffee and produced the photocopy.

'And you let her have it?' Bates asked adding sugar.

'Yes, staff had noticed that Julianna Hesseltolph had seemed a bit low lately. I discussed the matter with Gillian Dennerholm only this morning and she thought it would give the inmate a boost.' In one easy explanation Tierney had shelved the blame elsewhere once again.

Bates and the Sergeant examined the photocopy.

'Where's the original?'

'She must have taken it with her. Her cell's been checked and it is definitely not there.'

Bates nodded. 'She's going to meet her brother!'

'The postcard mentioned a place *winter haven*, could that be a pleasure resort, a holiday camp perhaps?'

Bates read it once again.

'We'll check it out. Did you hear through official sources that Jakub Hesseltolph killed the Psychiatrist at Ebenstatt and then a short time after that the village policeman in Kurlor went missing?'

'Do you mean dead?' Tierney asked.

'That would be my assumption. And from the information that I've read about Jakub Hesseltolph he doesn't take prisoners.'

Bates kept looking at the photocopy letting the sergeant take over the questioning.

'Word is that Gillian Dennerholm and Hesseltolph didn't see eye to eye?'

Ashton Tierney sat behind his desk as he made a spire bringing the tips of his fingers together, carefully contemplating his reply.

'They clashed at times, although in an establishment such as this there is always going to be an underbelly of tension gentlemen.'

Simon Travis pushed harder.

'Their coming together, could it have been a physical encounter?'

Tierney felt the small hairs on the back of his neck stand up.

'Are you suggesting that my staff would attack an inmate?'

'No, I'm merely asking if Julianna Hesseltolph had ever threatened Gillian Dennerholm.'

Bates observed. Tierney wasn't comfortable with the question.

'There are some events, incidents which take place sergeant without my knowledge. My staff are highly trained, patient individuals. They are selected for their integrity and how they can cope under stressful situations. Ashworth can be either a place of peace or a volatile jungle. It depends upon who we have here at the time, as a guest!'

'Somebody like Julianna Hesseltolph,' interjected Bates, 'I'd guess she would throw an injured rabbit to the wolves, then simply turn and walk away.'

'Yes, quite possibly. I thought we'd established that Gillian Dennerholm's death was merely an unfortunate accident, quite unusual, but such things happen.'

Bates nod was non-committal.

'And Judith Banks, do you think it was suicide or was she coerced.' Asked the sergeant.

'Not by my staff, definitely not!' Tierney replied vehemently.

Bates grinned, they were successfully putting Tierney in a corner and the governor, ruffled was coming out fighting.

Bates responded. 'I think my colleague was suggesting by another inmate not the warders.' They watched Tierney's shoulders relax.

'Hesseltolph was in the library at the time that Judith Banks took her life. Guilt playing a big part in the final moments I shouldn't wonder. Banks killed her mother!'

'Yes, we know,' replied Bates.

'I take it that airports, railway stations and ports have all been alerted?' asked Tierney wanting to divert the attention away from Ashworth.

'They've all been notified and as we were driving out of the back yard our Chief Constable was having a conversation with the Home Office. An official explanation will be given to the press later.' Bates took great delight in watching Tierney fidget in his chair.

'And the authorities in Melbourne will be contacted as well?'

'Yes, although it will take Julianna Hesseltolph some time to arrive there and even if she took a plane via Singapore, it'd still take a day, almost two. Going via Sri Lanka almost three. I shouldn't wonder that Australia is sick of our criminals, they have enough of their own!'

The two policemen left leaving Ashton Tierney to sort out his own reports. Standing outside the main gates they stood behind the Sergeants car looking back.

Bates scoffed. 'Tierney's like a rabbit caught in headlights, he's hiding something!'

Travis nodded in agreement. 'He's definitely protecting somebody on the inside, an inmate or member of staff, he'll sing if we lean on him a little harder.'

'I bet if he went to church on a Sunday he would tell others in the congregation that he was an atheist. When we get back to division have

Tierney's office fax across a list of all the staff on duty today Simon. We'll start running through background checks. I've a sneaky feeling that sooner or later something will leap out at us.'

He looked up at the first floor where the administrative offices were located and saw Tierney looking back down.

'I read Julianna Hesseltolph's file and she's one very clever woman. A qualified clinical psychologist she's not easily provoked or given to sudden fits of violence or rage. Whereas Gillian Dennerholm was a big woman, strong and more than capable of looking after herself. Something here at Ashworth doesn't ring true!'

They walked around the sides of the car and got in.

'Right Simon, let's go only there's a DCI Baines that I want to call.'

Chapter Twelve

Carving a way through the crowd of reporters that were waiting eagerly by the back entrance to the divisional station James Bates held his hand up to shield the left side of his face at the annoyance of the cameramen.

'After all these years in the job I've never understood how these bastards get to know what's going on before we do!'

Simon Travis parked the car as close to the rear doors as possible. 'As much I hate to say it, I reckon somebody here tips them off!'

Bates looked back at the press by the entrance. 'You could well be right. However much we paid our constables they'd always be the unscrupulous bastard on the take.' He remembered when he'd started and walked the beat, today's wage structure was more liveable and most had their own houses.

'I was actually thinking a bit higher up the building than the locker room.'

Bates laughed. 'You mean two pips and above.'

Travis switched off the engine and removed the key. 'There's plenty in the Masons that outrank our structure here. Favours are owed in all walks of life.'

Bates scoffed. 'You're probably right. I have to work bloody hard to climb the ladder of promotion.' He looked up at the top floor. 'There's some up there that have forgotten what it's like to fight crime. The hardest crime they solve is missing the hole on the seventeenth green.' He put his hand on the door handle. 'Come on, we won't solve what went down at Ashworth sitting here. I'll call Baines if you give Ashton's secretary a ring, that'll rattle his cage.'

Travis made sure that the car was locked and followed Bates inside. He liked working with the chief inspector, a no-nonsense detective he had solved a good many interesting and intricate cases in his time. Respected and admired throughout the force, the waiting list was long who wanted to be on his team. And like all in the current tea, Simon Travis had read the intelligence on the case known as the 'triangle with two sides'. Julianna and Jakub Hesseltolph were two and the missing Jason Chancery the third. Until recently brother and sister had been where the public were safe, but now they were both on the run. As for Chancery there had been no sightings in years. But Travis knew that psychopaths didn't just disappear. He was either dead or would surface at some time and start up again, the thirst to kill a habit that they could never kick. .

He charmed Ashton's secretary into faxing over the staff list and waited beside the facsimile machine for it to arrive. Not to waste any time he punched into the computer the details of the photocopy that he had taken from the top of Ashton's desk when the governor had been distracted by Bates. Travis watched the search engine number climb and reach nine hundred and eighty three million results. When it stopped searching - *'Climate's changed - going to see aunt at the Winter Haven in Melbourne'* – had the name of a fish restaurant in Melbourne. He wrote the details on a jotter and took them to James Bates.

'Get a call through to Melbourne Police and have them check out the restaurant, if it is still a restaurant. Either way Simon we had best be up front with them and let them know why we want them to check it out. If they ask, tell them the lot. There's no point us keeping anything back.'

'It could explain how Chancery's not shown up on the radar for ten years!'

Bates tapped the information into his computer bringing up an image of the fish restaurant in Melbourne it looked better than the one in the High Street.

'Would be nice to have all sides of the triangle at last. That's if prats like Ashton don't go losing them.'

Three quarters of an hour later Travis returned. 'Melbourne will do what they can, but they say they're over-stretched at present, only they have a homicidal psychopath snatching lone backpacker's and leaving them dead in the bush.'

Sexually motivated or marked?' asked Bates.

'Apparently not.'

Bates tapped his fingertips on the desktop.

'We'd be foolish at this juncture to speculate about Chancery. A psychopath he fits the bill, but he has sociopathic tendencies as well. Australia records so many missing backpackers each year and not all are found dead. It must be difficult knowing which are the genuine cases from those individuals who just wish to disappear and never be found.'

Bates discussed their next strategy regarding Ashton and Ashworth as he ran his finger down the list of staff that had been on duty that day, after which Simon Travis went to brief the rest of the team while Bates tried a second time to call Trevor Baines at Reading.

When he picked up the receiver of his office phone Baines had a gut feeling that it would be about Julianna Hesseltolph. He was surprised to hear that she had escaped.

'So there's no evidence to suggest that she was involved with either death?'

'Not at this precise moment in time, no.'

'You sound doubtful?' added Baines.

'The governor is a man named Tierney, I am not entirely sure about him.'

'I know what you mean, I met him when I paid Julianna Hesseltolph a visit shortly after seeing her brother. I tried to discuss Jason Chancery, but she refused to say anything about him. It was like she knew he was dead.'

'We spoke to Melbourne and they have a killer on the loose, taking backpackers. There's no sexual motive or cutting, just kills them and leaves them.'

Baines was thinking fast.

'If he is alive, he did kill at random although he had an ulterior motive, like he needed a boat and place to stay or money. Sex did come into it, but I've an idea because of the control he had over the female victims.'

He paused.'

'Gut reaction tells me that he's dead. I've always though he met with the people and they sorted what we couldn't, least ways not legally.'

'You mean the grandmother of the girl reporter.'

Trevor Baines stopped tapping at his computer.

'Yes, she had some big men in her family, all clean although I wouldn't want to cross any of them.'

Bates laughed. 'That's why they don't have police records. I think sometimes we'd do well paying them to resolve some of the crimes that can't get anywhere near.'

He studied the picture that they had on file of Julianna Hesseltolph, a studio photograph of when she had attained her masters in clinical psychology. 'She has a demure look about her,' he said speaking down the mouth piece.

'So does a jaguar until it pounces. Julianna Hesseltolph and Jason Chancery were an odd couple, like they didn't quite fit together, not your average Romeo and Juliet. Visiting her at Ashworth I got the impression from the little that she said about him that she used him, manipulated Chancery to fulfil a need.'

'A physical need?' Bates asked.

'No, something more capricious. Both men had a tendency to change mood like Jekyll and Hyde. Julianna was more controlled.'

He asked if Bates had read the interview notes that he had conducted with Jakub Hesseltolph at Ebenstatt. Bates said he had.

'Like his sister, Jakub is no fool. I would describe him as a very dangerous individual. I take it that you know about Alexander Koskovsky and the missing Albrecht Hartmann?'

'Yes.'

'I met with Koskovsky, eccentric type and arrogant, I didn't like him much. His ego seemed to be ahead of his reason for being at the sanatorium. I think he'd lost touch with reality himself, possibly being amongst so many different personalities and talking with them endlessly day in, day out. Koskovsky told me that despite numerous sessions, they'd made little progress in unravelling Jakub Hesseltolph's mind. They could not say what controlled him or how. I can't say that I'm surprised to hear that Koskovsky is dead.'

'And Hartmann?' Bates asked.

'I'd say he's long dead, although they may never find the body.' As he spoke he tapped away on the keyboard of his laptop. 'For the past couple of nights we've had a full moon.'

'Is that relevant?'

'Jakub Hesseltolph mentioned the moon and how the lunar cycle introduced uncertainty. When the moon was full Chancery would crawl out from under a stone and act out his atrocities. The woman Linda Cunningham, with whom Chancery lived with for a time, she said that he was at his most dangerous and unpredictable when the moon was big and bright, only he never howled.'

'They make a weird bunch, no wonder Australia were reluctant to spend time looking for them.'

Trevor Baines didn't exactly share the sentiment.

'Weird, I'm not so sure. Chancery I would say yes, but remember he had serious dysfunctional problems as a child, which were evident when he attacked his victims. The Hesseltolph's, they're a different act. They think alike, but not act the same. Julianna is controlling where Jakub will act then think. You mentioned a postcard?'

'Yes.' He read Baines the brief message.

'I agree and that's where she's heading. Australia however a big continent, finding them could be very difficult.'

Chapter Thirteen

The steak was exceptionally good, larger than anything that he had ever seen before and Jakub was struggling to eat it all. Pushing aside the side salad and fries he finally accepted that he wasn't going to get through it all.

Despite an excellent list of options on the steak specials board Elise had stuck with her original choice of fish. Red meat, especially steak always left her feeling cold.

'Do you get to see many crime scenes up real close?' he asked, the question appearing quite out of the blue.

'Some, but only if I am called in early enough. As a profiler we tend to say that it is vitally important to get a feel for what has taken place at a crime scene, collect the vibes that linger behind. Like a forensic examiner will seek out and identify the minutest particle of evidence, the scene itself can tell us a story. It's like walking through an open door and with the lights already on.'

'Sounds interesting.'

Elise continued. 'The victim had a sense of belonging because they were there for a reason, maybe a walk, to visit friends or just to unwind, who knows. Whereas the perpetrator chose to be there waiting, selecting a victim. Good versus evil. It's my job to delve, overturn the stones and look underneath where the answers lie waiting to be discovered.'

'But surely that's impossible. If I was sat opposite you, I could easily be lying. How would you know the difference between truth and deception?'

'I say I can see the truth in the eyes.'

Jakub smiled, he liked playing this game. So did the voices in his head.

'And outside influences, what about them?'

Elise was fascinated by Johann and his interest in her subject.

'Do you mean the other factors that could contribute to the scene, the attack or aftermath?'

'Yes, although I thinking prior to the attack. Is the victim drawn to a certain and the attacker too. Does the moon, a past event or expectations influence their unfortunate meeting?'

'Expectations?' she repeated. Elise was puzzled.

'Is there a common denominator in why, how and when?'

'You mean like murdering a prostitute working the streets at night. She had to be there and the attacker knew this.'

'She will do as an example, although I was thinking more along the lines of somebody with wicked intentions, when the victim is not as saintly as they seem and like their attacker they also have evil thoughts and their deeds are as destructive. Does not their coming together represent getting even, calling a spade a spade, making right all previous injustices.'

Elise parted her lips and raised a knowing forefinger.

'Ah, I see what you mean. Yes, there are many in society who would willingly turn a blind eye to a paedophile being murdered down a dark alley, but my argument is that the killing is vigilante and the intention different. It's a fine line we can cross to see justice served.

I had to look into the background of a victim recently. By the time I concluded my report I knew him better than his own mother. I knew all about his seedy little habits, hobbies some would say, but then I question their approval. My focus was solely on how his death had influenced the attack. His killer had time to watch, plan and pick the location where the attack took place. As innocent walking, talking members of society we can influence destiny. It's my job to determine how much.'

He thought about the six boys that he had tortured in the woods. Their abuse and intentions against Julianna had influenced his reaction.

'And what about supernatural forces?'

Elise put down her beer glass.

'Do you mean the occult, ghosts and ghoulies, things that go bump in the night, vampires?' His eyes didn't blink.

'I look at all aspects, influences when I'm building a profile. The moon has a great pull, a control over how a killer plans, works, kills.'

'And nightmares, you must have some?'

'Not necessarily nightmares, flashbacks definitely.' His eyes fascinated her. So dark like black polished tourmaline they would stare back at her, hardly blinking. If she didn't like him so much, they could be unnerving, like a demonic force they could suck the energy from your soul.

'Occasionally, when I can't sleep at night and I lie awake thinking, I would see an unrecognisable face, somebody that I have not come across before, but definitely that of a man. I try hard to memorise every detail so that I can give what I see to a sketch artist.'

'Does that work?'

'I'm not sure.'

The frown on her brow suggested that she wasn't a hundred percent confident it did.

'Something, instinct perhaps tells me that it is the face of a perpetrator, somebody I am yet to meet and perhaps a man the police are hunting. A female friend, a colleague told me that she had experienced much the same. When I asked a male profiler he said that it had never happened to him.'

'That could be quite mind blowing, don't you think?'

Elise felt a shiver pas through her.

'What I found disturbing was that a male perpetrator, possibly somebody that I had not met could invade my mind and have me feel threatened. I've never experienced that before.' She was interested to know what he thought could have caused such a reaction.

'Maybe because you're getting close, perhaps too close. I would imagine that somebody, a killer or not yet a perpetrator doesn't want you invading their personal space. You are delving into the realms of where, when and why. Opening up their book of secrets.'

Elise picked up her glass again.

'But that's my job, my professional aim Johann to delve, dig deep.'

'Then that is the risk that you take, doing what you do. You have a book secrets, things you want nobody else to know. You'd be mighty pissed if somebody, a stranger invaded your privacy and stole them.' His change of mood was noticeable.

'You asked about the supernatural. Do you think that could make the connection?' She had turned it back around to see how he reacted.

'Yes, I do. Although it's only an opinion remember.' He smiled, a reassuring reaction bringing her thoughts back to the meal. 'Do you want a dessert?'

Elise picked up the menu, her focus on the images in front of her, but her mind was still elsewhere. She chose ice-cream, nothing fancy, just two scoops. She wasn't ready to let it just rest there.

'So the image, the man's face could be a premonition?'

Jakub acknowledged with a nod wondering if Matthias Baumgartner had encountered bad dreams lately. To ease the mood he laughed.

'Did you see me appear before we met in the diner?'

A grin appeared, turning into a laugh. 'No silly, you're not a killer!'

That made him laugh all the more.

There was a sudden commotion from the other side of the restaurant as a diner grabbed the wrist of the waitress making her lose her balance and the tray of food that she had been carrying. When Jakub looked, the light that side of the room was slightly darker and the waitress had similarities to Julianna. A young man working behind the bar intervened hoping to calm the situation, but he was immediately assaulted by the confrontational customer. A family of four with small children exited the restaurant not wanting to become involved.

When the waitress tried to free herself of the man's grip he said something to her before slapping the side of her face. In an instant Jakub was out of his chair and moving fast between tables. Before Elise could utter advice Jakub had hold of the male customer's wrist, he gave it a twist yanking it back, he immediately let go of the waitress's hand. Standing up he was a big man, powerful and angry.

'Stay out of this,' he warned, *'unless you want to get hurt as well.'*

Jakub who had seen worse and bigger in Ebenstatt stood his ground glaring back. The man grabbed his steak knife from the table and began waving it back and forth menacingly, provoking an attack. *'I'm warning you little man, fuck off or I'll gut you like a fish and add you to the special's board!'*

Jakub grinned his eyes connecting with the bigger man's pupils. 'Put the knife down unless you intend to use it. If you do, make sure that you execute your move fast and that you know exactly how!'

Hearing the advice the customer laughed, his contempt apparent.

'You little prick, I'll carve you into small pieces for that!'

Helping the barman to his feet the waitress was heading for the phone to call the police. She had just gone behind the bar when the man lunged at Jakub with the knife. Grossly overweight and out of condition, his mouth was his bravado. With lightning speed Jakub blocked the advance twisting both knife and the man's wrist down hard until he heard it snap. The bigger man yelled out in pain as the radius snapped in two tearing the upper deltoid muscle for good measure. His companion who was sitting watching started to rise, but Jakub who still had hold of the man's injured arm issued a warning.

'Think wisely friend. Sit back down, don't get involved and you can tell the police when they arrive exactly how this happened.' Ignoring the cries of his friend the man sat back down. The injured man was now down on his knees holding his arm rocking back and forth with the pain.

Jakub felt a gentle hand rest on his arm as the waitress pulled him away.

'Thanks friend... now I suggest you get out of here. I'll sort this when the highway patrol arrive. Arnie's well known for throwing his weight around when he's had a few too many. He got what he deserved here this evening. Don't worry about the tab, me and Ben will sort that later... now please take your wife and go!'

Jakub took one last look at his attacker, thanked the waitress then went over to where Elise had witnessed everything.

'We'll take dessert elsewhere,' he said as he swallowed the last of his drink. Not too far away the sound of a police siren broke through the silence that had descended the inside of the restaurant. They left by the front door and walked across the parking lot to the sidewalk.

'I saw everything Johann and you acted in self-defence. You gave that thug every opportunity to put the knife down. I could smooth over everything here with the police you know, once they establish who I am.'

Jakub shook his head convincingly. 'No, they'd still drag me down to the stationhouse for questioning. It's best we just go. The waitress told me that the man is well known to the police so they'll deal with him appropriately. He also assaulted her and the barman, so let him spend a night in the cells rather than me.'

She looped her arm and together they walked seeing the patrol cars coming down the opposite side of the road. Pulling him into the nearest shop doorway Elise wanted to make sure that the thug was arrested. Five minutes later an officer unceremoniously dumped the man with the broken arm in the back of the patrol car and shut the door.

'My guess is that he'll spend more than one night in the cells.' Elise still had her arm looped through his. 'That was courageous and impressive what you did back in there. Where did you learn to do something like that?'

'Army cadets. It's called aikido, an ancient Japanese form of self-defence. Opponent size is immaterial and can hinder rather than help for the person attacking that is. Speed and agility is what counts. He fractured his arm because his own body mass worked against him. I just helped.'

'I know, I saw. It was a brave thing to intervene Johann, you saved that barman and waitress from being hurt by the drunkard. He reminded me of the truck driver.'

'I don't like to see women hurt and she looked like my sister.'

Elise didn't probe sensing that Jakub might clam up. They watched from the shop doorway as the two officers settled themselves back in the patrol car then headed back down the carriageway their side towards the stationhouse. None of the occupants took any notice of the couple looking at the window display in the shop doorway.

'Your sister is very lucky to have a brother like you Johann. I never had one and could definitely have done with a brother like you when I was in my senior years.'

When a second patrol came back up the street Elise grabbed Jakub and pulled him in very close finding his lips with hers. Jakub didn't pull away. When their mouths parted she was looking directly into his eyes. 'That was spontaneous… I'm sorry. It was all I could think of to prevent them stopping and asking if we'd just come from the steakhouse. They probably have a vague description of you and are out looking.' Jakub pushed her hard against the wall of the shop doorway and kissed her once again, only this time it was he taking the initiative. She felt his firm body hard against her own and responded.

Back in the motel room they shed their clothes dragging one another to the bed. For Elise it was nothing like she had ever experienced before. Oscar had never been this exciting or so appreciative of her sexual desires. Johann ticked all the boxes. It was gone three in the morning before she fell asleep content and exhausted.

As she slept Jakub stood at the window looking out across the vast water of the Buckhorn Reservoir. The waters were calm in the moonlight with only the odd ripple to throw an image over the blue water. Tomorrow they would head out again and down the ninety five where he had a strong feeling he would find Baumgartner.

He was still watching when the voices began talking. Some advised he should get dressed and leave before she woke, others told him to take her again, then leave her body for the maid to find. Slipping back into the bed once again he pulled her into him, his lips kissing the sides of her neck.

Chapter Fourteen

James Bates returned to Ashworth the following day with backup from his team so that they could question and take statements regarding the death of Judith Banks. It annoyed Ashton Tierney that they were insistent upon delving so deep into an obvious suicide.

'Is this really necessary,' he asked, 'my staff have a busy enough time watching and controlling the inmates here?'

Bates was used to belligerent obstruction, from Tierney it seemed oddly strange and only endorsed the policeman's suspicion that the governor had something to hide.

'We won't be long or get in the way and today, our being here will help the coroner rubber stamp the matter surrounding the Banks death.'

Tierney although frustrated didn't the coroner on his back as well, he was already feeling the heat from the Home Secretary's office.

'Are there any developments regarding Julianna Hesseltolph?'

'Not yet,' smiled Bates, 'that's nothing unusual. She'll go to ground for the first few days before she pops up like a spring rabbit.'

Tierney liked the optimism in Bates reply, although something told him that she was already long gone and already out of the country. Slipping the odd question in here and there about Gillian Dennerholm the team soon established that there was an underbelly of tension floating uneasily about the corridors and none were sorry to see the back of the senior warder. It was James Bates who spoke to Sammie Saunders.

'Why submit your resignation, you're in the clear?' he asked.

'Because of the shame.'

He looked her as she kept her head down, no older than his eldest daughter he felt angry. 'Was you coerced into the affair with Gillian Dennerholm?'

She nodded raising her eyes to meet his, he had the same friendly face that had once tucked her into bed and read her a bedtime story before turning out the light. 'Yes Sir, she cornered me almost from the first day that I arrived. Gillian told me that she could make things very difficult for me if I didn't co-operate, succumb. She threatened to tell the governor and make up stories that would wreck my probation and career chances.' She sighed heavily the stress of the relationship weighing heavy on her conscience. 'I'm not sorry that she's dead!'

And neither was Bates. He'd heard enough.

By the time that the investigation team convened again in the staff canteen the call had already come through from the Home Office that Ashton Tierney was being replaced. Three coroner enquiry's and an escaped prisoner would not be tolerated whatever the circumstances. James Bates watched as Tierney gathered together his private effects from his desk.

'The price of supervising some of England's most notorious insane comes at a very high price Chief Inspector.'

'What will you do now?' Bates asked.

'Take the pension that's been offered, go away for a while with my wife and children then consider my options when I come back. I might become a writer, just think of the stories that I could write about this place and its guests.'

With his departure there seemed little point in wasting any more precious time trying to unravel the dark secrets that were hidden in the fabric of Ashworth. Bates wished Tierney well and went to collect his team.

Stopping at a red light Travis turned to Bates.

'So going by what Saunders said, Julianna Hesseltolph might have been the last person to have seen Gillian Dennerholm alive.' He looked up, waiting for the lights to change.

'That's about the crux of it, although we'll never really know what took place when Dennerholm walked onto the ward. Dennerholm was a nasty piece of work and perhaps she deserved to die. That between you and me Simon. The only good thing to come out of this affair is that the daffy old girl in the middle bed is being transferred to an old people's home at the end of the week. Tierney told me that he room is being prepared and getting a fresh lick of paint before she takes up occupancy.'

Travis engaged gear and moved away when the light turned green. They gone a couple of kilometres when Bates took a call on his mobile. Minutes later he told Travis to head for the John Lennon Airport where they had a police helicopter waiting.

'How's your Irish?' asked Bates.

'As good as it's always been, why?

'The body of a young woman was found earlier today by a hotel cleaner in Dublin. Garda officers have checked the CCTV in reception and although the image is a little grainy they think its Julianna Hesseltolph. It would seem that victim and our escapee spent the night together.'

Travis gave a shake of his head. 'It seems that everybody's taking lovers these days, only the ones we come across end up dead!'

They were met at Dublin Airport by a regular patrol who took them straight to the Mermaid hotel where Bates met with an old colleague who he hadn't seen since walking the beat together. Francis Ryan was also a DCI. He extended his hand before introducing Simon Travis. On the way up in the lift to the fourth floor Ryan outlined the facts as known to him.

'It would seem that your missing lady came over on the ferry and literally walked off as cool as you like wearing a company uniform. It's still hanging in the wardrobe. Forensics are all over it, but more tests will need to be done when they get it back to the lab. We're hoping that the hair samples found match Hesseltolph. She's one cool lady under pressure.'

'The victim, how did she die?' asked Bates as the lift gently came to a halt.

'Suffocated with a pillow.'

Bates looked at Travis, then back at Ryan.

'We've just come from Ashworth where the senior warder allegedly suffocated having slipped and crushed her windpipe on a bed stay. Suffocation was said to be the cause of her death.'

Francis Ryan scoffed. 'Yeah right, and my Auntie Fanny won the two thirty at Leopardstown today riding a three-legged donkey.'

James Bates grinned, he had always liked the Irishman's wit.

'Hesseltolph swapped places with a dead inmate in the next bed, but not before she had dealt with the warder. As far as we know she hadn't killed until yesterday.'

Ryan was impressed. 'She took a risk. She could have permanently ended up on a funeral pyre or six feet under helping to fuel the ozone layer.'

Simon Travis grinned, either way would have been good. Ryan looked at the body on the bed. He thumbed his thumb at the dead saleswoman.

'And she would still be alive if Hesseltolph had never got free of Ashworth.'

James Bates went over to the bed side.

'She didn't have much chance to fight for her life!' He looked closely at the hose hold her wrists firm against the bed posts. Francis Ryan stood alongside.

'Surprisingly she was complacent until the last few moments. There's no sign of a struggle so my guess is that she was a willing party in being tied to the bed.'

The only sign of any struggle was where Melanie Smith had rucked the sheet down at her feet kicking out as the air had been sucked cruelly from her lungs.

'We'll swab for DNA, but I'd say that Hesseltolph's prints are all over this room. Forensics say they have two different hair samples in the shower tray, one the victims, the other the attackers.

'Do we know who she is?' asked Bates.

'Melanie Anne Smith, aged thirty three. She was a Sales Manager for a company that sells telecommunications space. Reception records offer an address from your neck of the woods. She was here on a four day seminar on advanced sales techniques. It was the course organiser who alerted hotel staff when she failed to show up. A statement has already been obtained from the cleaner, but management have given her the rest of the day off. It's not every day that you open the door to a guest room and find the guest dead wearing nothing, but a pillow over her face.'

Travis had seen almost everything possible, but at times it was the simplicity of death and how it was executed that he never understood. 'I'll have the team make enquiries at the home address, whoever answers can perhaps tell us more.'

Bates stood back up. 'She'd be about the same age as Julianna Hesseltolph, a bit younger perhaps. Have them check Hesseltolph's old client diary Simon. The two might have known one another professionally.' Travis went out into the corridor to make the call.

'Have you any idea where she's heading?' Ryan asked.

'Melbourne in Australia we think.' He told his counterpart about the postcard.

Ryan pulled open the wardrobe doors.

'Most of her clothes are missing, shoes, underwear, cosmetics and her handbag.'

James Bates listened as his eyes scanned the room. 'I noticed coming here that the rail station isn't far. Does it have a photo booth?'

Ryan chuckled. 'Same old James. I always knew you'd make detective one day. I've already sent somebody over to recover the kiosk discs.'

Bates liked working with Francis Ryan, he was a first rate detective, shrewd and not easily fooled. He gave told him about the brother escaping Ebenstatt, killing the doctor and about the missing policeman. He briefly outlined the Hesseltolph family history.

'Melbourne you say and possibly to meet her brother?'

Bates nodded. 'Quite possibly or the serial killer Jason Chancery.'

'Is he still missing?'

'Yes.'

Ryan walked over to the window to look out. The windows were dirty where the rain had collected the dust and grime in the air.

'That'd be a deadly combination if they teamed up. I don't suppose the Aussie's are putting up the bunting knowing that they could soon have all three on their patch.'

'No. They weren't exactly cheering down the telephone line. Travis made the call and he told me that the Aussie's have a nutter of their own running amok, snatching and murdering backpackers.'

'And when exactly did Chancery disappear?' asked Ryan.

'Back end of nineteen ninety nine.'

Ryan told Bates that all ports, bus stations and airports were being checked. Outside the sun had disappeared once again and it had started to rain.

'James did you know that there's a Melbourne in America as well?'

Bates stepped out from the bathroom. 'You're kidding me!'

'No. Siobhan and I took the kids to Florida a couple of years back. We rented a villa for three weeks staying at a place called Kissimmee. It wasn't that far from Melbourne down on the east coast.'

Bates muttered something incoherent under his breath. 'Great, one side of the world to the other. The FBI is going to love us.'

They stood aside as the medical examiner went about her business having changed her blue nitrile gloves. She pointed over at the box on the side.

'If you and your colleague would like to use my supplies Chief inspector you're more than welcome and I'd sleep a lot easier tonight.' Bates took two and thanked her.

Molly Flynn untied the victim's wrists having already taken all the necessary photographs.

Ryan and Bates stood talking watching molly and her team work methodically, collecting, tagging and bagging various samples. The room was comparatively clean except for the hair in the shower cubicle. Julianna Hesseltolph was no fool. He thanked Molly and her team then left to find Simon Travis as they had another call to make to the FBI at 935 Pennsylvania Avenue, Washington DC. They were not going to be amused to learn that they could have a couple of serial killers running amok somewhere in the states and with a woman no better.

Chapter Fifteen

The plane touched down on the tarmac a little after seven at Orlando International and taxied to the terminal in under five minutes. Looking through the compartment window she was relieved to see that there were no police lurking furtively about amidst the throng of waiting baggage and freight handlers. Taking her hand luggage from the overhead locker Julianna stood in the centre aisle and straightened out the creases in her trousers wanting to look her best when she stepped onto American soil. Taking her turn at the exit door she was wished a pleasant onward journey by the cabin crew.

Along with other passengers she boarded the waiting relay bus to the arrival centre slipping beyond the terminal and through customs. The immigration control officer, a woman checked her photo and details several times.

'And the reason for your stay Miss Smith?'

'Business, I'll be gone in a few days.'

She looked one more time then endorsed the entry.

'Have a good stay.'

'Thank you.'

Julianna walked clear of the terminal building and took a cab. Outside and on the drive through there were more police, but none paid her any attention. So far the police in Dublin hadn't worked through the crime scene or established where she was heading.

'Where to lady?' the driver asked, not looking.

'Melbourne Beach.' She replied adding a fine layer of lipstick.

The driver, an Asian American didn't converse much which pleased Julianna. He dropped her at the junction of Ocean Drive and Fifth Avenue where she exchanged English currency in the purse for American dollars to pay the fare. Later she would have some money transferred from a secure off-shore business account that the police didn't know about. Registered under a different name and her as the sole account owner, she could make her stay last as long as she liked.

At a local convenience store she purchased hair colour, a pair of scissors and sunglasses before finding a small family guest house where she took a shower, dyed her hair a different colour, cut and styled it shorter. In under two hours, she was no longer recognisable as Julianna Hesseltolph or Melanie Anne Smith, but anybody she wished to be. Outside of the guest house the sun was still incredibly bright for the time of day and her stomach was beginning to rumble despite having had a meal on the plane. She had a hot meat roll and fries with a drink at a fast food bar opposite the beach where she sat watching mothers with children getting ready to go home. Florida was a far cry from Merseyside and Dublin.

When the traffic died down and the beach looked relatively deserted Julianna crossed the coastal road and descended the few wooden steps down onto the sandy beach. Slipping off her shoes the sand grains were soft and warm to the touch. She bent down and scooped up a handful letting it sift through her fingers. It felt good, therapeutic. Walking down the beach she came to the water's edge where before her all she could see was a huge expanse of blue water, tipped gently with the white of the surf as it rushed towards the sand. She turned and walked letting the warm water wash about her feet. In the distance two dogs ran and jumped at one another playing in the shallows. Behind them, but some way back were the owners, two women engaged in a conversation. At this time of the day and almost deserted Melbourne beach was her Shangri la.

Stepping back from the water she sat down on the soft sand to enjoy the view, have the sunshine warm her through and wash away her thoughts. Since Kurlor her life had been out of control, a spiral staircase forever going down and with no end in sight. She took the postcard from her pocket and read the message again – *'Climate's changed - going to see Aunt at the winter haven in Melbourne.'*

Julianna was still deep in her thoughts when a dog, a beautiful Labrador suddenly appeared. It sat itself alongside wagging its tail. As she stroked it head she became aware of a tall shadow blocking the sun.

'I'm am terribly sorry,' the owner said apologising, 'Emily Lou didn't mean to startle you, but she must like you to come sit beside you, ordinarily she's very fussy who she sits next too.'

Julianna continued to gently stroke the dog's neck as the older woman stood to one side allowing the sun to shine again.

'She's a really beautiful dog. So is the beach.'

The woman smiled.

'You've not been here long, have you?'

Julianna didn't feel threatened by the observation.

'Does the lack of a suntan give me away that much?'

The woman grinned. 'No, not really. More intuition, and that I have not seen you down here on the beach before. Emily Lou and I walk this beach every day, early morning and evening, and we know most of the people who visit. We were on the last leg of our return back home when this old girl decided to introduce herself. Would you like a coffee?'

Julianna stood up, picked up her shoes and dusted the sand from the backs of her trousers. The woman was slightly shorter, but she had a reassuring look in her eyes, a soft look that told Julianna she could be trusted.

'Yes, thank you I would like that.'

Realising that it was time to go the Labrador stood and walked towards home sticking to the sand rather than the water.

'The old girl used to like paddling home, but the vet told me only recently that she has a touch of rheumatism. Nothing to prevent her walks each day, but enough for us to realise that she should really stay clear of the water. Unfortunately, she's like the rest of us and she ignores good advice.' She pointed to a white house further up the beach. 'That's ours on the corner of Cherry Drive. Just follow Emily Lou she'll show you the way.'

Walking alongside Julianna felt that she could not lie to the older woman. There was something about her, an aura of spiritual energy that she identified with that of a mother, not her own, but perhaps with somebody she wished had been.

'I'm Julianna.'

The woman threw a ball for Emily Lou to fetch. The dog didn't run, but she walked instead and collected.

'I'm Mary… Mary Peterson and it's just me and Emily Lou at home, but we make a good team.'

The dog brought the ball back only she dropped it at Julianna's feet.

'It won't matter how far you throw it, she'll get there when she can. The old girl and me, we have a habit of not rushing anywhere in a hurry, but arriving in one piece and with the same heartbeat that we had five minutes earlier. Life's too short to be constantly catching up with shadows.'

Julianna threw the ball, only not too far up the sand, but far enough away to instil confidence in Emily Lou knowing that she could still fetch it. She watched as the dog sauntered across the beach wondering about the shadows that she herself had been chasing lately. Maybe it was time to stop.

Standing before the gated entrance to the front garden she remembered the house at Kurlor being full of flowers and looking as good as Mary's. The architecture was colonial and the timber whitewashed with a long wooden veranda and at either end, slowly creeping up the supporting posts were tendrils of a lilac wisteria. It was as Mary had described, a simple succinct house, comfortable and convenient for the beach walks. Julianna liked it, it was the kind of house that you visited in a nice dream. Mary invited her guest to take a seat on the veranda with Emily Lou while she made the coffee. Several minutes went by before Mary reappeared with a tray of coffee and iced-tea, accompanied by a tin of homemade biscuits.

'Here we go,' she said, putting down the tray, 'we always have refreshments after a long walk and Emily Lou won't go without a biscuit. We always sit here and watch the evening walkers down on the sidewalk or the beach. Thankfully the view never changes, only the people.' She gave the Labrador her biscuit. 'Tea or coffee?'

'Coffee, black with one sugar please.' She thought the caffeine would help her get over the flight.

'This is so beautiful here Mary, the view, house and garden. I would image you have a lot of envious residents in Melbourne.'

The older woman gave Julianna her coffee then sat down with iced-tea.

'There are some that regularly check the obituary column hoping that they'll see my name in the listing and for the past nine months I've had a persistent real estate agent approach me about selling the place.

'My late husband and I, we bought this house soon after our marriage. It was our dream and our children were born in the house and their memories live on here, I could never sell it.' Mary sighed. 'I'm no fool Julianna and I know that time is against me.' She raised a hand to stop any interruption. 'They would come home from school, change into their beachwear and spend the afternoon down in the surf. I know this beach front property is a sought after location and any principal agent would give their right arm to get their mucky hands on it.' She poured more coffee into Julianna's mug. 'I am so pleased that you like it. Where do you call home?'

'Kurlor in Austria. It's so small that it would fit in one block of Melbourne. I used to think that it was idyllic nestled neatly with the mountains one side and waterfalls the other. The air is fresh and the smell of pine trees rich, but things change Mary. The magic disappears overnight. England has been my home and consulting room for a few years now.' Julianna sipped the coffee, it was good. She wondered how Mary could influence the truth so easily.

'Austria sounds wonderful.' Mary offered more biscuits. 'At my physician appointments, the doctor tells me that the biscuits are bad for my health and that too many will kill me.' She laughed. 'I don't tell her that Emily Lou eats more than I do and she doesn't get the same hassle from the vet.'

Are you diabetic?' Julianna asked.

'Perhaps, maybe I am never sure. The tests are always so border line, up one quarter then down the next. They said that next time they'd give me one of those home kits so that I could monitor myself. I thought that I'd test Emily Lou and send in the results that should throw the medical centre into a frenzy.'

Julianna really liked Mary's carefree attitude and approach to life. It was a perspective she had thought about on the plane over to America. The postcard from Jakub had made her think that life was going around in circles and like a vortex the end of the tunnel had no lights. Julianna felt that she was being sucked into a black hole. She took another biscuit which she gave to Emily Lou.

Mary continued. 'I'm sixty nine years of age and I've had a wonderful life. I have a beautiful family, although I rarely see them because they have their own lives, careers and families. They all have healthy bank balances and the house on the corner of Cherry Drive hasn't been visited in the past three years.'

'I thought this place held their memories?'

'Yes, it does, but since the death of their father they say the house has lost its' appeal. As you say Julianna things change.' She stroked the dog's ears. 'When my time comes and I knock on the pearly gates, I would somehow like to leave the house to Emily Lou.' Mary smiled and chuckled. 'I've not put my affairs in order yet and Greg Youngman, my lawyer will wet himself when he reads out the conditions of the Will.' Mary ruffled the Labradors head. 'Just think girl you'd be the envy of all the real estate agents and they couldn't do a thing about it.'

They sat of the veranda, sipping fresh ground coffee, iced-tea and munching on homemade biscuits. The sun which was at one end of the beach cast a long warm glow over the sand. It was a sunset that Julianna had never seen.

'I was born at the end of the summer of forty two when the Japanese attacked Pearl Harbour. My father was drafted into the army, did his basic training and sent to France, he never came back Julianna. Survivors of his unit told my mother that he was killed in a place called Poitiers. There's a cemetery there and one day before I die, I would like to visit his grave and have him know that I love him.'

'Poitiers is a beautiful place. Eleanor of Aquitaine became the French Queen when she married Louis VII, but when the marriage was annulled she wed Henry Plantagenet, King of England becoming the English Queen. She had eight children, one being Richard the Lionheart. I hope your wish comes true Mary and you do go.'

Mary was staring at the waves which had settled after the tide was fully in. Everything seemed so calm. As peaceful as it was every evening.

'Growing up without a father was like losing a limb that I never had and even though I never knew my father I feel a strong connection with his soul. I felt that same connection when I saw you down on the beach, so did Emily Lou. A friend of mine who went to Poitiers visited the cemetery, she told me that the French had planted so many trees around the wall of the cemetery so that when they grew the branches extending out would represent the arms of our loved ones, as though they still reach out to us, even now and let us know that they're always around. Even in death Julianna the love never dies.'

'I have never looked at trees in that way before,' replied Julianna, 'it's an interesting spiritual hypothesis.' She looked at the trees lining the beach road and wondered if either of her parents would ever reach out to her.

Mary poured herself more iced-tea. 'Are you in some sort of trouble?'

Julianna looked her way, not unsurprised. Mary had been insightful from the moment that they had met. There was a look in Mary's eyes that was trusting.

'I've done bad things Mary. I thought coming to America would put to bed some of troubles.' She continued to stroke the dogs head. Down on the beach a group of teenagers, boys and girls were playing volleyball. 'What made you ask?'

Mary gave a shake of head, not an admonishment, but in agreement.

'Walking the sidewalk of life Julianna hasn't always been an easy route for me neither. Without a father figure I was the original wild child. The trouble is that when you are so young, you never consider the emotional rollercoaster that a parent has to control. In the end my sins caught up with me. I got off lightly, but the three months in detention with hardened criminals, women who would kill for just looking at them shook me from my selfish, uncontrollable narcissistic ways. The day I walked free from that detention centre was the day I changed my outlook on life. I hoped that my mother would one day forgive me all the heartache that I had put her through.'

Mary paused to sip her tea.

'Whatever the crime, however big or small we all walk a fine line between good and bad. Abraham, my late husband was my guiding white light whenever I got depressed, wanted the excitement of my former life, he'd hold on tight and never once did he let go. His resolve got us through the bad times. He would say to me that he only ever saw the good in me, how I never understood, but eventually the nightmares disappeared. The day that he proposed to me, I cried all night long and I gave my thanks to God. Never a religious woman, I was also thanking my father as I felt his presence throughout that terrible period in my life.'

Julianna looked at the tree branches and wondered, were they there, watching.

'Abraham was my miracle, my angel of the light. We had a wonderful marriage that lasted for forty seven years until the angels came and took him one night. He died peacefully in his sleep. A gentle man all his life he was my strength, my rock. I have five grandchildren and each possesses a beautiful quality of their grandfather. If my marriage to Abraham taught me anything Julianna, it was to never to stop believing in hope.'

'I am really not sure that the Lord would forgive me my sins Mary.'

Stretching over Mary placed a motherly hand on Julianna's arm.

'I wasn't consciously talking about any religious beliefs that I hold sacred, I was referring to the spiritual soul inside of you. That magical thing that we none of us ever see, but which makes us love, laugh and at times cry. Abraham would say to me late at night when I'd had a bad day *'shut the door, come to bed and don't look back, only when you open the door again the next morning the view will look that much different'*. A wise man he was always right, it always did. The back yard never changed, but the light was different, full of promise.'

Emily Lou repositioned herself at Julianna's feet laying over them. The action made Mary smile.

'She's a good judge of character, she knows. I often say Abraham left some of his soul in Emily Lou so that she would look after me. She obviously likes you Julianna.'

'Regrettably Mary I can't turn back the clock and hide the mistakes.'

Mary shook her head adamantly.

'No, that's right, none us can. Time however is an unpredictable phenomenon. Ticking on second by second it sees all. Destiny had Abraham waiting outside the penitentiary when the doors opened again for me. He told me that it was our time to be together. I never argued with him, ever. Take the time that you have left, look only ever forward and never back.'

The conversation ended there as they each sat on the veranda soaking up the late evening sunshine and listening to the laughter coming from the youngsters playing on the beach. Julianna was quite happy to sit back in the chair with Emily Lou at her feet and just watch. When she looked sideways Mary had fallen asleep in her chair. She looked so peaceful, at peace with herself. Maybe, thought Julianna coming to America had not been a waste of time.

It wasn't until a sudden change in the breeze blew gently over Mary that it made her open her eyes again. She looked at Emily Lou and Julianna surprised to see that they were still exactly where she had left them before she had fallen asleep.

'I'm sorry my dears, I must have dozed off, it must have been a longer walk than usual today.'

'You looked so peaceful and you were smiling.' Julianna remarked.

Mary grinned. 'I was strolling down the beach arm in arm with Abraham and Emily Lou had run on ahead. We were just about to kiss when I woke, don't you find that so annoying!'

'Does it happen often?' Julianna asked.

'Nearly every time we go to kiss. There must be a hidden message in there somewhere only I'm damned if I know what.' Mary touched Julianna on the forearm, her fingers were like ice. 'There was somebody else in the dream too, somebody on the beach that Abraham recognised.'

'Do you know who?' Julianna asked.

'Yes... you!'

Julianna felt her skin prickle as the cold sensation swept down through her body. 'Me, that's impossible. I only arrived today.'

Mary grinned. 'Remember what I told you about closing the door, not looking back and seeing everything different the next day.'

'Are you telling me that Abraham is reaching out to me as well?'

'Somebody is Julianna. Just out of interest where are you staying?'

She told Mary about the guest house to which the older woman suggested Julianna collect her belongings and use her daughter's old room instead.

'It never gets used and I would welcome the company. I know Emily Lou would definitely like somebody different to talk too.'

An hour later Julianna returned to the beach house, she had with her a brown paper shopping bag which she gave to Mary. Inside was a miniature bonsai in a dish.

'My way of saying thank you Mary and that the trees reached out today!'

Chapter Sixteen

Senator Matt Baum, formerly Matthias Baumgartner and magistrate from Kurlor, Austria sat comfortably behind his desk made of walnut and leather having pushed aside a pile of papers that needed his attention.

'There are times Ed, when being a member of the senate stands in the way of private enjoyment and the demands can be over bearing.'

Edward Samuel Nathan Jackson, a descendant of Andrew Jackson and seventh President of the United States of America stood patiently the other side of the desk observing the man sat behind. He would like to have told him what a privilege it was to be elected senator, but Baum wasn't the type of man to take criticism good or bad lightly. Ed wondered if his boss really appreciated the values of his office and serving the people came first to his private life. As tactful as ever Jackson kept his opinions to himself, he pushed instead a file across the desk top.

'If we can take a positive hit on these papers, there'll be enough time left to get in a round of golf before the sun goes down.'

Baum looked at the documents, official letters and government amendments that needed his attention begrudgingly pulling them back. 'You're right of course Ed. Yeah let's plough on through this lot and then we can have that wager as to who wins on the green today.'

Ed Jackson stood opposite waiting for the first paper to be passed his way. It had become the practice for Baum to read papers first then pass them across to Ed, who would give an educated opinion upon which Baum should sign. History predicted that Ed Jackson had more respect and knowledge concerning the principles and precedents of the senator's office than Baum would ever have. Signing the third stereo-typed letter Baum added it to the mail box. Baum continued not looking up.

'With your ancestry Ed, I sometimes wonder why you've never run for president. You have the biological stock of America running through your bones and the portrait of the former president staring back at you every time you arrive home. You would make a damn good president one day.'

'Maybe I like a wager on the golf course too much.'

Baum laughed, he was easily amused.

Truth was Ed Jackson was happy with his life. He had a beautiful and clever wife who he adored. Four years younger than him she was a Harvard graduate and lawyer with a well-known law firm. Juggling the balls between family and work commitments they had successfully raised their family living under the roof of a respectably comfortable residence, which backed onto a fresh water river in Old Tampa. Giving up everything that he held dear to him for a term in the White House didn't appeal. Ed stopped grinning.

'On the more serious side, Sandra has enough at work to keep her happy and Vanessa and Andrew are reaching that time in their education when schooling is becoming important. I wouldn't want the media hounding them day and night.'

Baum who saw himself as Marlon Brando in the role of Godfather rolled his head around on his shoulders feeling the tension of the day craving to be elsewhere. Married to Adelina and with two adult children of his own, things were very different whenever he walked through the door of his home. There was no smiling portrait of Andrew Jackson to greet him and Adelina was indifferent to whether he came home or not. The kids were away at university and as long as the bank balance remained healthy they weren't that bothered neither and certainly not in his political aspirations. More recently Adelina had made it known that she much preferred the snow-capped mountains of Austria than the fake Florida lifestyle.

Set in its own grounds with gardeners looking after the lawns, shrubs and flower beds Adelina had always considered the house her prison. Life had become more unbearable when the children had left home and each and every day she seemed to rattle about the place with no real purpose. Privileged with her own purse of credit cards she would visit the shopping malls, coffee shops and gym where she would meet up with friends, women as bored as herself and many that she knew because of her husband's business interests.

Adelina yearned for the smell of fresh air and would willingly give up the sunshine for the peace and quiet of a country lane without a bodyguard following at her side. Lately the late night arguments at home had grown with intensity and the wall beside the door in the bedroom needed a new coat of paint where she had launched a flower vase at Matthias's head. She detested the name Baum and longed for the day that she could regain her independence.

Matt Baum on the other hand liked and adored Florida, loved America. It had everything that he wanted, vast wealth, a land of opportunity, America had welcomed him and his family with open arms. Devious and unrelenting in his quest for the top job he had used his underhand dealings and wealth to attain the office of Senator.

Where his wife desired peace and quiet, Matt Baum revelled in the noisy adulation of the huge crowds that gathered at rallies and fund raising events to greet him and hear what he had to say up on the stage. Matt Baum thrived on the adrenalin rush. When Adelina had launched the flower vase at Matthias she had accused him of effectively ending her life. If he could have found a bullet-proof way of making that happen sooner than later, he would have willingly made the arrangements himself, whatever the cost. He looked up at his aide after signing the last of the documents requiring his attention.

'Well Ed, I'd be lost without you.' He dropped his correspondence into the sorted tray. 'Let Mary deal with that lot later. Now what about that round and a cool beer at the Seven Valley clubhouse only the back of my throat feels like a crocs arse having laid in the sand all day.'

Ed Jackson closed the diary dropping it in his case.

'A few holes and a beer sounds perfect only I promised Sandra that I would be home in time to take Vanessa to her dance class. She likes me to watch.'

Matt Baum locked his desk drawer and slipped the key into his suit pocket. He thought about the times that he had watched his own daughter at her dance classes, but it was such a long time ago that the memory had become cloudy, hazy. When he thought about it many of his memories with what he had done with his son and daughter had become a blur.

'I had best not be too late tonight as I promised Adelina that I'd take her to that new fish restaurant down on the waterfront.'

Lying at the side of the pool in her one piece gold and black swimsuit Adelina watched the young gardener at work through the lens of her sunglasses, his bare arms flexed as he trimmed the hedge at the deep end.

Like an artist he skilfully clipped, cleared away and shaped the hedge just like Monet would have added oils to his canvas. The young man could not have been that much older than her own son, but she didn't care anymore. Adelina checked the time with her wrist watch, it would several more hours before Matthias came home before they went out to supper, plenty of time to ask if the gardener wanted a lemonade and ice.

Stealing a glance whenever he thought she wasn't watching Adam Slade continued to cut and clip the leaves of the topiary hedge, taking his time as he was in no hurry to get it finished and there was still a way to go before the dolphin took shape. The senator's wife was alluringly sexy in her swimsuit as she soaked up the afternoon sun on the lounger. He had to be careful though because with her dark shades it was impossible to know if she was looking his way.

When the sun moved around and behind the shortleaf pine it was a good indicator that it would be at least another hour before it passed by the tree and reappeared in full. Putting the book down on the lounger that she had been reading Adelina walked around the edge of the pool to where Adam was clearing up.

'You've done a great job. It must be exhausting work in this heat, would a lemonade and ice help cool you down?'

Adam Slade looked up, smiled and took a clean rag from his back pocket where he wiped the sweat from his hands.

'I would like that very much, thank you.'

Adelina grinned, feeling the sudden rush of rejuvenated blood dash from her head down through the stitching to the bottom of her swimsuit. It had been a long time since Adelina had felt as excited as she gestured with her index finger to follow.

'Leave the tools where they are, you can collect them after.' She gave his arm a gentle tug of reassurance. 'They're safe, nobody will come here for at least another hour.'

'Won't I get in trouble with the body guard?'

Adelina chuckled.

'No, I told him that he could have the afternoon off, he's in the movie room.'

Chapter Seventeen

FBI Special Agent David Hunter rapped lightly on the door, entering when invited in. Sat behind her desk and expecting his visit was Helen Montgomery, the Section Chief of Behavioural Sciences. She lay down her pen and gestured for David to take the seat opposite hers.

'How far have we got David?' she asked, her eyes meeting his.

'Nothing that will light up the parade. Homicide in downtown New York report the body of a male as having been washed up under the jetty near to the Keansburg Amusement Park, north west of Sandy Hook Bay. First impressions are that the deceased had been in the water sometime.'

'Do they have a name or any other details?'

'He'd been marked him up as a John Doe, but forensics ran a scan of body tattoos through the system that the fish hadn't destroyed. NYPD believe they belong to an Adam Jankowski. He had a condominium over in Chelsea. One of those upmarket new places, all mod cons and overlooking the river.'

Helen Montgomery sucked in then breathed out.

'I doubt Jankowski sees the attraction now!'

Hunter continued. 'Adam Jankowski had a couple of rap sheets for minor misdemeanours involving same sex offences. Nothing heavy and times have changed along with public opinion. It was different fifty years back, but not now.'

Montgomery wasn't sure.

'That could complicate the investigation. Gays tend to be very fussy and house proud. I doubt NYPD will find much to help in the apartment not unless the killer overlooked something.'

'Jankowski's car is missing.' Said David. 'The usual bulletin alerts have been issued, although there's nothing to say that the vehicle isn't at the bottom of the river or reservoir.'

'We're losing the initiative here before we begin on this one.' Montgomery stood and went over to look at the view beyond the window. 'You need to read the bulletin on my desk David, it only arrived ten minutes before I called you to this meeting.'

David Hunter picked up the communique which was from Dublin police. It gave details about an escape from Ashworth high-security psychiatric hospital in Merseyside. The escaped inmate was named Julianna Hesseltolph. She was the suspect in connection with a suspicious death of the senior warder and a woman named Melanie Smith. He continued reading about the brother's escape from Ebenstatt, the torture and murder of Alexander Koskovsky and the missing policeman Albrecht Hartmann. The last line mentioned Jason Chancery who had not been seen since nineteen ninety seven.

'And the police in England initially thought Melbourne was Australia.' She turned to face him.

'If this trio has somehow managed to slip through the net and they've landed on our shores, we're going to be busy David. Call it a gut feeling, but my opinion is that Adam Jankowski was only the beginning.'

David went over to the window to join her.

'Do I get any help on this?'

'Yes.'

From nineteen seventy two the induction of the Behavioural Science Unit at the FBI's Training Division at Quantico, Virginia had grown in stature, developing with every new case understanding the mentality of violent crime and offenders. Every piece of information however small which would help the agents in the field.

Interstate and worldwide Interpol cooperation had successfully seen the arrest of numerous suspects, some from terrorist factions that were not known to the public and the new buzz on the block culminated in the profiling of serial killers and psychopaths. The BSU was a highly trained unit, sent out to learn as much as possible, infiltrate and work in conjunction with police to keep the public safe from offenders. David Hunter and other fellow agents worked the streets, talked to gangs, visited prisoners doings serious time behind bars. At times they were called ghosts because they operated without being seen.

He thought Helen Montgomery looked pensive.

'I'll have the boys and girls down the hall search through security videos of rail, plane and port arrivals that should help free up some time for you. I'll make sure that you're the first to know if they uncover anything interesting.' He thanked her. 'One thing is for sure David and that's that these three haven't come here for the sake of their health or a holiday. We need to find out why and fast.'

Her computer screen saver was the same as his, a circular gold and blue emblem with the words *Fidelity, Bravery and Integrity* in the centre.

'I'll need to go home and pack a bag first.'

'Take Alvarez with you David. His languages could be useful. I'll pull together a backroom team.' She touched his arm the first time for a long time. 'Promise me that if you find anything, you'll keep me in the loop.'

Both were experienced to know that that first forty eight hours were the most important and anything beyond that and the trail started to go cold quickly.

'We'll need petty cash.'

'I'll sort the budget with upstairs, but try to keep it under control David, the last case involving Chester Miller almost blew our annual expenditure.'

'That was his fault, he was like a Jack Rabbit and wouldn't sit still. We had to cross a dozen states until we nailed him.'

Montgomery grinned.

'I know and the department got the credit for bringing him in.'

He was about to close the door when Montgomery had a parting shot.

'Oh and David, please be careful out there, I still care even if you think I don't.'

'I know.' He smiled, he meant it.

'I will try my best to control the media from this office, but if you encounter anything out in the field throw it back my way and if you have to, lie, let's leave integrity aside for this trio.' He looked at her knowing how strong her values were for the department and him.

'I never lie, unless I'm cornered.'

'Just be extra careful. I've a bad feeling about this case that it won't end well.'

She back down at her desk and picked up her pen not looking up as the door clicked shut. When it did then she looked. *'Fuck it...'* she whispered to herself. It was getting hard sitting opposite David. She still loved him and even six months down the line after they had mutually agreed to end the relationship, they had somehow managed to keep it hidden from anyone in the department. Writing the time and date of their meeting in the file she realised that her emotions had not gone away.

It had been a mistake to finish it, but how they felt about one another was in danger of wrecking both their careers. During that time Helen Montgomery had got promotion to section chief. It had been another nail in the emotional coffin. Taking a small photo of him that she kept hidden in the folds of her purse she rubbed her thumb affectionately over his image. *'Please take care David, I am always with you, wherever you go!'*

Walking down the hall he passed between the other offices his broad six foot frame reflected in the glass made him look taller and wider. He wore a deep blue, two-piece suit with white shirt and tie. Sporting a neatly styled cut his brown hair and chiselled features had the woman agents and researchers turn and look.

'Inch-for-inch David always reminds me of a well-honed running back for the Redskins rather than a bureau agent.'

The woman standing alongside sighed silently.

'Inch-for-inch he could investigate me any day!'

They poked their heads around the door frame to watch his butt disappear as the hall curved.

Alvarez Mendes saw the women looking and laughed. He closed his desk drawer and locked it retrieving the jacket from the back of his chair.

'Do we have anything good?' he asked.

'Yes and no.'

Chapter Eighteen

The next morning neither made any reference to the events that had taken place having returned to the motel each accepting that what had happened not only felt right, but had been right and that no explanation was necessary. They found a small diner in the opposite direction to the steakhouse for breakfast before heading out again on the road. Sitting next to the window seat Jakub made the conscious decision to be honest with Elise and the alias Johann Roebers had served its purpose, but now he felt that he could trust her.

'Why did you say that it was Johann?' Elise asked, leaning forward over the table so not to attract the attention of the other diners, 'I rather liked Johann, although Jakub suits you just as well.'

'At school the other kids would taunt me about my name, they would call me Jakub Hubbub, the name of a simple man from an Austrian nursery rhyme. For years I struggled academically and I wasn't the brightest in the class. When the opportunity presented itself to be Johann, I adopted the name. I like change.'

It was a plausible reason and Elise seemed satisfied.

'You can use either,' he implied, 'I don't mind.'

'Jakub... I like Jakub, it has that biblical ring to it, like the saint!'

Jakub laughed, a saint nothing could be further from the truth.

'I'm glad that we got that sorted.' He kept the surname Roebers knowing it would stop her delving too deep into the past if she knew he was Hesseltolph. Finding out his true identity could end up disastrous for them both. Heading back down the ninety five they stopped off at Florence for bottled water and sun oil. Jakub had stopped smoking on board the freighter over from Rotterdam choosing a packet of mints instead. Elise had said that she liked the fresh smell that the mints gave his mouth.

Driving with the sun chasing close behind they were relaxed and Jakub found himself looking every so often at Elise, there was something that he liked about her, something that not even Julianna possessed although as yet he didn't know what. With the radio on low as background drive music Ebenstatt had stolen the chance of being close and in a relationship. He liked sex, had enjoyed the special moments spent with Julianna, but Elise was different. She was a mature woman, sexually experienced and she had proved it the night before. He was keen to know more about her.

'You said that your parents were killed in a tragic car crash, was you with them at the time of the accident?'

Elise didn't look at him.

'No, I was at school when it happened. It was some years later that I read the official reports which said that the brakes of a commercial heavy goods truck laden down with a cargo of quarry rocks had failed to react quick enough and stop the truck at the junction. It made no mention to say whether it was illegally overweight, not that the outcome would have made any difference.

"My grand-pere was really loving and very kind. He told me that my parents would not have suffered as death would have been instantaneous. He was a gentle soul and had a way with words that I always found soothing. Losing them so abruptly still hurts even to this day.'

Elise paused to let the memory catch up.

'Irrespective of their death being instantaneous, I am still of the belief that in that split second an individual realises the inevitable horror that is about to befall them, unless they are struck from behind. I think we carry those thoughts with us into the next life, a sort of street-wise catalogue of events that make us that much wiser each time that we're reborn.'

She scooped a mint from the dashboard, opened the packet and popped one into Jakub's mouth.

'There are times when I've attended a scene. Forensic have taken the evidence, taken photographs, but I take my own. Often I get the impression that the victim's soul hasn't left the body, but he or she is staring up at me. It's as if they are daring me to begin profiling, like they're saying *'go on then prove your worth, are you good enough to find this attacker.'* I feel a heavy weight on my shoulders and it remains there until I close the file and the perpetrator is behind bars. In my dreams I see a face suddenly loom out of the mist and come at me. I know that I am asleep, but I can't escape. I know it's the murderer and that he also knows I am getting too close.'

'Nightmares can do that. Why is that?' he wanted to know.

'The brain is the most complex computer ever designed, receiving and discharging commands to limbs, senses, muscles and organs. It can trigger a reaction that tells us something is about to happen. Some call it sixth-sense. Psychologists however refer to it as reflex mechanics, the infinity of a single moment where the brain defends the victim from an attack, like raising an arm defensively when you know you are going to be hit. My parents might have experienced that a second before they saw the shadow of the truck, a second before it killed them. I call it the shadow of death. I find myself at a murder scene looking for the shadow. I know it'll be there somewhere.' She turned to face him. 'Why did you ask?'

'No specific reason. I was just thinking knowing the nature of your work how you might have dealt with your parent's death.' Really he wanted to know how deep she would go until she uncovered the truth.

Elise crunched down hard breaking the mint in half.

'Reading the official report, it was just words, but the truth brought me closer to them again. The only battle I had was with myself. I still ponder over fate and destiny. I'm not sure about God and heaven or hell. Is there a split infinity that divides our living with death and takes our soul to be reborn, who knows. I feel that I've lived before so I look at death as a chapter coming to an end before some greater force turns the page and we start the next chapter of our existence. I look at that way and that my parents turned the page. I feel that I'll see them again one day. That is how I deal with their going so abruptly. '

She swallowed the last of the mint. Her mouth felt fresh.

'Professionally, I hear so much crap from madmen, psychopaths who commit any manner of heinous crimes that I admit, there are times when I could willingly pick up a gun hold it to their head and pull the trigger, walk calmly away and feel no remorse.'

'Like the truck driver?' he was pushing her harder. He overtook a delivery truck. He liked the idea of her firing the bullet.

'I'm not sure. There were no witnesses, so I cannot say categorically who was to blame.'

'And the madmen, the psychopaths, what about them?'

'They tend to live in a bubble of ignorance and their appreciation of suffering belongs to somebody else. Taking a life is so easy, keeping a victim alive is much harder.'

Jakub took a swig of his water. Elise had her own bottle.

'A sort of torture?'

She spilt some of the water looking his way. It was strange how it saw the scenario as torture for the offender.

'Tied up with a hood over your head in constant darkness and only your senses of hearing and smell left, yes torture would panic the mind. I cannot answer for the offender, they are permanently tortured by the thoughts that make them do bad things to others.'

'Like voices inside the head?'

Again Elise looked, she wondered where he was going with the conversation.

'I guess so. We all hear them now and then. A moment's indecision is resolved by a voice in our mind. Negativity is replaced by a positive solution and we react accordingly. Do you hear voices?' she asked adding a chuckle.

'Only when I'm with negative people!' He thought about Koskovsky and Hartmann if only they could have heard the voices then they would have known what was going to happen next.

An audible alarm on the dashboard sounded and flashed red letting Jakub know that they had an additional fifty miles before he needed to pull into a gas station and refuel. A mile further up the road he saw a sign for the next station. The fuel alarm had brought an abrupt halt to the conversation and Elise put her head back on the headrest thinking about happy times that she had spent with her parents before the crash.

Pulling onto the dusty forecourt of the gas station it had definitely seen better days, the petrol and diesel pumps together with the concrete base were rusted and marked with old spills. To protect them from the elements the owner had erected a makeshift corrugated tin roof.

Switching off the engine the attendant appeared almost immediately emerging from a timber shack that served as both the pay desk and accessories shop. The single window that overlooked the forecourt was in need of a wash, scratched by dust and road particles. Wiping his hand clean down the front of his blue overalls the male attendant had a few missing teeth. He was as tatty as the gas station.

'Good day to you folks. Nice day for travelling.'

He came up on Jakub's side, although he was clearly interested in Elise, her long bare legs disappearing up her shorts and her cleavage had jumped clear of the of her tee-shirt the front of which was emblazoned with a Quebec University logo. Jakub handed over the key for the petrol cap then got out of the vehicle to stretch his legs.

'Regular do you?' asked the attendant as Jakub kicked the tyres to check the pressure.

'Yes, please.'

He watched the gauge spin on the drum as the fuel filled the tank.

'You want me to check under the hood as well?' the attendant asked.

'That would be good.' Jakub responded, adding a smiling. It was a nice day, sunny and warm.

Inviting polite conversation the attendant sniffed and asked if they were on vacation.

Jakub watched the regulator slow as the fuel neared the top of the tank. 'Yes, we're doing the East Coast before we cut across to Las Vegas.' In the car Elise smiled at Jakub. The pump stopped whirring and registered at thirty two dollars. Replacing the hose and locking the cap the attendant moved forward to the front of the Chrysler catching sight of Elise who had reached down to retrieve her bottle of water, the mounds of her breasts evident as her tee-shirt fell forward and free of her chest. When she sat back up he was smiling at her. She didn't respond there was something about him that she found creepy. Adjusting the top of her tee-shirt she folded her arms over her chest.

Popping open the hood the attendant had noticed the registration plate.

'Hell, if I don't remember this plate,' he said tapping the metal plate with his fingertips. 'The driver, a different guy to you stopped here last year on his way down to the Jacksonville Pride. He needed a tyre changed having picked up a tack.'

'What's the Jacksonville Pride?' Jakub asked, coming around the car and between the attendant and Elise.

Pulling the rag slowly down over the rod of the dipstick the attendant hoped Elise was watching.

'It's the old queen's parade for them queer folk, you know the type all hand flicking, hip bending gays, lesbians, transgender you name it, it goes. When I get the chance I close the garage and go along just to see the sights. Damn if it's not a laugh just standing there, watching.'

Bending down to rehouse the oil rod he winked at Elise.

'For the sake of a weekend I would claim to be one of those gender-bender types just to get me near some of them horny lesbians.' He leant in closer to Jakub. 'Why is it that a lot of them lesbo woman are so fuckin' good looking. What a waste for a straight guy like me.'

He closed the hood and tapped the number plate again.

'Yep, that's the one alright. Chelsea insignia with the statue of liberty top left corner and the initials AJ. I remember because they were my late mum's initials when she was a single woman.' He rubbed his chin not realising that he left behind an oil smudge. 'I never thought that gay would sell the car. It was his pride and joy.' He winked again at Elise when Jakub watched a police cruiser go sailing by. 'Pride and joy, I bet he had his engine decoked after the parade!'

Elise refused to look any longer, the attendant was as crude as the trucker that had tried to force himself upon her. She shivered at the thought. Jakub followed the garage attendant to the pay desk. Elise would like to have used the bathroom, but she crossed her legs and would wait until later.

Jakub took out his wallet to pay for the fuel, but the attendant instead of ringing up the amount reached under the counter and pulled out a ledger. Running his finger down the entries he turned it around for Jakub to see.

'There you go mister as I thought, it were the autumn of last year and one rear tyre puncture repair. The guy paid cash and he had plenty on him as well. I remember telling him that it was foolish to be carrying so much in his wallet only them kind of parades always attracts pickpockets and druggies ready to shake you down in a dark alley.'

'Did he pick up a repair invoice? Jakub asked, turning the ledger back around.

The attendant opened a metal drawer behind, he withdrew a wad of invoice copies.

'There you go - Adam Jankowski from Chelsea, New York City. I remember the guy because he had a foreign twang to his tongue, similar to your own. Polish bloke I think.'

Jakub had seen and heard enough. He handed over four ten dollar bills before walking over to the accessories shelf, where there was an assortment of vehicle spares, cans of oil and confectionery.

Ringing up the change the attendant sniffed.

'We've got most things here, you looking for anything special only if it ain't there on the shelf I can root around out back and find you an alternative. Maybe something nice for the pretty lady out front!'

Jakub suddenly bent over clutching his back, it had the attendant rush around the counter and come to help, out of sight of the forecourt.

'Are you alright there mister?' he asked.

Jakub rubbed his back hard. 'I broke some ribs paying soccer a way back and they hurt every so often. The pain can kick like a mule and be as irritating as a woman nagging in your ear, only worse.'

The attendant laughed. 'Nothing worse than a woman nagging, let me know what you want and I'll reach down for you.'

Jakub pointed to the cans of oil. 'I had best take one only that car eats oil.' He straightened up arching his back and raising one arm above his shoulder as the attendant bent down to select the correct oil. Chopping the back of the attendant's neck hard the man immediately went to his knees. Before he lost consciousness Jakub had his hands positioned around the man's head back and front, with a swift twist he snapped the man's vertebrae. He let the attendant fall to the floor dead. Dragging the body through to the stockroom out back he closed the door and secured the hasp lock. It would be sometime before the body would be found by the fire service.

Dropping the wad of invoices into the waste can he added lighter fuel and a small butane cylinder. Jakub raided the till, took more bottles of water together with confectionery then lit the match dropping it into the waste basket. He walked casually back to the car where Elise was waiting passing over the water and chocolate bars.

'I thought we might need a little extra for the journey.'

Elise smiled, she was pleased to see him back. 'That guy really gave me the creeps Jakub, he was constantly undressing me. It made me shiver. I could positively feel his hands all over me especially when he popped the hood and checked the oil.'

Jakub started the engine, dropped the gear into drive and released the handbrake.

'Forget him Elise, he's not worth thinking about and depraved men like him get what they deserve.' He thought about the boys in Kurlor had teased and concerned Julianna following her home when he had been held back at school and she had to walk home alone. He put a reassuring hand on her leg giving it a squeeze. 'Shall we try and get ahead of the sun once again?' he asked.

'Yes please.'

Three kilometres south of *The Lazy Bend* service station Elise had again relaxed back into her seat listening to the music on the radio. She was so relaxed that she didn't hear the popping noises coming from behind and neither did she notice the rising plume of black smoke that was growing in intensity. Several minutes later a fire truck sped past them going in the opposite direction, even then she wasn't interested. Looking instead at Jakub she put her hand gently on his forearm as he took the Chrysler around the bend.

'I hope that bastard garage attendant burns in hell one day, along with the truck driver!'

Chapter Nineteen

Walking out onto the veranda Julianna was met by Mary who had been out front tending to the deadheading of the flowers. Julianna was surprised to find that May had already walked Emily Lou up and down the beach. Occupying the vacant wicker chair she poured herself a coffee.

'You obviously needed that sleep, Mary smiled, 'I'll make us some breakfast soon. Do you like croissants or toast?'

Julianna felt the warmth of the sun surround her. She loved the easy existence of the beach and being with Mary and Emily Lou.

'Whatever is easier, do you want some help?'

'No, you're a guest. Sit and enjoy the view.'

'Is it always this beautiful, peaceful?' she asked.

Mary stretched relieving the aches and pains from where she had been bending. 'More or less, I've had a reason to complain, not in all the years that I've lived here.'

Mary sipped her coffee.

'You were tossing and turning, mumbling a lot in the night. I would have come in, but I didn't want to intrude. It's best to let a nightmare run its course.'

'I'm sorry, I didn't want to disturb your sleep.'

'I never sleep for long. I would rather be talking with Abraham than sleeping. I was awake when you had your nightmare.'

'That's exactly what it was Mary, a nightmare.'

'You've something dark troubling your mind Julianna, that much is obvious and for somebody so young and beautiful you shouldn't be consumed by the past. I try to put the demons to bed when I lay my head down on the pillow.'

Julianna sighed. 'I'd like to do the same Mary, but they keep coming back night after night!'

Mary poured herself another coffee, topping up Julianna's cup.

'Do you miss your mother?'

Julianna gave Emily Lou a biscuit.

'Yes, although I thought I never would.'

Mary chuckled. 'I miss my mother. I can never forgive myself for the heartache that I caused her and yet she stuck by my through thick and thin. Mother's do that regardless. I sensed, felt your mother close last night. Abraham told me that they had talked, but he didn't divulge what they had talked about.'

'She appears in some dreams although she never talks to me, but she's there on a street corner or sitting in the room watching.'

Mary stroked the dog's head. 'I always used to think that they could never be the same waves returning day after day, but they are, maybe longer or shorter they are still wet and just as beautiful. Life is like that Julianna, coming and going in waves of happiness and disappointments. We have to learn to ride the waves and find the balance. If you sit here in the dead of night, you'll hear them talk to you, the waves I mean. They bring messages.'

Julianna sipped her coffee, it was good as ever. Some would think Mary was flying with the fairies, but she was the most grounded person that Julianna had ever come across.

'Nightmares are there to pull us back, to have us reflect and to tread carefully the coming day, the next week or in the future. I've found that thinking positively I don't have so many. I cast aside the dark cloud that followed me around Julianna, you have to do the same.'

'I've hurt so many people Mary, I don't think I deserve another chance.'

Mary wobbled Emily Lou's chin making the Labrador wag her tail.

'Causing the pain of others is an inevitable vexation that we learn early on in life. I had a friend Missy at kindergarten, you call them nursery. I would lock her in the children's playhouse and make her climb through the window to escape. I lost count of how many times I got chastised for that. Poor Missy she grew up to be an architect. I sometimes wonder if she put extra windows in a design, just in case!'

'I see Melanie Anne Smith walking in and out of doors in the dream, she's searching for a way to escape, only I beg her to take me with her Mary.'

'Horologists say that turning back time will eventually help break the winder. Abraham talked about Melanie, she's in a good place now Julianna. You need to be as well.'

For the first time for a long time Julianna started to cry, really cry. She was relieved to know that Melanie wasn't in any pain. Maybe the doors would stay shut now. Mary came over and put her arm around Julianna as she would with her own daughter. Julianna let the tears flow as Emily Lou edged in closer laying herself over Julianna's feet. She felt their love sucking out the negativity. When she was done crying Mary gave her handkerchief.

'Prison is a harsh place to begin the healing and you've been there,' said Mary, 'but feeling the healing is paramount, only then can you believe in yourself. Marrying Abraham became my salvation and *Whispering Echoes* my bolt hole. Even when I leave here, I'll leave my soul here because this is where it belongs.'

'I feel calm here Mary. This house has a heart that beats, I hear it!'

'That's what Abraham used to say about the place.'

Giving her biscuit to Emily Lou, Julianna could only nod her response.

'I was locked up Mary, I was labelled mad and dangerous. Maybe the things that the authorities said about me were true. Here, right now at your house everything seems so far away. I'd do anything to prove them all wrong and right the sins, even if it meant giving up my life.'

Mary shook her head.

'That's a little too extreme. Life is a gift. Abraham told me once that I was being selfish when I had similar thoughts.'

Julianna told Mary about Kurlor, her parents, Gillian Dennerholm and Jason Chancery. When she was finished Mary still had her arm around Julianna.

'Coming to America was a gamble, you could have been picked up anywhere en-route!'

'Time was on my side.' She showed Mary the postcard. 'I came here to find my brother although now I'm not so sure. I have lived in Jakub's shadow for so long that I dare not open my eyes in the dark in case he's looking over me.

'I cannot condone his evil ways and I am to blame as much as he, but I found a way to survive only my survival was through manipulation and control. I help a killer escape justice. The staircase to hell has marked where I went down so low. Jakub is coming here solely to seek revenge.' She told Mary about her relationship with her brother. 'Now do you understand why it would be easier to die, than to seek absolution?'

Mary held on tighter. 'Here's coming here, Jakub's coming to Melbourne?'

'Yes. He seeks a man called Matthias Baumgartner and he will kill anybody that gets in his way.' Mary felt the breeze blow up and across the front garden, knowing what it meant.

'You must not meet Julianna, you and your brother I mean. It will destroy you if you do. And my path also cross with Jakub's, I will not be able to lift the curse.' Emily Lou stood up, stretched her front paws forward then changing position nestled herself even closer to Julianna. It made Mary smile.

'Dogs don't have complicated lives, they always settle for the easy option. They are also good judges of character. Emily Lou sees only the good in you.'

Julianna reached down and stroked the back of Emily Lou's neck.

Mary continued. 'Love comes in many forms. Love for a husband, a wife, grandparents, our parents, siblings and our children, and their children. Love transcends the generations and we include friends who are loyal. At times it becomes necessary to sacrifice a little of yourself to secure that love.

'You have to love yourself first Julianna before you can give love. Emily Lou is different from us in that she can love us both and not have to worry about any silly consequences as long as she is fed and watered each day, along with the odd biscuit.

'Maybe now the time is right to break the connection of the past and go on alone. Perhaps it's time to stop holding on so tight. Maybe destiny bought you here not the message on the postcard. Fate works in mysterious ways. I suppose the burning question is what do you want to do with your life, now that you are here?'

'Before I tell you that, what did you mean you wouldn't be able to lift the curse?'

'Every day Emily Lou and me, we hike up and down the beach twice a day. Invariably she runs ahead walking beside the spirit of Abraham, you see she was his dog. They both wait for me to catch up. We talk and my late husband tells me that he's waiting until we can pass together. A long time ago he sacrificed everything to lift the curse hanging around my neck. We talked last night, he would do the same for you.'

Julianna felt the full weight of Emily Lou's head on her feet as the Labrador changed position in her sleep.

'And like you Julianna, I'm not crazy. I feel my late husband's presence on the beach and in the house here. Friends don't visit as much as they used to do, mainly because word got around that I was talking to myself. If they had the love that I had for Abraham, they'd talk to their dead husbands.'

On cue Emily Lou raised her head, looked at them both as though giving her opinion on the matter before closing her eyes and laying her head back down.

'She always tells me when Abraham is around. You asked how it was possible to lift the curse. With Abrahams help we can make things right with your soul, but only if you believe it possible and you break your ties with evil.'

'You mean my brother.'

'You have a choice Julianna. Your parents have begged the beyond that you be given one more chance!'

Julianna nodded that she would.

'Can I stayed one more night Mary, then come tomorrow morning I promise to pack up my belongings and leave you and Emily Lou in peace, there would be no trace that I was ever here. I'm good at disappearing.'

Mary Peterson stood arching her back and stretching her arms high.

'We're late for breakfast, but what the hell. I'll make another pot of fresh coffee and you can help with the croissants and toast, I feel like both today.'

She placed her hand over her forehead and watched a young female surfing the waves beyond the sand.

'Later, will you take Emily Lou for her walk? The beach is over two kilometres long and by the time you reach the end and turn around I guarantee that your head will clear of thoughts. You'll know what to do.'

Julianna picked up the used coffee cups. 'Of course.'

'Nobody will come looking for you here Julianna not at the white painted house where the mad old lady lives.'

She turned away from the beach and walked to the door leading inside.

'You are welcome to stay here for as long as you want and if I do see any of the friends that I have left, I meet them in town not here. Here you're safe and we have Emily Lou to stand guard over us. Stay a while and let the early morning sun wash over you and the evening light suck out from the past that you want to let go, keep only the good bits. And we have a good stock of wine down in the cellar as well only Emily Lou gave up the drink the night my Abraham died.'

Chapter Twenty

Narrow and windowless, illuminated by a range of blue ceiling lights the room known as the *'brain'* was functional, without decorative pictures unless you wished to include the suspect photos. The room was stuffy, kept warm by the heat generated from the computers and screens and some complained, but it was workable because of the air conditioning system. Along one wall were a set of copiers, printers, facsimile machines and heaped in the corner boxes of photographic paper.

Alvarez Mendes accompanied David Hunter into the intelligence room keen to see how the progress board was shaping up and if there had been any new bulletins on the information screen. When Mendes checked the in-tray, Hunter talked to the technician drawing up the memory chart.

'Anything new Michelle?'

'We have no new leads on Jakub Hesseltolph and his sister has literally vanished. We know she landed at Orlando international, but from there the trail goes cold. It could be she's still in the area or if they've met up they could be moving back inland.'

On the progress board two names had already been added - Melanie Smith and Gillian Dennerholm. Against each name was the method used to kill them, the *modus operandi*. Under that were photographs taken when the bodies had been found. Michelle was compiling a check list to ascertain every piece of information they could on the two victims, first of seeing if they were linked by ancestry, work place or schools. Nothing would be left to chance.

'And we still have no recent photograph of Jakub Hesseltolph?' he asked.

Michelle pursed her lips together as she shook her head.

'I pushed it over to Dave, he's good with graphic profile. I asked him to age the one we do have, adding aging around the eyes and hair styles. We should have something in about an hour.'

He thanked her and asked that the digital printouts be shown to Helen Montgomery. Mendes stood alongside Hunter looking at the various bits of information and photographs.

'It's not a lot to go on, is it?'

David Hunter the eternal optimist nodded and they stood back to allow the technicians space to move about and work.

'Michelle has Dave working through some forensic character building, at least then we'll have something to work with.'

Mendes compared what they did have.

'They have haunting eyes. They follow you around the room.'

'Dark like that of a wolf you mean.'

Mendes looked again. 'Yes.'

They watched as a technician added the names of Alexander Koskovsky and Albrecht Hartmann. Alongside the policeman they wrote 'missing'.

'And the body washed up at Keansburg,' asked Hunter, 'can we add that to Jakub Hesseltolph's tally?' From the far end of the room a female researcher called out.

'Dental records has positively identified the deceased as Adam Jankowski.' She went over to the facsimile machine and punched the incoming button with her fingertip, giving David Hunter a lingering smile. 'The coroner's report is coming down the wire now.'

Mendes nudged David's arm.

'Do the women working here have an extra daily dose of androsterone or is it just you?'

Michelle looked up and smiled, but said nothing.

'There's your answer.' David walked away and over to the facsimile machine where he read the coroner's report.

'Adam Jankowski died from a single stab wound, administered from behind puncturing the heart which caused a massive internal haemorrhaging. Death was instantaneous. Drowning was not a contributory factor, merely secondary during the disposal of the body. The coroner believed the knife used was from a common kitchen set.'

Mendes read the fax in the tray from forensics at NYPD.

'The condo had been meticulously washed down and work surfaces, sinks, taps and door handles didn't have a single print, not even from the occupant. Forensic tests revel the knives in the block were cleaned by pouring meths over the blades and then setting fire to them. Tests show traces of denatured alcohol in the sink.'

Hunter inhaled and filled his lungs. 'Our killer knew what he was doing. We can assume that he took the car, the clothes, the deceased's wallet and his identity.' He looked across to where Michelle was marking up the chart with lines, making connections. 'We have to add Adam Jankowski to the board, but as possible player. A dead man walking the streets or driving his own vehicle.'

'Anything else?' asked Mendes.

'There was only one message on the ansa-machine and that checked-out as being from a lady friend who Jankowski was supposed to meet later that day. NYPD cleared her, she doesn't even have a parking fine against her name. We had best pack our Bermuda's and sunglasses, we're heading for Florida.'

Mendes was as convinced. 'And we know for sure that's where they're heading and that Jankowski isn't the work of a jealous lover?'

Hunter showed Alvarez the copy of the postcard sent to Julianna Hesseltolph. 'Come on let's go see the boss and let her know where we going.'

They were about to leave the room when a shout stopped them in their tracks.

'You might want to look at this agents. It's just in.'

Gathering around the monitor, outside broadcast units were reporting the mysterious and tragic death of a fire and explosion at the *Lazy Bend* gas station. A fire chief told the reporter that a body had been found in the back storeroom which was believed to be that of the owner. There were no further details, not until the coroner's autopsy.

'It's Jakub Hesseltolph, I know it, feel it. He's heading down to Florida on the ninety five.'

Alvarez nodded. 'The car shouldn't be too hard to find.'

Together they checked the road map, calculating time, distance and average speed, taking into account motel stops, eating and refuelling.

'Hesseltolph's covered a fair amount of the journey already.' Admitted Mendes.

David said that he would update Montgomery and Alvarez call NYPD to make sure that they had everything and that nothing had been left out of the initial fax.

'Are you packed?' she asked as David closed the door.

'I will be soon.'

David remembered their last trip away when they had been to the lakes going camping. They had picked a remote location where the days had been long, but fun, the evenings relaxing and the nights great. With the sun on her back Helen looked amazing sitting the other side of the desk.

'And it's your hunch that he caused the explosion at the gas station?'

'Yes. Obviously something took place there that had him kill the owner and torch the place.'

'And is that a hunch too?'

'When the coroner does the post-mortem they'll find that the garage owner was murdered. I'll bank my pension on it!'

Helen Montgomery didn't argue back the possibilities recognising that David was rarely wrong.

'You can still get there ahead of Hesseltolph if you take the plane!'

'No, I'd rather drive thanks and if he takes a detour we can be on him quicker.'

'What about the sister, any word on where she could be hiding up?'

'None. She's gone completely to ground. I've a strange feeling about her too.'

'Like what...?' asked Montgomery as she looked directly at him, wanting to go around the other side of her desk and have him hold her again.

'Like she's here, but we won't know it.'

'You mean not meet up with Chancery or her brother?'

'That about sums it up nicely.'

'That's a big hunch David. I hope you're right for your sake and the public. Is Alvarez ready?'

'Yes, he's just talking to NYPD and then we'll be on our way. We'll take it in turns to drive and cover as much ground as possible. I'll keep you posted.'

'And you think he'll keep the Chrysler.'

'Yes, he's already made progress and he's almost there. Taking another vehicle would only complicate things and maybe give him an extra hour before the authorities start searching, but from I've learnt about Jakub Hesseltolph already he likes the thrill of the chase.'

She shook her head in admiration of his positive stand.

'Forever the optimist David. That's what I always admired about you.'

'Was that all?'

A smile creased the sides of her mouth. 'You know it wasn't and the nights out at Tahoe should have told you as much.'

'After this assignment is done and the dust settles would it help if I put in for a transfer?'

Helen Montgomery looked shocked. *'Why...?'*

David leant forward resting his palms on her desk. 'So that I can see you again!'

'Where and how would you go?'

'Far enough to keep them upstairs off our backs, but close enough that I can travel back at weekends and spend time with you.'

She knew him well enough to know that he was serious.

'But the unit David, it means so much to you and much of the success here is down to you.'

'Maybe, it's time for somebody else to shine at BSU, somebody like Alvarez. He's really good at what he does.'

She was quiet, an unusual quality and at times Helen could be difficult to read.

'Maybe, the time has come for me to also take stock of my life and look ahead, at the future. This should have been you sitting here this side of the desk instead of me.' She replied.

'No, I enjoy it in the field too much to be pushing paper around all day and you fit the chair better than I ever would.'

She laughed. 'So that's all I do all day, push paper around,' she put her hand over the back of his, 'come back safe from this assignment David and we'll talk it over.'

David grinned and gave a shake of his head.

'Always leaving a little of the mystery hanging in the air, that's what I found attractive about you!'

She watched as he shut the door wishing she had told him just how much she loved him. How much she too wanted to settle down and have a husband and for it to be David, to have a family and to have most of all somewhere where she could call home. Time was marching on as was her body clock and for too long the FBI had been her only family. Perhaps now it was time to get a divorce.

Hitting the freeway they received a communique from the 'brain' to say that another report from the police at Wilson had just come in regarding a disturbance that had taken place at a diner restaurant where a man had his arm broken. It was an everyday defensive assault, but what alerted the team to the report was the accent of one of the men involved. They did the sums and guessed it could be Jakub Hesseltolph. The details were sketchy, as was the description and there was no CCTV, but an eye witness had said that the man had left the steakhouse with a woman.

'It could be his sister and like we thought they could have met at Melbourne and now be travelling inland.'

David wasn't convinced.

'No. I told Montgomery that I had a hunch. I don't think the woman is Julianna Hesseltolph, but somebody else.'

Alvarez laughed. 'You like to mix things up and make them complicated. I like my plate clean and keep the menu easy.'

David who was sat in the passenger seat had been thinking about Helen, agreed.

'Michelle did some digging on our behalf and found the motel that Hesseltolph and the woman stayed at. Again no camera images to help, but in the register it had been signed RM.'

Alvarez changed lane adding a little more depression to the accelerator.

'Using RM as an alias is the obvious choice although translated from French, it would read: *'eu le bon – rm'* which could also be interpreted as *'got the right one – rm'*. And the initials RM can signify *'remake'* – to do something different.'

David was impressed with the way that Alvarez was thinking and unravelling, looking at the variables. If he did transfer Mendes would do well at BSU, very well.

'My hunch is that Jakub Hesseltolph has already found himself a target. Our job is to find him before we discover who exactly.'

Chapter Twenty One

Jakub and Elise covered the remaining mileage to Melbourne stopping overnight at another roadside motel, eating at nearby diner where the choice of food was good and relaxed. This time there was no rowdy diner or need to help some beleaguered waitress. Returning to the motel room they passed the time naked and pretty much as they had twenty fours earlier, until physically exhausted.

With Jakub sleeping soundly beside her Elise stared up at the stars beyond the window. His desire to satisfy her sexual needs had been as exciting, but Elise had perceived, felt a difference from the night before when they had been intimate. It was as though Jakub had something heavy weighing down on his mind.

He had been happy with her insistence to try different positions, have some fun, but she could tell that his participation had been rougher, almost desperate as though he needed to be elsewhere, needed it to be over with. Looking up she wondered if the stars had the answers. She also wondered whether or not she was looking too deep into something that wasn't actually there. Oscar had once accused her of being oversensitive and when she had questioned him as to why the sex hadn't been as passionate, his excuse was that he was tired. Of course Oscar had been tired, he'd been banging some other woman that day before her.

Elise gently stroked Jakub's hair making him murmur. She wondered if he had been hurt by love in the past and did that account for the way that he had held her from behind and pushed hard. From her interviews with suspects she knew that most men had a desire to prove themselves, to be macho especially in front of a woman. She had catalogued the varying emotions before the thoughts arrived down at their dick. During the intimacy there had been a moment when Jakub had looked up at her, his dark eyes fixing on her breasts. It was the same look that she had received from the garage attendant, it had made her shiver. When Jakub had asked why, she blamed a cold draught.

'Maybe I'm over analysing too deep,' she thought, only nobody answered back. Jakub moved in his sleep and his arm came to rest over her abdomen.

She watched a bird, a large bird fly across the sky, probably a barn owl remembering a lecture that she had attended in Washington on the *sexual practices and subsequent abuse* between consenting adults. The words of the female lecturer were still clear as she drummed home the point that there was a fine line which could be crossed at any given moment during intimate moments. Oscar had never crossed that line, he had simply rubbed it out.

She continued stroking as she thought of how the garage attendant had continually undressed her with his eyes. Why she wondered were there were so many vile, sexual predators around who wanted nothing more than raw meaningless sex. Jakub had been right when he had said retribution would be swift. It did make her wonder how he knew.

Elise had originally intended leaving Jakub after the first leg of the journey and heading west taking in Tennessee, Arkansas and Oklahoma, Nashville, Memphis and Broken Arrow where the Creek Indian Chiefs had once settled their wandering tribes on the grassy plains. Pre-planning the end of the journey through the state of California, moving north up along the west coast before returning home. The horrible, scary incident with the trucker however had her made her take in a diversion where she had come across Jakub.

She really liked him, thought she trusted him, but inside of her despite feeling safe with Jakub there was an odd feeling that was gnawing away at her confidence and a voice inside her head was telling her to be careful. Was he all that he seemed and she had only known him a few days. Elise wanted to disbelief her doubts, but the way that he had dealt with the diner in the steakhouse had left doubts.

When the moon appeared in the window Jakub stirred again muttering incoherently although what he said was annoyingly too quick to understand. Elise couldn't be sure, but she believed his mutterings had been about a female. Groaning in his sleep his arm slipped away from her abdomen as Jakub turned onto his back. She used the opportunity to ease herself from the bed and walk naked to the bathroom.

She left pulling the flush of the system and stood at the sink rinsing cold water over her face with the inexplicable feeling that it was important to stay awake until daylight. The towel smelling nicely of a laundered lavender powder felt good as she wiped her face dry, like a soft teddy bear that she'd had a child, a bear that her grandfather had bought her as a special gift for no particular day, just because he saw it and knew that she would like it. When she took the towel away another face was looking at her. Jakub was stood in the doorway of the bathroom looking at her reflection in the mirror.

'Are you okay?' he asked.

'Yes, I'm fine, I needed to pee and wash the perspiration from my face. I'm sorry did I disturb you?'

He shook his head. 'No, I was dreaming… I think it was a nightmare. When I woke you weren't there. I thought you'd packed up and left without saying goodbye.'

Elise feigned a short chuckle.

'No way, what and leave in the middle of the night. All there is out there on the freeway in either direction are sex starved hungry truckers!'

He walked over to the toilet and positioned himself ready to relieve his bladder. Elise exited the bathroom and climbed back into bed where the moon had moved again only now it wholly occupied the room illuminating the rumpled sheets.

The next morning the conversation at breakfast was chirpy and Jakub was different again. Having climbed back into bed they had indulged in one another again only the second time it had been more intense, equally balanced and without the desperation or roughness. Elise wondered if Jakub's demons had been present the first time around until the nightmare when he had banished them altogether. They hit the freeway early wanting to cover as many miles as possible before the sun was at its highest. Stopping only for more bottled water Jakub refuelled wanting to keep the tank full covering all unexpected eventualities. An hour later they arrived in Melbourne. They had not seen one police patrol.

Elise ran her fingers through her hair, she liked the ocean.

'Do you think that your sister's already here?'

She purposely tipped a sliver of water from the bottle down the front of her tee-shirt, feeling the cooling effect disappear between the crease of her cleavage. Jakub watched as the thin veil travelled down the fabric of her top. 'There's no real way of knowing unless I see her. Julianna had further to come than me.' It wasn't a lie.

Not far down the beach Julianna sensed intuitively a strong a presence close by, but she managed to block the thoughts from her mind.

'I'd like to meet your sister, do you think that we'd get along?'

Watching the surf roll in and up to the beach Jakub continued staring ahead. Elise was good in bed and fun to be with, but Julianna was special would always be very special. Having arrived he had a decision to make about Elise. 'She's always been easy to get on with, I'm sure it'd work out fine.'

Elise let her head fall back against the headrest as she relaxed. 'That's good. Are you hungry, my treat then we can decide how best to start looking for Julianna.'

He looked at her curious to know why she had stayed so long knowing that she had originally planned to weave her adventures across to California. Was it just to be safe or to be with him, he wanted to ask, but for the time being he would play along until it was time to say goodbye.

As she soaked up the sun her hands behind her head pulling back her hair and pushing forward her breasts he wondered how many times she had analysed like she would a suspect. Was she playing along building a profile like the voices had said before they climbed into bed the night before. Pushing open the passenger door she stepped onto the sidewalk where she could see the water and beach much better. Looking her up and down it would be a pity to kill her.

Sitting herself on the edge of the car bonnet Elise had never asked about the car, how or where he had acquired the Chrysler or indeed why he had so much ready cash. Ordinarily Jakub would deal with a problem and walk away, but there was something about Elise that fascinated him. Holding nothing back she had been honest about past relationships, her work and her ambitions. He liked the sex, liked touching her, being intimate with her, but there was something else, something that had him ignore the voices that held his interest. *'She's playing cat and mouse with you,'* they had warned him the night before, *'and soon you'll fall into her trap and how do you know that she's not already been in touch with the police when you've been in the shower?'* Locking the car he joined her having spotted a fish bar a block down from the front.

Elise was keen to sit outside under the shade where she could watch the children playing down on the beach and see the bathers in the water. Jakub sat to the side of the table pulling the peak of the cap that much lower.

Melbourne had come alive hours before they had arrived and it wasn't until the bakery five doors down pulled down the metal security screen that it signified just how late they had arrived. Wiggling her wrist the watch had died somewhere along the journey.

'The damn battery is always giving up the ghost. I should invest in a new one.'

They shared a crab and salad platter washed down with a cool beer. Unlike breakfast the conversation seemed stilted. Elise was beginning to wonder why.

'Have I annoyed you in any way?' she asked.

Jakub looked up over the top of his beer.

'No, I just have a lot on my mind, that's all.'

'Your sister?'

He responded with a half-smile. 'Amongst other things.'

'Am I somewhere in that mix?'

This time the smile was more convincing.

'No,' he lied, 'only annoying events from the past although nothing important.'

Elise returned the smile, although she didn't believe him.

'I am grateful Jakub that you got me this far safely, but if you'd rather we could part company here and still be friends. I know finding Julianna means a lot to you?'

Jakub adjusted the shades so that she could see his eyes.

'No. I like you around.' It wasn't a lie, he did. Saying yes, thanks for the sex and going their separate ways would have been the easy option, but the voices in his head were now indecisive, juggling the balls of indecision between letting her sty and letting her go. Jakub broke the back of a king prawn venting his anger. He repeated himself. 'No, really I like your company Elise, I'd like you to stay.' He caught a whiff of the warm salty air coming up the beach and across to the restaurant. 'It's nice here.'

Elise agreed. 'Yes, I've always liked the sea, the beach and sunshine. I like the way that the tide washes away the footprints left in the sand as though the beach had never been touched in the first place.'

'If only life was that simple.' Jakub replied. The remark was a surprise.

'There is something troubling you?'

'I was just thinking about an old friend who I had heard moved to America a few years back. I was thinking how nice it would be to catch up with him again and we would have a lot to talk about.'

Jakub grinned. Somewhere out there Matthias Baumgartner was probably about to sit down with his wife and teenage children and enjoy an evening meal. It could well be his last.

'You could kill two birds with one stone!'

Jakub looked at her over the top of his sunglasses.

'How's that?'

'Finding Julianna and then visiting your friend.'

He nodded, breaking another only larger prawn in half.

'Trouble is... I've no idea where both are?' He caught the waiters attention behind the bar ordering another two beers.

At the table next to theirs a large man in a loud Hawaiian shirt left some money under the bread basket, got up and left the restaurant leaving behind a newspaper. Jakub reached across and took the paper. It would help give the impression that he was relaxed and enjoying the evening to any passing patrols. Growing a designer stubble since New York he looked nothing like his teenage photo. He flicked through the pages stopping at the centre fold where there was a large scoop on the potential candidate for up and coming elections. Staring back at him, larger than life itself was Matthias Baumgartner, only now he was called Matt Baum. Elise recognised the change in Jakub's mood.

'Seen something good?'

This time his smile was genuine, full of interest. 'Things are suddenly looking up again.' He turned the paper around so that she could see the centre fold. He tapped his fingertips on the image of the man. 'That's the man I just told you about. How about that!'

Elise liked it when he was happy.

'The pulling power of the moon,' she replied, 'it must have sensed that you wanted to find him.'

'You believe that?' he asked.

'Yes, I do and that it's not just there to invite the loonies out at night. There is so much about the planets and our universe that we don't know about. I know from experience also that a lot of my psychopaths and serial killers operate when the moon is full.'

'You fool, you should have killed her last night after you'd had the sex,' reproached the voices, whereas a few had other ideas, *'no, keep her by your side only she could prove instrumental to your plans and prove extremely useful.'*

He took another look at the picture in the paper. Baumgartner had lost a few pounds since he had seen him last. The hair on top was a little thinner and the sun had given his face a glow that had never been there before. A senator indeed, Jakub wanted to scoff, but kept his contempt to himself. Soon they would discuss the future together. He continued reading. Baum had recently sold his large stock holding in a marine engineering take-over, bought out by a much more powerful conglomerate organisation although unbeknown to other shareholders the new board had secretly made Matt Baum a silent director. Not even Adelina Baum knew.

Elise studied the photograph that stared back at her. 'He has very shifty eyes, although that's about right for a politician.'

Jakub didn't respond, he wasn't really listening. His head was full of laughter. First Koskovsky, then Hartmann and now Baumgartner. Julianna would be so pleased with him.

Flying high over the shade of the screen umbrellas the seagulls were on the search for scraps of food.

Tossing an untouched prawn onto the sidewalk the frantic squabble that ensued for the delicacy was fun to watch. Soon Matt Baum would become the unfortunate prawn and the buzzards would gorge at what was left of his corpse.

Picking up the menu, he read down the choices.

'I still have room for some cheesecake, what about you?'

Chapter Twenty Two

Jakub booked them into a shared room approximately two kilometres out of Melbourne with direct access to the freeway. He parked the car down the side of the motel rather than out front where it was too inviting knowing that by now the NYPD would have begun putting together the death of Adam Jankowski. So far his luck had held out without any serious problems except for the moron in the diner, but to come so far and to be thwarted by a stupid oversight such as leaving the car where it could be easily spotted was insane.

They spent the evening going to an art gallery and checking out the price of property in the windows of local real estate shops. Jakub was happy to tag along with Elise getting a feel for the streets, junctions and important escape routes. Staring annoyingly back at him from every street corner were posters of Matt Baum his insidious smile grating on Jakub's nerve endings. Elise saw him looking.

'Your friend is a popular guy, he has a damn good press agent.' Bottom of each poster was printed the address of his campaign office. Elise wrote it down on a notepad. 'That will help.'

'Help with what?' asked Jakub, his focus on a police patrol crossing the junction two blocks down from where they were looking into a shop window.

'Now you have the details of the senator's campaign office. It's highly unlikely that he would be there, but there is always the odd chance he might. I'm sure as an old friend they could make the necessary arrangements to get you two together.'

'I guarantee he will remember me.' The police cruiser had disappeared.

'Just remember Jakub that Matt Baum is an American Senator and they are powerful people with serious protection.'

'Thanks, I'll bear that in mind.'

Jakub felt the resentment growing inside of him as he looked at Matt Baum. After all these years the ex-magistrate was still looking down on him and smiling, laughing in his face. Somehow he would find a way around the security problem.

They returned to the motel where he opened a bottle of wine that they had purchased from a late night convenience store. Coming in close Elise was aware that he was still pensive from their walk, although Jakub was hiding it well. His voice, like his touch was sensitive and meaningful.

Around one in the morning she sensed a vacant space beside her, stretched out and found Jakub's side empty. She found him on the balcony looking into the distance at the lights illuminating the beach road.

'I didn't hear you get up. Can't you sleep?'

'No. It's nothing, probably just the reality of being here at last. I can feel my sister is close although I have no idea where. I guess I'm just excited as it's been a while since I saw her last.'

'Do you fancy going for a walk down on the beach?'

Just shy of two they were sitting on the sand. In front of them the water looked dark, like a black carpet tipped white by the occasional wave as it wrinkled up to the water's edge. Overhead the sky was full of stars and the moon had reappeared behind the clouds. Standing Elise suddenly stripped naked and ran into the surf, it was cold, but exhilarating as covered her breasts where the nipples had gone hard. *'Come on, do something daring,* 'she cried, *'something we'll remember forever!'*

Leaving his clothes where they fell he joined her pulling her arms away to reveal her breasts. Jakub came in close. Elise reached down and took hold of his penis. 'Don't lose that will you!' she begged.

He scooped her up into his arms and carried her back to where the surf met the sand then laid her down where the water just covered the lower half of her legs. They made love in the water, neither talking just feeling the need to be together. When it was over Jakub rolled away and lay beside her. The water was still cold although neither really noticed.

'That's the first time that I've ever done it in the sea, it was amazing!'

Jakub caressed her abdomen, drawing circles with his fingertip. He remembered making love with Julianna in the stream at the back of their house in Kurlor, but there had been no stars nor moon present, only the excitement that they should not have been doing what they were doing.

*****

Not more than half a kilometre from where they lay in the surf, Julianna lay on top of her bed the many thoughts going around and around in her head refusing to let her sleep. With the window open she could hear the waves moving the pebbles along the shoreline. Every so often the breeze coming up from the beach would dance the drapes. She was still watching the drapes sway back and forth when she thought she heard somebody move over the boards of the veranda, slipping from the top of the bed covers she went to the window and looked out, but there was nobody there, except damp footprints. She thought about calling Mary, but decided to not disturb her peace. Julianna wondered why Emily Lou hadn't heard somebody walking outside. Did *Whispering Echoes* really have a ghost she wondered, Mary's husband Abraham?

When she turned away from the window she noticed that Emily Lou wasn't in the room. She was sure that he had been there earlier when she was thinking. Since arriving the Labrador had taken to sleeping in her room rather than with Mary. Julianna felt guilty that she did, but Mary dismissed the importance saying that Emily Lou recognised when somebody needed help. Taking a shawl from the wardrobe and wrapping it about her shoulders Julianna felt at peace not just with herself, but the world.

Sitting on one of the wicker chairs on the veranda, she saw Emily Lou push the gate open with her nose and pad up the path. She came and sat beside Julianna where she noticed that her paws were wet.

'Did you go for a night time paddle girl?' asked Julianna.

'She does when Abraham's about.'

Julianna turned to see Mary holding a tray of hot coffee and biscuits. Protecting her shoulders she also had on a shawl.

'When Abraham died, we'd sit out her until very late just listening to the ocean. It's how the name got its name.' She gave the dog a biscuit. 'We would sit out here all night if we could and watch the sun rise on the horizon, seeing the shadows disappear.'

'Shadows, what shadows?' Julianna asked.

'Why the Souls of the Angels. They come to watch the sunrise every morning, don't they girl.' Mary stroked her head. 'When she was younger Emily Lou would race across the sand and join them. She would sit amongst the shadows and watch the sun rise. I've even see them stroke her head once in a blue moon. That's how I reckon Emily Lou can recognise when somebody needs help.'

'I never known anywhere so beautiful Mary, so peaceful. Even in the dark, it has a feel about the place as though protected by magic. It's the only way I can describe it.'

Mary smiled.

'That's what it is… magic.' She poured the coffee. 'And before you ask you didn't wake me, Abraham did. He said we had to talk!'

'The wet footprints, I saw them.'

'I thought you might. He told me that he had come to watch over us both.'

'But we have Emily Lou to look after us.'

'He came because there was a bad force close by, he told me on the beach. He said that the screams were echoing up and down the sand.'

'Jakub…' Julianna whispered, 'he's close Mary, Jakub's arrived. I felt him earlier this evening, but I managed to block his thoughts.'

Reaching down and under the table Mary withdrew two blankets then opened the lid of an old sea chest where from within she pulled out a brandy bottle and two clean glasses. She poured two good measures handing one to Julianna.

'Abraham's treasure we used to call this. He introduced the idea when we bought the house when we would stay awake all night before the kids arrived. We'd make love down at the water's edge then come back for a brandy. The water can be mighty cold at night. *'A Melbourne Tonic'* he called it. Abraham always had good ideas.'

Julianna sipped the brandy it was good.

'Nowadays we keep the chest stocked for emergencies or the nights that Emily Lou and I spend out here on the veranda. Some nights I would fall asleep although waking much later the glass would always be empty. I'm sure that this old girl licks it clean.' Mary ruffled the dog's head approvingly and poured some of the brandy into the dog's bowl. 'It helps keep our ticker pumping, don't it girl!' Emily Lou looked up and licked Mary's hand before diving into the bowl.

Julianna sipped her own.

'I remember my grandmother giving me a brandy once for a toothache. I don't recall if it worked, but I liked the taste and I know that I slept well that night. The next morning the toothache had gone. I like the idea that the old sea chest is put to good use.'

Mary ginned.

'What annoys me is that Emily Lou never suffers a hangover, unlike me!'

The coffee was excellent, as good as ever and although darker than other nights the stars were plentiful. Every so often the moon disappeared behind a cloud, but it did nothing to mar the beauty of darkness. They sat in silence, sipping the brandy and each with their own thoughts, Mary was the first to speak again.

'Since the death of my husband, I see things much differently. I threw away the rose tinted glasses and I accept that our time here is brief, hopefully much longer on the other side who knows. But here, at Melbourne at Whispering Echoes time dictates what we can achieve in the countdown to death. When I saw you first on the beach, instinct had me know you were lost, not physically, but spiritually. I sensed you searching for your soul. I'm no mystic and I don't possess magical powers, but I recognise pain when I see it.'

She offered more brandy and Julianna allowed an additional refill.

'I think of life as a butterfly initially shedding aside the outer casing of the pupae so that it can spread its wings and fly away free. You'd do well to think of your current circumstances the same. Shed this current skin Julianna and take the opportunity to fly free of the past. A chrysalis without wings is going nowhere. Be who you want to be, not who or what Jakub wants you to be.

'After Abraham I would wander aimlessly up and down the beach with Emily Lou cocooned in a tunnel of darkness until I saw the light again. My children accused me of being distant and unpleasant when we spoke on the phone. My pain hurt them too only I didn't consider their feelings. Abraham was their father. Because I didn't know mine was no excuse to have them not remember their father. Whatever trouble befall us, and they do, there is always a solution Julianna, always!'

Mary held her chest with her free hand feeling the rise and fall of her heart as the blood was pumped around her body.

'The reason I invited you to stay with me here at Whispering Echoes was not only because my husband told me it was right, but selfishly because I thought that we could help one another.'

Julianna looked from Mary to Emily Lou back to Mary.

'You see the inevitable is drawing near for me. The day before we met I had been to see my doctor. She had some alarming news to tell me perhaps more so for her than me, although we managed to laugh about before I left her consulting room. Not beating about the bush I'm dying. There's no time scale it will just happen. My system has decided that enough is enough and no amount of decoking the engine or adding extra oil will help. It could be tomorrow, next week or whenever, but I go I need to put my affairs in order and that includes Emily Lou and this grand old house. My son and daughter and their families have been well cared for financially, but neither want the burden of the house.

'Call me a scheming old hag if you wish, but Abraham and I believe that Whispering Echoes is where you need to be right now. This lovely old beach house has been a good home to me and my loved ones for many decades and we've enjoyed many happy times here, but the magic needs to be cared for, loved. In the past forty eight hours I have watched you, observed you and seen the darkness disappearing from your eyes. In its place is a light, a radiance that only ever appears when there is hope. This is a once in a lifetime offer Julianna to stay here indefinitely with Emily Lou and bring some of the happiness back into your life.'

*****

A short, abut safe distance from the white painted house the darkened outline of two figures stood up, dressed and walked from the shoreline back up to the sidewalk. Neither took any real notice of the sleeping properties along the beach front. As they stepped back up and onto the sidewalk Mary replaced the brandy bottle back in the chest and closed the lid.

'Probably only youngsters, their introduction to love on a star-lit night.'

Julianna nodded still coming to terms with what had been offered.

'I hope that I've not offended you?' Mary asked.

'Offended, most definitely not Mary. I am speechless. You hardly know me.'

Mary rubbed the rim of the brandy glass across her lower thin lip.

'Life is about chance Julianna. I see in you something that I once saw in myself. Don't think of my offer as a hand-me-down, instead consider it a chance to start all over again. Like the stars you alone can change your destiny.'

Flashing through her mind her thoughts were unravelling.

Images of Kurlor, her parents. Images of her and Jakub together, naked in the stream. Images of the bullies at school and Jakub being taken by Albrecht Hartmann and never coming back.

She tried hard to dispel those of Jason Chancery and Ashworth. She didn't think about Gillian Dennerholm as she deserved to die.

Julianna did think about Melanie Anne Smith and she didn't deserve to die. She should have just walked away and taken her chances. Mary was right, very few chances ever brought good luck. Could she turn her life around it was a really big ask.

The one thing she did know was that nobody would ever giver her another opportunity like what Mary and Abraham had offered. She stood up went over to where Mary was folding the seat blankets and hugged her tight.

'Thank you Mary, you do realise that it could be sometime until I can repay your kindness.'

Like a mother hugging a daughter who had been long lost Mary Peterson gently patted Julianna's back. 'Just knowing that you'll be happy here and looking look after Emily Lou is reward in itself.'

It was sometime after first light before they all went to bed again. As hard as she looked Julianna didn't see the angels down by the surf, not that it mattered because she was convinced that they were there. When she did close her eyes with Emily Lou already asleep at the base of the bed she heard a voice appear, a familiar voice as her mother whispered *goodnight.*

Chapter Twenty Three

Returning from the beach Elise had crashed down onto the bed exhausted leaving Jakub to do his own thing on the balcony outside. She had considered asking him to join her, but it was obvious that he wanted to be alone. Once again, despite what had taken place in the surf with only the stars overhead as their witness his mood was pensively deep and thoughtful.

Leaning back in the chair with his feet up on the balcony wall Jakub could only think of Julianna and Matt Baum. Walking away from the beach he had felt her presence close, but there was an unusually a strong force blocking his thoughts. Oddly too the voices in his head had been unusually quiet offering no help.

When Elise stirred he pulled the curtain aside to look. She was naked and asleep her pose the dreams of artists. He felt a stirring in his loins again remembering how Julianna had slept the same, naked in the moonlight.

Clenching his fists he tried to resist temptation wanting to concentrate on Matt Baum instead. First he needed to think through how he was going to get to the magistrate from Kurlor then later he could climb alongside Elise.

Sucking hard he felt his lungs inflate as he looked up at the moon. 'Soon, very soon, you and I will have a coming together Baumgartner.' He threw a single kiss at the moon, sealing the senator's fate. An idea was forming in his mind.

A short time later, Elise stirred again only this time she sensed somebody lying beside her, his erection stabbing her from behind. Reaching behind she held him as she turned and pulled him on top. Taking her wrists he held her down as he thrust back and forth wanting her like he had on the beach. Elise moaned, groaned with pleasure as Jakub nuzzled the side of her neck.

'I didn't think you had anything left,' she gasped.

He didn't reply, but continued thrusting hard his eyes on hers as he unleashed the last of his energy intensifying the urgency. With every kiss, bite and caress he was taking Julianna again, wanting her, needing her. He would show her just how much he loved her.

Sitting out on the balcony he had perceived a disturbing sense of abandonment from his sister. With every thrust he was putting it right. Beneath him Elise was gasping, holding on tight. Jakub was stronger than ever, bigger than ever. His eyes, dark and penetrating were burning into her. Unable to resist she felt his passion going deep.

Walking back to the sidewalk he had expected police to jump out from the shadows at any moment and surrounded him, but although they had seen the cruisers patrol the beach front, they had paid no attention to the couple in the surf. Whatever it was blocking his thoughts had been very powerful, stronger than anything that he had ever encountered before.

Reaching the peak of their climax they looked at one another breathing heavily then fell apart totally spent, gasping for extra air as the curtains across the balcony door started to dance nervously without any rhythm. They felt the cool air sweep over their naked bodies licking at the beads of perspiration as they lay side by side staring up at the ceiling.

Elise held her breasts as her chest went up and down. She didn't think that the intensity of the beach could ever be matched, but Jakub had just proved that it could.

The next time that they woke from a deep sleep the traffic outside seemed constant. Rising from the bed Jakub went to look. Sitting up Elise felt the ache in her groin and there was a bruise on each wrist where Jakub had held her so tight.

They took breakfast at a small diner across the street, but neither mentioned the night or the sex. Elise watched as Jakub eat the last of his waffles covered in maple syrup, she was becoming acquainted with his mood swings, but they were so unpredictable and like the moon they would appear then vanish behind a dark cloud. She was keen to know how many women he had made love with, waiting until his mouth was empty before she asked.

'Have you had many girlfriends?'

Jakub stared back at her wondering why she wanted to know. Before he met Elise his life had been a closed book. He continued looking sensing the pages were revealing too many secrets. He was becoming wary of her questions.

'Some, although I cannot remember really. They were a long time ago. None recently though.'

He studied her eyes looking for signs of suspicion. Was she probing, profiling, he wasn't sure. They were the same, soft and genuine, but he wondered if they were part of her façade. Whatever, she had not been the force that he had felt down on beach. Elise wasn't that strong mentally. He grinned. 'Why, are you wondering how many times I've had sex with them.' He exhaled. 'I'll tell you, only one before you!'

Elise wanted to say that the first must have been very good, taught him a lot, but something told her to keep her thoughts to herself.

'I have never done anything like happened on the beach before or back at the motel. At college I was always known as the shy geek, with ten thousand hang ups. It wasn't that I didn't want to do it, I just needed to be sure that was all. Last night I threw caution to the wind. Last night was amazing!'

'It was good,' was all he was prepared to admit before he cut another piece of his waffle.

He didn't tell her that at one point when they lay half in the sand with the water swirling about their upper body that he had considered holding her head under the water and drowning her. It would have been the ideal solution and he could have got on with finding Julianna.

Going over to where there was a rack of tourist brochures Elise picked up one that looked interesting.

'There's a zoo not far up the coast do you fancy that today. It would help kill the morning than later when the campaign opens we can make some enquiries about the senator.'

Jakub dragged the breakfast tab towards him reaching for his wallet.

'Okay, that sounds good.' He liked the idea and zoos were places where accidents could happen, as much as they could the beach.

Going back up to the motel room where she wanted change her clothes, Jakub went to the local newsagents for more gum. Talking with the owner he tapped into knowledge about the senator, finding out as much as possible before he stepped foot in the campaign office. Brad Denison had read all the tabloid write-ups, followed the campaign and reckoned that what he didn't know wasn't worth knowing. Jakub left with a smile on his face.

Brevard Adventure Park was easily found and they arrived the same time as a school bus, the children exiting their mode of travel eager to see everything beyond the turnstile gate. They had with them rucksacks and books.

A large arched board over the entrance was painted with artistic images of the animals inside and the eye-catching slogan told visitors that the park was a haven of adventure. Jakub noticed that the attractions included a kayak safari experience.

'I'd like to try that,' announced Elise as she released the seat belt from the safety catch.

They held back letting the school trip go first before approaching the ticket booth. On either side of the small wood shack entrance there were photographs of the animals sent in by previous visitors. Jakub especially liked the image of the black panther best. Powerful and with sleek lines their muscular body could move through the branches of trees undetected, moving close to their prey before they leapt. Dark and mysterious Jakub had stalked Albrecht Hartmann then pounced going in for the kill. Elise caught him smiling, she was happy to see that he was enjoying the prospects of the adventure ahead.

At the kayak centre the ranger clipped their tickets before issuing them with a fluorescent life-preserver.

'Can we have a kayak each?'

Elise had thought that they might share a two seater craft, but she was happy to show Jakub that she could cope with her own kayak. The ranger made sure that they knew how to corner and stop before he helped them get in and shoved them away from the wooden jetty.

'Have fun guys!'

Elise waved and smiled, but Jakub was already several metres ahead. She dropped her paddle into the water and began back thrusting hard to catch up.

At the first bend they encountered the giraffes. Tall and lanky the beasts were standing close to the water's edge. Moving her kayak in close to the bank the nearest giraffe lowered its head from the branches where it had been feeding on leaves to lick the back of her hand. Jakub liked the adventure park, but he didn't like that the animals were penned in with high fencing, many of the wire surrounds electrified. They reminded him of Ebenstatt where the fences served the same purpose, keeping the inmates from leaving.

With its natural Landscape the kayak adventure covered a total of twenty two acres and the water course was completed in under three hours. Bringing the kayaks alongside the jetty on their return Elise felt that she could paddle no more even if her life depended upon it. Every muscle, fibre and joint in her body ached. The ranger helped them back onto dry land, tied off the two kayaks then walked off to where he had other duties.

'I need something to eat and drink', exclaimed Elise as she stretched her limbs upper and lower, 'that was harder than I imagined it would be.'

Jakub who was fit and had an athletic build agreed that food and a drink would help replace the lost energy. Joining the queue in the restaurant Elise offered to do the counter run suggesting that Jakub find a table before they were all lost as the room was filling fast. To one side of the restaurant the school party were already tucking into their packed lunches. Jakub found a table near the emergency exit and where he could observe the children as they swapped sandwiches and drinks. It had been a very long time since he and Julianna had taken similar trips back in Kurlor. He was still watching and smiling at their excited chatter when Elise came back with a loaded tray.

'They seem to have had a good morning.' She said sorting the purchases.

'We did as well,' he thanked her for getting them lunch, 'they should make the most of these years, they disappear fast and we all grow old too quick...'

'The way you handled the kayak this morning, you've a long way to go before you're old.'

Jakub grinned. The kayak adventure had invigorated his senses and he felt good, alive.

They were enjoying their lunch engaging in small talk and listening to the excited chatter of the children when a shadow suddenly moved across the table top and stopped. Instinctively Jakub placed his hand over the knife that Elise had taken from the tray to cut the rolls. He looked up as to who had caused it.

Standing beside them was a zoo attendant dressed in a green uniform.

'I know you,' the man enthusiastically proclaimed, his stammer made worse by the recognition, *'you... you're... you're Jakub Hesseltolph.'* With agitated movements his finger started to rise and point at Jakub. *'I thought Baumgartner recommended that you be locked you up for good!'*

Elise who had watched Jakub's hand clutch the knife stopped chewing. She was bewildered, looking first at Jakub then at the zoo worker trying to quickly work out what the man had implied, locked up for good, locked up where she wondered. And Jakub whose eyes who were naturally dark, had narrowed like that of the panther. Remembering how he had looked moments before dealing with the unruly customer at the steakhouse she knew that an attack was imminent. She reached across to put her hand over the one covering the knife, but Jakub smacked it aside.

He recognised the man making the wild accusation. No longer a boy, but a man like himself the zoo attendant was heavier and older, and had less hair, but the eyes, the facial features had not altered.

'Stefan Van Linden. I remember you.' He relaxed his grip on the knife. 'You were one of the reasons that I ended up in Ebenstatt. You made my sister's life a living hell.'

'Jakub, please tell me what's going on?' Elise sked, but he ignored her.

'You were one of the animals who molested her, touched Julianna and it was you who expressed what she was to do to do when you were both naked. She had nightmares every night because of you Van Linden, nightmares that I had to help her get over.' Jakub rose from his seat making the edge of the table rattle as he did. *'How fortuitous to bump into you today!'*

Stefan Van Linden saw the look in Jakub's eyes, taking a step back he began edging away knowing that in recognising Julianna's brother he had made a huge mistake. Understanding the evil that bubbled away inside the monster from Kurlor Stefan suddenly turned and ran, crashing and banging into tables as he tried to escape, knocking over drinks and food as he went. As the children stopped talking, adults watched as Jakub gave chase taking with him the knife from the table. Several children, girls mainly began to whimper.

'No Jakub,' Elise cried out, but it was too late. Stefan Van linden was already running down the path outside and Jakub was hot on his heels.

The teachers quickly ushered their charges together where they could protect them better as several members of the restaurant came over to assist as the manager frantically called for security. Picking up her bag from the from Elise apologised then ran from the restaurant not knowing what she was going to do when she caught up with Jakub, but she felt she had to do something.

Outside of the restaurant she asked a young couple in which direction the two men had run.

The man pointed. 'The man chasing was really incensed. He shouted after the man that he was chasing saying something like today was his last day alive!'

It was what Elise had feared. She thanked the couple then took off again, hoping that she would arrive in time to prevent Jakub doing anything that he might regret later. Running hard her legs ached from the kayaking adventure. When she reached the last bend before the path straightened she stopped running coming to a halt. Next to the wall of the crocodile enclosure Jakub had caught up with the zoo employee. Holding the bigger man by the scruff of his uniform shirt Jakub was clearly the stronger of the two.

'Please… let me go,' begged Stefan Van Linden, *'I pro… pro… promise, that I won't tell a living soul that you were both here, or who you really are Jakub!'*

Down below the high wall basking in the midday sunshine were several mature American crocodiles their mouths open wide to catch a cool breeze and chill their bodies. They each had been alerted to the commotion above and had their eyes trained on the man who was backed against the wall.

'You really are as pathetic as the day when we met and how quickly you've forgotten the fun that had together in the wooded glade Stefan. Don't you remember?' Jakub grabbed and tore aside the open neck of Van Linden's uniform shirt to reveal the scars beneath.

'I… I remember Jakub.' Replied the terrified keeper, unable to prevent his body from trembling, the fear squeezing at his heart.

'Look at you, Jakub spat venomously back, 'after all these years you still squeal like a pig on the way to the slaughterhouse. Have you no pride in yourself, no backbone.' Jakub sensed that he was being watched, he turned to see Elise standing beside the bend where it split two way, his way and to the crocodile enclosure and the other to where they had left the kayak adventure. He smiled, ignoring the look apprehension in her eyes.

'You sealed your own fate Stefan when you stood by my table and announced to a packed room that I had been locked away. You have not only sealed your fate, but hers too!' he thumbed at Elise.

The look of shock registered on Elise's face as she began backing away. Looking about there was only the three of them. Her legs felt heavy, very heavy, but she realised that if she didn't take the opportunity to escape she never would. Jakub was quick on his feet, could run faster than her and he was way too powerful for her to fight him off. Jakub saw her turn and run in the direction of the kayak adventure, he called out after her, but his main focus was still on Stefan. Now his eyes blazed angrily.

'You piece of shit... you have tried to destroy every wall that I build in my life. First Julianna and now Elise. They'll be no trees to save you today, no simple warning for the future, only a swift retribution. You made a big mistake besmirching my sister Van Linden.'

Stefan stammered badly keeping one eye on his attacker the other on the crocodiles who were moving forward to the edge of the pit wall.

'We... we we're only young boys Jakub, looking to have some fun, we meant no real harm. Your sister she was beautiful and desirable. I just wanted to see her naked that was all... to touch her.' He swallowed the excess saliva that had collected at the back of his throat. 'Please Jakub show some mercy. After this you'll never hear or see from me ever again!'

Jakub laughed out loud, the laugh of a madman and applauding loudly inside his head so did the voices.

'Mercy was a word that they never used at Ebenstatt.' He pushed Stefan ever harder against the wall. 'Why choose America, why come here?'

'Matthias Baumgartner lives here in California. I am a good friend of his nephew.' Stefan tried to slow his speech to prevent the stammer, but also hoping that the longer he talked help would arrive any second and overpower his attacker. 'The senator got me this job at the zoo. I needed to get away from Kurlor. They put you in Ebenstatt Jakub, but when they did the rest of us that had been in the woods that day were treated like lepers. I had to escape for my own sanity.'

Jakub grinned, it pleased him to think that they had suffered as well. 'Where does Baumgartner live?'

Stefan hesitated, but the grip on the shirt collar tightened around his neck. There was also a hatred in Jakub's eyes. Coming in close, almost nose to nose Jakub was in no mood to be messed about. *'Answer the fucking question or you feed the crocodiles below right now!'*

'He's got a big place down Palm Beach way. I can't remember the exact address... but it would be easy to find, it's only one with a security detail at the gate.'

'And that's it... no name on a wall, no number?'

Stefan Van Linden shook his head. 'No, that's all I remember about the place I've only ever been there the once. Please let me go Jakub, I'll leave the zoo, go anywhere if it would please you. I'd tell security and the police that today was just a big misunderstanding amongst old friends.'

Jakub relaxed his grip leaving Stefan gasping for breath as the relief washed through his entire body. *'Thank you Jakub!'*

When it came, the fisted blow was hard and low connecting like a hammer hitting a nail against a stubborn plank of wood. Stefan doubled forward in pain clutching at his stomach as Jakub stepped forward. In less than a second, maybe two he reached out pushed a shoulder and lifted up a leg.

Stefan Van linden fell backwards his hands flaying frantically either side of his bulky body as he tried to grab the top of the wall, but the rounded stone was too smooth to get a grip. Moments later he crashed into the enclosure the impact breaking several bones, not least his lower limbs. In no time at all the huge crocodiles were on him, yanking, tearing indiscriminately at anything that moved. Soon the screaming ceased as one of the reptiles came from behind and tore clean from his shoulders Stefan's head. Watching from above Jakub smiled as the voices all cheered.

What was left of Stefan Van Linden the beasts dragged to the water where they would bury the headless dead man deep in the mud. Looking around Elise was nowhere to be seen and in the distance the sirens were getting louder and louder cutting through the warm midday air. Jakub looked at his options and the best way to escape and avoid capture. He was too close to Matt Baum now to be caught, at least not until he had dealt with the senator.

Back at the kayak station Elise grabbed and donned a life preserver, jumping into the nearest kayak she pushed herself clear of the jetty and paddled hard ignoring the ache in her muscles. The adrenalin pumping around her body forced her to yank the paddle back over and over again knowing that her life depended upon how much distance she put between Jakub and herself. From the direction of the crocodile enclosure she had heard the screams as the zoo employee had fallen and then as the crocodiles had attacked. When it went silent she felt her heart pumping hard and fast.

Elise wanted to find somewhere to release the bile that was rising in her throat, but she swallowed hard concentrating on the first bend ahead keeping her attention focused. Her thoughts were a battlefield of mixed painful emotion. She had trusted Jakub, she had been intimate with him and even considered having a future with him. The realisation of how foolish she had been once again came back to haunt her.

Chapter Twenty Four

The breaking news on CNN about the horrific death of the zoo employee was immediately picked up by the researchers working in the *brain* room along the corridor from Helen Montgomery's office. Michelle drew a line down from New York cutting through the gas station and on down to the zoo. She took it to Montgomery where both women agreed the link put Jakub Hesseltolph at all three locations. When Michelle left the office the head of BSU picked up her mobile.

'It has to be Hesseltolph,' she said convincingly, 'and we think he was definitely connected to the garage owner's death as well. A fire truck attending the scene remember a silver Chrysler going in the opposite direction prior to them arriving at the incident.'

Hunter agreed. 'He's not like any serial killer that we've dealt with before. I still feel that he has a primary target, but his kills so far has been out of necessity. Did NYPD find anything else at Adam Jankowski apartment?'

'No, it was as clean as whistle.' She looked at the images that had been sent to her office from CNN. 'Hesseltolph knows exactly what he's doing David and the manner in which he terminates life is completely cold blooded. You and Mendes need to tread carefully in your investigation.'

'I know I saw the news reel. I doubt there's much left of the zoo employee. Interesting that they didn't mention the woman he was with at the steakhouse and yet eye-witnesses say he was definitely with a female in the zoo restaurant.'

'How far away are you from Melbourne?'

'We'll be there very soon.'

'That's good.' There was a pause only seconds long, but long enough.

David laughed. 'I know, I will, he replied. 'We'll have dinner somewhere quiet when I get back.'

Alvarez Mendes who emerged from the gas station pay desk slid back in behind the wheel pushing the e-cigarette vaporiser to one side of his mouth.

'Have you heard about the breaking news on CNN?'

'About the dead zoo employee. Yes, Montgomery just called as you were paying. Did you remember to get a receipt?' Mendes held it up before hiding it in his pocket.

'So can we assume that Jakub Hesseltolph is in Melbourne?' He selected a gear pulling away from the forecourt.

'The killing has his hallmark, cold and calculated. Including todays' victim he doesn't leave behind a lot of evidence. We'd best cut across to the zoo and see what is left.' David observed Alvarez as a plume of fake vapour fanned the inside of the compartment. 'Do those things work?'

Mendes laughed. 'Of course not, it's all in the mind. I inhale which sends a signal to my brain to tell me that I am smoking only I'm no longer clogging my lungs with toxic waste.'

Hunter scoffed. 'You're as environmentally unfriendly as the Hesseltolph's.'

Arriving at Brevard Adventure Park, the first thing that they wanted to visit was the crocodile enclosure before they took their investigation elsewhere. Like the circus had arrived in town and parked at random were a number of marked police units, a cordon holding back news reporters and outside broadcast vans. Mendes parked next to a patrol car where he showed his credentials.

'They didn't take long in getting here,' he said making small talk with the patrolman.

'They're like vultures hanging about for a decent kill, still I don't suppose getting ripped to shreds by crocs is your everyday killing.'

They went through the turnstile ignoring the shouts from the reporters for a comment. Inside the zoo everywhere seemed deathly quiet except for the odd sound made by a caged cockatoo.

'You think the other animals know,' Mendes asked.

'What when something bad has taken place. Yes. It's like when there's a kill on the Serengeti. All the other animals can relax and rest a while until the next time.'

Mendes offered Hunter a mint. 'You sound as though don't like zoos?'

'Not much. Everything that lives and breathes has a right to be free, unless you're a killer like Jakub Hesseltolph.'

They didn't go down into the crocodile enclosure which had been zoned with tape so that forensic examiners could do a thorough search. Instead they went back to the control room to watch the CCTV recordings.

'That is definitely not the sister,' said Mendes zooming in and out.

'We'll send a copy through to Washington, have them run it through the system. Maybe they'll come up with a match.'

They read through the statements that had already been taken including the couple who had directed Elise to the crocodile enclosure. When a female keeper appeared and introduced herself Mendes was greeted with a wide smile.

'I'm Elle Hawkes, I look after the crocs.' She held out her hand and shook theirs.

'Was it you who got to the enclosure first?' asked Hunter.

'Yes, although there wasn't much going on, not least on dry land. Most of the activity was in the water and from the blood splatter I knew that poor Stefan had been taken under. Crocs go deep with a kill where they bury it for later. The mud at the bottom is very cold and like a deep freeze.'

'Have you been in the enclosure?' asked Mendes standing alongside.

Again she smiled. 'You've got to be kidding, not after a kill. No way, they're hyped like a junkie snorting on a fix. No, even after feeding time we always leave the crocs to do their thing until they're settled.'

'How long have you been their keeper?'

'A little over five years.'

'Where are the crocs now?' asked Hunter.

'Back inside so CSI could get to work.'

Elle Hawkes took them to the enclosure, ground level. She left them there to check on the beasts under her care.

'She's young to be doing such a dangerous job,' remarked Mendes.

'And pretty too,' joked Hunter, 'perhaps you should find out more about the habits of an American crocodile.

Mendes grinned and said maybe he would. 'That's a hell of an effective way to destroy evidence.' He added stepping where the markers as laid down by CSI said he could walk. Mendes was talking to an examiner when David Hunter read a text message from Helen Montgomery.

'Tread carefully, victim at zoo was known to Baum.'

He was called over to where Mendes was crouching down beside a member of the forensic team. They were knelt before a thick shrub. Reaching in the CSI examiner withdrew what was left of an ankle and foot still attached to the inside of Stefan Van Linden's boot. 'I'll make sure that somebody bags and tags it.' Said the examiner.

*****

Elise stooped forward feeling the last of her energy draining away, happy to let the kayak drift towards the grass bank having been paddling hard for the past half an hour. There had been no signs of Jakub ever since running from where he had hold of the zoo employee beside the high wall of the crocodile enclosure minutes before he killed him. Drifting with the natural flow of the river she put her head in her hands and wept, shocked and dismayed at how quickly Jakub had changed and become a psychotic monster. Letting the tears fall Elise felt shallow, used and abused. What frightened her the most was that her naivety had almost cost her, her life.

Straddling the grass bank she stepped ashore holding the paddle ready and besides Jakub snakes were her biggest concern. Florida had big snakes, the biting, crushing variety. She wedged the kayak into a grove in the bank where it would be found. She went east guessing that eventually it would take her to a perimeter of the adventure park and a way out.

Using a large tree that had fallen across the fence she climbed up and dropped safely down the other side never knowing if it had been electrified.

In the distance she saw the red tiled rooftops of what looked like a country club or commercial office block, using the paddle to push aside the long grass Elise made her way towards the buildings knowing there would be lots of people about.

She used the cover of the hedgerow to check for signs of the Chrysler, but most of the vehicles in the parking bays were luxury cars, sports and four wheel drives. Around back in the garden there was a hubbub of laughter and voices suggesting a large gathering of people. Elise went closer dusting herself down she noticed the board outside of the entrance announcing the wedding of the bride and groom at two thirty that afternoon. Making her way across the lawn she nodded at the surprised expressions of the guests before entering the hotel. At the front desk she found a foreign gentleman, an Italian she thought dressed smartly in his concierge uniform.

'Good afternoon madam. How can I help?' he asked. She was right definitely Italian.

Elise showed him her police identity that she always kept in her back pocket and leaned over the counter top. 'Please call the police or the FBI and I am not really fussed who gets here first, but tell them that this is a matter of life and death. Tell them I know who killed the man at Brevard Zoo.'

Knowing it was better never to dispute such a request the concierge did as he was asked. With a flick of his hand he caught the attention of a young waitress and asked that she escort the criminal profiler to the manager's office where she could be watched and not escape. He suggested also a fresh pot of coffee. If nothing else nobody could say that the hotel were not professional, polite and courteous.

Slipping the gold band on his bride's finger the groom was about to kiss his wife when suddenly the front of the hotel drive was filling with police units and overhead a black and white helicopter hovered low. Soon the place was swarming with uniformed armed officers, some with dogs. Leaving their car out front nearest reception Hunter and Mendes ran to the check in desk. They were met by the concierge and shown to the manager's office where they found and exhausted, but relieved Elise Theroux. The concierge called for a brandy and more coffee. Mendes jumped straight in eager to not waste time.

'Was it Jakub Hesseltolph?'

'Yes,' Elise replied, 'only when I met him he introduced himself as Johann Roebers.' She looked at Mendes then David Hunter. 'I swear that I didn't know that he was a wanted fugitive or that he was a killer.'

Taking the seat opposite Hunter was reassuring.

'Don't worry, you're safe now!'

Mendes stepped outside to call Helen Montgomery and to inform her that they had Elise Theroux in safe custody.

*****

Sitting in the room with both doors and windows open wide to allow the breeze to blow through Mary was flicking through the TV channels when a news bulletin took up half the screen. The news team went immediately to an outside broadcast at Brevard Zoo. Mary turned up the volume.

Enjoying the sunshine outside with Emily Lou, Julianna heard the volume go up. Running back inside she and Emily Lou found Mary staring at the screen.

'What's happened?' Julianna asked standing in the doorway.

Mary pointed.

'The Adventure Park and zoo is only thirty kilometres from here!'

A CCTV image captured in the restaurant at the zoo was clear and showed the face of both suspect and victim.

Julianna put a hand to her mouth. 'That's Jakub, that's my brother.' She admitted quietly.

'He threw a zoo worker into the crocodile enclosure.' Mary looked shocked. Julianna went and sat down alongside, putting her arm around Mary's shoulder.

'I was aware that my brother had a vengeful streak running through his body, but he is out of control.'

Mary felt the shiver run through Julianna. 'You should stay here at the house until he's caught. You don't want to get mixed up in this Julianna. You have the chance to begin again, to wipe the slate clean, don't let Jakub ruin that for you!'

Mary walked over to the TV unit and turned it off.

'It was when the security camera captured that look in his eyes. I had seen the same look when Jason left my consulting room to return to London. I am so ashamed of what I have done, but I am also scared Mary. I don't think that I could ever see Jakub again.'

Mary went momentarily outside onto the veranda, returning with the brandy bottle and two glasses.

'I know its early afternoon, but think you and I need a drink.' She smiled when she looked down at Emily Lou. 'What you too girl, okay I'll fetch your bowl.'

Chapter Twenty Five

Matt Baum had enjoyed his time spent with Ed Jackson, knocking back a cool beer and talking about the coming NFL game, anything but politics. It had been too hot to play on the fairways so they had decided instead to stay in the clubhouse of the course to which Ed had an annual membership. When the time came for him to collect his daughter and take her to her dance class Baum decided to move onto the Summer House which he owned and where most of his business transactions took place.

Ed Jackson knew of the Summer House, but had declined the free membership having heard the rumours wisely distancing himself from any future scandal. Baum had accepted Ed's refusal knowing that the Jackson's had a stake in the clubhouse where they had enjoyed a drink together.

Aide to the senator, friend and confidante Ed was no fool. He knew about the sex that took place at the Summer House, knew about the Baum's marriage and that the ship had floundered on the rocks and bit by bit the hull was coming apart. So far he had managed to keep the lid on their private lives carefully wording the press office releases to show that all was harmonious in the Baum household, but whenever they were together Matt and Adelina Baum was rarely together.

Adelina had also heard about her husband's involvement and the orgies that took place at the Summer House. Keeping the marriage alive had been for his political progression, not because of love. Shortly after arriving in America Matthias had changed, changed their name and his outlook on life. Wanting a stab at the Whitehouse her husband would do anything to make it happen, legally or illegally, like Ed Jackson she distanced herself as much as possible. More recently the rumours were that she had acquired a liking for bourbon.

Around a quarter to one in the morning Adelina heard him climbing the sweeping curve of the staircase as his hand gripped the wooden handrail for support. They were supposed to have gone to dine at the new fish restaurant down on the waterfront, but Adelina knew where her husband had been instead.

Taking the stair treads cautiously Matt Baum steadied himself, grinned to himself then launched an attack on the next three steps. When he reached the landing he punched the air triumphantly. Like his political ambitions one day he would reach the top. Stumbling towards the bedroom door his head hurt and his body ached. Pulling her lace night gown over the matching set nightie Adelina watched for the turn of the door handle.

Resting the palm of hand on the door frame Matt Baum held his head in his hands massaging his temples where it hurt most. His left kidney hurt to and the physician had warned him about his over indulgence of rich food and mixing his drink. The romp in the bedroom after dinner had helped, but it had been fun. Belching, his stomach felt easier.

Standing up straight he made a concerted effort to focus. He even straightened his tie.

Twisting the brass handle the door started open. Immediately the scent of lavender oil hit his nostrils. Adelina had an annoying habit of scenting the room at bedtime and she knew that he didn't like it. He pushed the door open and stepped inside to see her waiting, her hands down on her hips. It made him smile.

'And through the gates of hell I descend once again!' he laughed, only his wife didn't join in.

Standing in front of the bed, Adelina looked to him like angel only somebody had stolen her wings and the expression that masked her face was without any pity or compassion. Standing where he could hold onto and be supported by the open edge of the door she noticed the lipstick smudge on the collar of his shirt.

'I see you've been with another cheap tart!'

Matt Baum looked back outside to the landing in case the girl was standing behind him, but there was nobody there. He focused again on his wife.

'If you were more attentive perhaps I'd not have to find pleasure elsewhere!' the response was sharp and venomous.

Adelina mocked him shaking her head remembering the afternoon that she had enjoyed with the young gardener. Her hips were still aching and her lips ached for his again.

'Ever the silent down-trodden beleaguered maiden from the Austrian mountains.'

He went to move towards her, but he was unsteady on his feet as the effect of the alcohol swept angrily through his muscles and senses. 'I would say categorically Adelina that there are times when you wish that you had never left Kurlor!'

Knowing that he was drunk and she was safe she stepped forward and put her arms around his waist so that she could support him over to the bed. Like a bear caught in a trap Matt Baum spun her around and tore savagely at her nightclothes, ripping the top open and exposing her breasts. Adelina quickly covered herself where the gardener had left her marked.

'Kiss me...' he demanded, but instead she stepped backwards. *'I'm a state senator, kiss me you fucking whore!'*

Adelina took a step forward and slapped the side of his cheek hard.

'How dare you insult me, I am not one of your cheap tricks that you have at the Summer House. I am your wife.'

Rubbing the cheek he raised the back of his hand to retaliate, but Adelina stood defiantly before him, her eyes blazing and she was ready.

'At least they know their place,' he replied angrily.

Adelina laughed as she mocked him.

'Any woman without self-respect would go down on her knees. I am not that kind of a woman Matthias.' She pulled together the torn nightwear across her chest and knotted the ties.

Matt Baum rubbed the sting from his cheek. Inside his mouth his tongue rolled from side to side. The sting of the slap having cleared his head slightly and steadied his legs.

'How dare you strike me, you are nothing without me and you would do well to remember it. I can and will take any whore I like as and when I feel like. At least they're willing. You forget Adelina that I own this state and you are only here because I knocked you up all those years ago and your father demanded that I marry you.' He flicked together his forefinger and thumb. *'When we're in the Whitehouse you will do exactly as I say!'*

She went to strike him again, only this time he was quicker as was his strength. He held her with one hand and went to hit her with the other, but he stopped short. Again Adelina didn't flinch. She was calm and unflustered.

'Go on Matthias hit me, I would welcome it. Come the morning my face will appear on the front page of every tabloid newspaper up and down the state. Later, I would tell my story to the world. Come lunchtime your reputation, your career and your precious ambitions would be in tatters. Some the afternoon your support would fall as flat as the soles of your feet and your chances of ever conducting affairs in the Oval Room would vanish as quick as a morning mist.'

She paused to let him absorb the enormity of her threat.

'I would blow the whistle on how you embezzled funds from Austria to help set up your political career here in America. I would tell the members of the press how you own and support a whore house and how the righteous senator is despised by his own children.'

Baum let go of her wrists. She rubbed the skin where he had held her so tight.

'If you doubt anything that I have said, go ahead and do your worst, but trust me that not only will the president know, as will the country, but our children will know everything. I will take away everything which you hold dear and treasure most, and more, much more!'

Matt Baum watched as she moved away from him. This time he realised that he had gone too far. He had known Adelina long enough to know that she would be true to every word said.

'What is it that you want?' he asked, defeated, knowing that he was cornered.

'Nothing from you as a man, however as a husband everything. I am going back to Kurlor where I will live in our house there.' She walked across to the door. 'I will sleep in one of the guest bedrooms tonight and I will lock the door.

'In the morning you will make the arrangement to deposit ten thousand euros in my account every month and you will do the same for each of our children.

'And you will never set foot on Austrian soil ever again. As of this night we have a marriage in word and document only, but I will not divorce you Matthias. Do as I say and I will let you chase your dream without suffering any indignation or embarrassment. You can tell America that I had to go back home because of our elderly parents health.' She raised a warning finger. 'I warn you though, that if you renege on any part of this deal, you and your precious political career will come to an abrupt end. That is not a threat, but a promise!'

Baum watched as she quietly closed the bedroom door. The girl that he had known ever since their time at school together had finally found a voice. A girl who had never answered back, had never asked for anything, until now. The years of humbly walking two steps behind him had finally come to an end.

Come eight thirty the next morning her suitcases were filled and lined up at the front door ready for the cab to take her to the airport and her airline ticket had been arranged electronically. Her husband had not come down for breakfast.

After decades of servitude to Matthias, Adelina Baumgartner was at last leaving the house that she despised. She hated the lifestyle, the constant hordes of false people who had walked in through the doors and been entertained on the lawn or at dinner. Men just like her husband, ruthless and arrogant and stereo-typical women with their breast implants, hyped lips and salon painted nails. Pulling the front door shut she walked to the waiting car, she did not look back or up. Had Adelina looked up she would have seen the lonely figure watching from the upstairs window.

Two hours later the announcement came over the public address for passengers travelling to Austria to proceed to gate number ten. Minutes earlier, leaving it as late as possible she had contacted Ed Jackson and told him about her decision and why. Ed wished her well and said that he would miss her, Adelina believed him. Before talking to Ed she had spoken briefly with her son and daughter who were not surprised at her decision and promised to visit Kurlor during their next semester.

At the end of the covered walkway only metres away from the open door of the Boeing 737 Max she took one final look through the window at the blue skyline. Adelina didn't say anything she just looked. Her time in America was done and at last she was going home. She was free of Matthias and his desire for power at any cost.

When the flight attendant asked for her boarding pass, she smiled back. 'Economy class, seat E2,' she added.

Chapter Twenty Six

Elise Theroux put her hand above her eyebrows to protect her eyes from the sun that was penetrating powerfully between the gaps in the blind. A force of habit had her check the time. It was early and surprisingly it had been a peaceful night.

Her room was directly opposite that of David Hunter and Alvarez Mendes and they had given her their mobile numbers in case she needed them. They would have put her on the next flight out and had her safely back in Washington, but by the time she had told them everything from when she had first met Jakub at the roadside diner it was getting late and she was too exhausted to travel. Reluctantly Helen Montgomery had agreed to the overnight hotel room.

Beyond the window everything looked exactly as it should so she decided to take a shower standing under the water for much longer than usual. The warm droplets felt good, really good running down over body, helping to wash away the memory of where Jakub had touched her and been intimate with her. She let the water run down over her face for ages hoping it would wash away the negative thoughts. She had just finished dressing when there was a knock on the door. She jumped startled by the knock grabbing her cell phone.

David Hunter knocked again. 'Elise are you awake?' Elise opened the door with her foot against the base panel. 'Are you okay,' he asked, 'only Mendes has already gone down for breakfast, I said we'd join him.'

'Hi, I'm fine. I'll just grab my bag and come down with you.'

In the lift David told Elise that a night patrol had found Adam Jankowski's Chrysler parked down a side street near to the motel. Armed tactical officers had rushed the room, but Jakub Hesseltolph had already left. Her effects were at the local police department being dusted and checked by forensics. She would get them back when the tests were concluded.

They crossed the foyer heading into the restaurant where they found Mendes scrutinising the breakfast menu, he had with him a female guest, although Elise could not see as the woman had her back to her. When she did see who, it was a face she recognised, but could not add a name.

'Hi remember me Elise, I'm Monica Jordan from Internal Affairs, based in Quebec.'

Elise remembered. 'I thought I would be seeing somebody from your department at some stage, only not for breakfast.'

Monica Jordan smart, professional and with crisp lines dressed in a dark pinstriped trouser suit didn't react. 'Look upon it as a two-fold visit Elise. Initially we needed to establish that you are safe and secondly establish why you had an association with a wanted psychotic killer.'

The atmosphere was suddenly cut in two. Hunter detected that neither woman liked the other.

'I don't make a habit of hitting the road with a serial killer alongside!' Elise replied, but it fell on stony ground.

Realising that the conversation had got off to a bad start Monica Jordan raised her palms to placate the atmosphere. 'Nobody's accusing you of being involved Elise, just that you were perhaps the victim of circumstance.'

The agents liked the different approach.

'You must understand Elise that you have a high profile role in Quebec that sits publically under an umbrella of scrutiny. I am here to fend off any knives coming your way.' It was an inept choice of phrase, but Elise let it go. Jordan continued. 'You have an excellent record with the department and we would like to keep it that way.' She looked at Hunter and Mendes for back up.

Hunter helped. 'It goes with the territory Elise and not everybody in this crazy rat-race sees the bigger picture. Your dedication and professionalism is not in question, but the press can destroy you overnight. Miss Jordan is here to prevent that from happening.' He looked at his partner. 'That why we work together, covering one another's back.' Elise could see the sense in what he was saying.

'I've come to rescue you Elise, not push you under.' Added Jordan.

They ordered breakfast and waited until the waitress had refilled their cups before talking again. Monica Jordan told Elise that Oscar Calderthorpe had heard about her situation and he sent his blessings that she was safe.

Elise eyed Jordan warily. 'Strange that he should send a message as personal as that through you. He could have done it via my cell phone.' She noticed as did Hunter and Mendes that the reply had made Jordan uneasy. Suddenly Elise glared at the other woman.

'You pompous bitch it was you… wasn't it!'

Hunter looked at both women then Mendes who shrugged his shoulders. Hunter detected a history emerging.

'For the moment Elise, we should put aside any personal feelings. Once we sort this mess then we can deal with private matters. The agents have an extremely important agenda.'

Elise realised that she suddenly had the upper hand. 'I can wait, I've waited long enough. As they say, what goes around comes around and the truth will out!' She stirred the sugar in her cup. 'You and Oscar are perfect for one another.'

Cards on the table both men realised what was going down. David Hunter stepped in once again to diffuse the situation. 'Let's get back to why we're all here and Jakub Hesseltolph. Is there anything Elise that you can remember that will help our investigation, something that we didn't discuss last night?'

Standing under the shower with the water running down her body Elise had gone over everything that she knew. There was nothing she had left out. 'Other than the sex… no!' She had wanted to see if the revelation shocked Monica Jordan, but the woman from Internal Affairs was thinking of other things.

'Why Melbourne,' Mendes asked, 'was it only to find his sister and the senator?'

'Yes, the man at the zoo was in the wrong place and definitely at the wrong time. If he had not approached the table and recognised Jakub, he would almost certainly still be alive.' She looked at Monica Jordan. 'And we wouldn't be here having breakfast together.'

'And Baum, did Jakub tell you what he intended doing when he met with the senator?' Mendes pushed.

'No. Although going by events yesterday, I would say that they weren't looking favourable for Matt Baum.'

Hunter watched, listening. Elise Theroux had got over her initial shock. She had found a way of dealing with the anguish and embarrassment, anger and resentment. Sat opposite Monica Jordan she had regained a good measure of her confidence as well. He believed her story and that she was the innocent party in a trail of death and destruction. With nothing else to add he thought about Helen, wondering if she would give it all up for him, settle down and start a family. He was still swimming upstream with his thoughts when Mendes repeated his suggestion. 'I'm sorry?'

'I think Elise and Monica should leave today. I'll call Montgomery and have the Lear jet sent down.'

Hunter nodded agreeing.

'Yes, do it. Gut feeling tells me that it would be better with you both out of harm's way.'

Mendes left to make the call and David followed soon after giving the two women the opportunity to talk.

Jordan jumped in first. 'Maybe now that we're alone Elise this would be a good time to clear the air.'

Elise scoffed. *'You gotta a fucking nerve coming here to check on me. Irony or intent, I am still trying to fathom which. Was it rub salt in wound?'*

'That's not how it works Elise. You should know that.'

Elise responded quickly. 'Like I should have known that you were being busy banging my live-in partner.' The look in her eyes told Monica Jordan that she wasn't done. 'Don't worry, I'm long past and over Oscar and after this short fucking escapade with Hesseltolph I am over men for a very long time. Whatever you put in your report or whatever the department decides I'll be the one to decide my future and recoup some of the six years that I lost being with Oscar.'

'I wasn't with Oscar for six years, only two,' Jordan admitted.

*****

Nobody took any notice of the maintenance worker in his blue overalls and peaked cap as he emptied the bins into the waste disposal containers. Watching and patiently waiting Jakub knew that Elise was inside. He had seen her looking out of the bedroom window earlier. It was easy identifying the agent's car, black in colour, a four by four they all looked official. When he saw Elise walk into the glass fronted foyer with another woman he put down the bin and pushed the trolley to one side.

Opening the door of the rented car Monica Jordan settled herself in the driver's seat and was about to put the key in the ignition when she realised that two other doors had opened, Elise getting in alongside her and the other at the rear. A second later she felt the blade of the knife press against her throat. Closing her door Elise could only watch in horror.

'Melbourne isn't as big as you think, is it Elise.' He pushed Jordan's jaw up a notch to emphasise the point that he had control. 'Do exactly as I say or I'll leave you slumped dying over the steering wheel before I deal with Elise.'

Elise put her hand on Monica Jordan's forearm. 'Please, just do as he's say's, he means it!'

Jakub nodded, only the smile was missing. 'I was disappointed that you didn't elect to hang around at the zoo yesterday. You more than most should know that every story has two sides. We could have talked Elise and cleared the air.'

'I heard you clearly say that I was next Jakub.'

The voices cheered.

'I only said that to frighten Stefan. I wanted to see him squirm like a worm dangling on a fishing hook.'

'And what about the others, the psychiatrist at the sanatorium Jakub, the village policeman, the copy writer in New York, the gas station mechanic and…' she paused, 'and your parents. Why them?'

Jakub shook his head. He hated his life being discussed like it was the pages of an open book.

'The FBI have been busy.' He lowered the knife blade. 'Start the engine. We're all going for a ride along the coast road and take in the sights.' He watched as Jordan engaged a gear, released the hand brake and the car started to move. 'Just three ordinary people out to enjoy the sunshine, what could more innocent.'

Transferring the blade of the knife from her neck he poked it through the back of the seat until the tip broke the fabric positioning it at the base of her spine. Monica Jordan arched her back when she felt it touch her skin. Jakub pulled it back a little so that she could drive.

'It's just where I want it. One false move and I will shatter your spinal cord. You might not die, but you will never walk again!'

Elise had known violent men nearly all serial killers, but there were none like Jakub. Watching him intently and his hand on the handle of the knife his dark eyes were difficult to penetrate. She wanted to know his thoughts, his intentions, but he was in no mood to answer questions.

Monica Jordan did as she was told reversing the car back from the parking space. Sat in the passenger seat diagonally to Jakub, Elise felt trapped. If she jumped out now and ran back to Hunter and Mendes she would be safe, but he would kill Jordan. If she stayed, it was inevitable that they would both end up dead. Jakub read her mind as the car stopped, then went forward.

'*I will find you Elise, wherever you run and hide!*'

Elise could only nod back that she understood.

Standing in the reception Alvarez Mendes saw the car reverse. His keen eyes caught sight of the shadowy figure in the rear seat, reaching for his gun he ran towards the door. David Hunter heard the shout '*Hesseltolph*' as Mendes ran outside his gun hand raised. Taking off at speed the hire car hit the freeway without stopping at the junction. By the time that the two agents joined the traffic the black Honda was already a long way ahead and difficult to see. Sat alongside Monica Jordan, Elise thought about Oscar, wondering if she had tried harder in the relationship she would not be hostage in a car with a psychotic killer.

Chapter Twenty Seven

Despite a frantic chase by Hunter and Mendes the car ahead had left the freeway and tucked around back of a disused work shop the occupants watched the FBI agents drive on by. Florida police had scrambled their eye in the sky, but even the helicopter was unable to spot the car.

When the way ahead seemed clear Jakub told Monica Jordan to drive again. Elise watched the people relaxing, playing and having fun on Daytona Beach as they drove on by, the long stretch of golden sand seemingly endless. She tried hard to not think about how they had rolled about in the surf, wanting forget the memory. Every time she looked at him, Jakub grinned. When they went past a road direction sign for Bulow Creek, Elise looked back to check.

'What's at the creek?' she asked.

'Destiny,' Jakub replied. He told Jordan to proceed until the next turning. When it did appear he pushed the blade slightly forward so that she complied. 'Good, now we can all go sightseeing!' Monica Jordan glanced sideways at Elise.

'Bulow is a state park with historic ruins, old oak trees and nature trails.'

Elise wondered how she knew, but she didn't ask. Instead Jakub laughed. 'That's right and people get lost there sometimes.'

He touched Elise on the shoulder.

'What you and I had, was good and there were a few times that I had the opportunity to kill you, but I let you live. You should have left when we arrived in Melbourne.'

She didn't feel fear although she knew it was there lurking in the background. She looked back looking directly into his dark eyes wondering what he had planned for them both. 'Life doesn't always pan out as we like Jakub.'

Monica Jordan expression, looking at Elise was one of disbelief. Was she being brave or incredulously downright plain foolish. Either way it was a dangerous game to be playing and especially as Hesseltolph held all the trump cards.

Passing the brown painted signs that announced they had arrived Bulow Creek was pretty much deserted during the week with just the odd visitor here and there, pensioners mainly who were happy to avoid the hustle and bustle, noise and children at the weekends. Jakub told Jordan to park in the corner where it would be under the shade of the trees. There was only one other car in the spaces provided.

'Switch off and give me the keys.' She did as he requested.

Climbing between the seats he placed the knife on the underside of Jordan's throat. He looked at Elise. 'Get out and wait. If you run I'll slice her and catch up with you. You know I can outrun you.'

Elsie stood beside the door and waited for them to come around her side of the car, Jakub had his arm around Monica's waist with the blade pointing at her heart.

'Now we're all going for a nice walk in the sunshine.' They took the yellow trail heading towards the historic ruins. Elsie went first.

Besides the threat of the knife against her ribcage Monica Jordan didn't like his arm around her waist. 'You do realise that the FBI and police will be crawling all over this place soon looking for us. A rental car will stand out a mile.'

Jakub made her walk a little faster. 'And so do dead bodies. Now keep up with Elise.'

Glancing either side of the path Elise searched for something that she could use as a weapon against Jakub, anything that would give her and Monica a fighting chance of staying alive. Cold and calculating he read her thoughts.

'It would be unwise Elise to annoy me!'

She stopped walking and turned to face him.

'Why can't you just leave us here Jakub, you have the car keys. You would be long gone before anybody found us. Killing us serves no real purpose and it's just another lot of pain that will one day catch up to haunt you. Did I really mean nothing to you?'

He looked at her, then at Jordan whose eyes were full of fear. Elise continued.

'Leave us tied to a tree if you must. This place is virtually deserted and it could be tomorrow morning before they find us. You'd be long gone.'

Jakub was thinking, ignoring the voices arguing inside his head.

'And what about her, she's involved now.' He sniffed, like a wolf would pick up a scent of its victim. 'Just think of the profile that this would make, should you survive.'

Elise was also thinking, only perhaps faster than Jakub. She wasn't ready to lie down and die, and neither did she want Monica Jordan dead.

'What could we possibly tell our rescuers? That we took the beach road past Daytona before arriving at Bulow Creek. It's hardly going to blow fuses and light up the Christmas tree. Not killing us would help you too Jakub.'

He frowned. 'How exactly?'

Jakub could feel the heat transferring across from Jordan's thigh to his and her waist was as slim as Elise's.

'There comes a point Jakub when you have to stop running. A point where there is nowhere else left to run. Letting us live would sit favourably with any judge and jury.' She was using every ploy she knew, knowing that the longer she had his attention the less likely he was to act rashly. What Elise didn't know about were the voices inside his head.

Understanding what Elise was trying to do Monica Jordan nodded her support. 'I'm not FBI, I'm Internal Affairs and I work with Elise. What Elise say's makes sense and my word holds a lot of clout with the men who pull the strings.'

Jakub laughed out loud.

'Another puppet, there are so many.' He was of course referring to Albrecht Hartmann and Alexander Koskovsky. Coming around the bend of the parallel trail a middle-aged couple waved. Jakub told them to wave back and smile as he jabbed the point of the knife in a little closer. When they were gone and out of sight, he eased the blade back.

'Alright...' he said, 'I'm feeling compassionate today so I won't harm either of you. But I need something to secure you to a tree. I'm not leaving you here untethered.'

'There are boats down by the lake,' Jordan suggested, 'I've been here before. There's bound to be twine or rope around the lake.' Elise wondered if she meant with Oscar.

They passed the ruins or what was left, time and weather having been unkind on the brick and stone. Covered over in moss and vegetation, it reminded Jakub of a giant's graveyard. Somewhere, no close cockatoo shrilled. Jakub liked it at the creek, it was full of mystery and was foreboding like the woods at Kurlor.

They found the boats as Monica Jordan said they would. He switched his attention to Elise holding the knife below her ribcage. Upturned and in need of repair a rowing boat had a long length of rope attached.

Jakub looked at Jordan and grinned. 'Strip down to your underwear and I mean now, or I'll plunge the knife in and then come for you!'

Monica Jordan did as he asked, half turning away to cover herself. Jakub made Elise do the same. As she removed her clothes she looked at Monica Jordan. Not as shapely as herself, she wondered what it was that had attracted Oscar. When she was down to her underwear Jakub held her close again, she could tell that he was aroused.

'That night at the beach, rolling in the surf. I won't ever forget it Jakub!'

Monica Jordan's eyes grew wide. *'What was the hell was Elise suggesting, that they all lay down on the grass bank and have sex?'* She noticed the rope attached to the boat.

'Do you want me to untie it?' she asked.

Jakub nodded.

'I won't neither, but somewhere out there Julianna is waiting for me and she will always come first.'

Monica Jordan looked up. 'You're in love with your sister, don't you find that a little bizarre!' She realised her mistake when Jakub's eyes narrowed.

'Matthias Baumgartner and Alexander Koskovsky said pretty much the same, only I left the good doctor stretched between two trees, naked and to the mercy of the woodland creatures. The senator's fate will be much worse.' He eyes the trees nearby. 'They were trees very much like these here.'

Monica Jordan edged back, but Jakub pulled Elise with him. 'Pick up your blouse and hand it to me.' Jakub tore the sleeves from the blouse using them to tie Elise's arms behind her back. Making her lie down on the grass he did the same to her ankles. All the while he had the knife between his teeth. Jordan knew that if she turned and ran he would aim it at her back.

'I thought we'd agreed that you'd leave us tied to a tree?'

Jakub made sure that the knots were tight on Elise's bonds. 'The plans changed.' He made Monica Jordan lay down next to the broken boat where he lashed her wrists together with the rope. He left her feet untethered. She was nowhere as pretty as Elise, but she was still desirable. Putting his hand on her thigh he caressed the top of her leg. Monica Jordan stiffened.

'Once the dogs get the scent of you, they'll soon come barking your way.' Not far away on the bank a beaver who had been watching slipped into the water, vanished then reappeared much closer. Jakub grinned as he ran his hand down her leg. 'There is however, always the chance that the creek creatures will find you first.' His hand travelled up to her abdomen. Jordan clenched her teeth together and sucked in air.

'You're a sick fuck Hesseltolph. When the authorities catch up with you, which they will, you'll be heading for a quick fix of potassium chloride.'

He grabbed at her breasts cutting away her underwear, wanting to see her naked. She spat at him receiving a fearsome slap in response which made her head spin. On the other side of the upturned boat had no idea what Jakub was doing. She called out, pleaded with him not hurt her, but Jakub ignored her. Seeing her attacker undoing the belt of his trousers, she kicked out hard catching his shin. Jakub punched her hard, but she snarled back angrily.

'I'll die first before you fuck me, you sick bastard!'

Rubbing his shin Jakub laughed.

'Don't flatter yourself Internal Affairs. I might take you later, but first I am going to do something much better than shag you.' He tore another strip away from her damaged blouse and stuffed it in her mouth. He did the same to Elise, but she was more cooperative and didn't fight back.

Slicing left and right, in circular movements he patterned Monica Jordan's flesh until she could take no more and passed out. When it was done, he casually wiped the blade of the knife on the grass and stabbed it into the ground. Going around the other side of the boat he removed the gag from Elise's mouth, kissed her and stroked the side of her cheek.

'We found one another by accident and that's how we should part.' He gestured at the other side of the boat. 'She's not dead, she's just sleeping.'

He stroked her abdomen, but Elise didn't flinch like Monica Jordan had. He made circles on her flesh and grinned. 'I know how investigations go and they never end well. Life is a one-way street Elise and there's no turning around. I'll do what I have to do then disappear. I promise you will never see me again.'

He stood, turned and walked away not looking back. Elise watched until he was no longer in sight. She was convinced that having changed his mind he would kill them both. She would never know why he had a change of heart. Rolling herself around the end of the boat she saw the bloodied body of Monica Jordan, it was difficult to tell if she was asleep or dead.

*****

A patrol of Park Rangers found the two women having been out on the lake looking for a colony of beavers. Finding Elise conscious one untied her bonds as the other went to check on Monica Jordan. Grabbing his radio he asked for urgent assistance, although he knew that it was probably futile. Rubbing the circulation back into her limbs Elise sensed that something was wrong.

'Is she going to be okay?' she asked.

The ranger nearest Monica shook his head. 'I can't get a pulse.'

'Oh Jakub… why, what have you done.' It came out as no more than a whisper, but inside her head it sounded like all the cries from hell had erupted as one.

She looked at the ranger who had freed her bonds. 'Why didn't he kill me as well?' she asked.

He pointed over to where Monica Jordan lie motionless.

'It wasn't the cuts that killed her. She has two small puncture wounds on her left thigh. A snake bite. Most probably an eastern diamond rattlesnake that was asleep under the upturned boat.'

'But the venom can take a day, maybe longer to kill.' Elise added.

'That's so in most cases, but fear makes the heart pump much faster than normal. It probably bit her when she was unconscious. She wouldn't have known.'

Elise wondered if Jakub knew. Feeling her stomach react she ran to a nearby bush. The rangers looked away giving her the dignity of vomiting alone.

Much later she would learn why Jakub had cut Monica Jordan so badly. The same as she would discover how being involved with Jakub would ultimately change her life. A post-mortem would reveal that Monica Jordan was probably dead before he had walked away knowing that the snake had bitten her. Distressed that the woman from Internal Affairs had died in such awful circumstances, Elise was silently happy that was Oscar Calderthorpe would also suffer, having now lost two lovers.

What would puzzle Elise was why Jakub had removed the gag kissed her, not hurt her and then calmly walked away without looking back. The answer would come two months later and as a result of a pregnancy test. Sitting on the floor of her bathroom at home, she watched the parallel lines turn blue knowing that it was a clear indication that her chorionic gonadotrophin levels had increased. Elise was pregnant with Jakub's baby. She cried until there were no more tears left to cry.

Later that night she lay awake on her bed looking up at the stars wondering what to do. Elise was no murderer and she could not kill the child growing inside of her. Her anxiety was what gender the baby would be. Either way, it would have some of the DNA of its father.

Chapter Twenty Eight

Unstable to stay away any longer Helen Montgomery had flown to Melbourne wanting to lend her support to David Hunter and Alvarez Mendes at Bulow Creek.

The trio were shown to where the body of Monica Jordan lay untouched and covered over by a forensic tent.

Under sedation and with an armed police guard at a secret location Elise Theroux would tell her story when she was awake. Hardened to most crime scenes Helen Montgomery was horrified by how her killer had marked the dead woman from Internal Affairs.

'We need to catch him and put an end to this evil.' She said, looking down at the patterns where the blood had congealed. 'Killing is one thing, but cutting like this is barbaric. Do we know why?' Montgomery looked at Mendes.

'Most serial killers leave their mark at a scene, a signature. This is more than that!'

'Do we know if he raped her first?'

David Hunter shook his head.

'Initial investigation suggests that he cut her, that's all.'

He didn't touch, but he pointed to the two puncture wounds that had turned blue.

'Shock, plus the venom probably was enough of a cocktail to kill her.'

'And Elise Theroux, how's she holding up?'

'She's tough. She's under sedation at present and we planned talking to her later.'

Helen Montgomery knelt down and checked the dead woman for herself.

'That was a hell of a risk snatching them at the hotel and from under your noses.'

David Hunter knelt down beside her.

'We've been asking ourselves the very same question.'

'Was Theroux marked in any way?' she asked.

Alvarez Mendes replied. 'No. That's another unanswered question.'

Montgomery stood up.

'Maybe he did feel something for Elise Theroux. Whatever it was, it certainly saved her life.'

Exiting the tent they saw a beaver in the water nearby, it was lying on its back enjoying the afternoon sun and watching them.

'I bet he could answer some of our questions.' Said Mendes. Hunter smiled.

'On the flight I read the file on Jakub Hesseltolph. He had been interviewed by a DCI from England, a Trevor Baines. In his notes he made reference to a disturbed family, describing how Jakub had marked his sister's body the same way as the deceased. It was to save her from the abuse of men. It was what sent him to Ebenstatt, having tortured and marked the boys similarly who had attacked Julianna Hesseltolph.'

'A revenge punishment.' Exclaimed Mendes. 'Christ, when I was a teenager, I would protect my sisters using my fists not knives or violating their body.'

Montgomery continued looking at Hunter, her eyes burning into his.

'The victim at the zoo was apparently one of the ring-leaders who sexually abused Julianna Hesseltolph. The rest we know.'

'Now we have a motive.' Hunter added.

Montgomery instinctively knew that there was more.

'Next you're going to tell us that he only operates when the full moon is highest is the sky.'

He grinned adding a nod.

'The front cover of his medical file was stamped *psychotic-schizophrenic – delusional*. I guess we can add a few of our own. She looked back at the forensic tent. 'He apparently had a fixation with nature and wide open spaces, which might suggest why he brought them here. Has the detail guarding the senator been advised?'

Hunter replied. 'We called when we were giving chase, just before we lost sight of the car.'

'Let's hope that they take this threat seriously. Jakub Hesseltolph is resourceful and not afraid to take risks.'

Montgomery asked Mendes to give the all clear and to have the body removed to the morgue. She asked Hunter to walk with her.

'Was Hesseltolph and Theroux close?' she asked.

'If you mean intimate, yes... several times. She certainly didn't hit it off with Jordan, only I don't think she would have wished for this to have happened.'

'No, I guess not. The missing policeman from Austria we received an update earlier. A pig that went to slaughter yesterday, coughed up his wedding ring. I don't know how, but the ring had a partial print for Jakub Hesseltolph.'

Hunter shook his head as he grinned.

'That didn't do a lot for the pig's digestion.'

Helen Montgomery stopped walking.

'Before I left Washington David, I asked Forrester to run some background checks on the senator. Adelina Baum boarded a plane this morning bound for Austria. She had purchased a one way ticket. My opinion is that she's not planning on coming back.'

'That's interesting and especially as he's running for the Whitehouse.'

'On the plane I called the US Marshalls, they will arrive soon and help bolster the numbers.'

Hunter agreed knowing they would be a useful addition.

'And you what about you,' he asked, 'are you going back to Washington?'

'No, why... I've only just arrived. This is still your investigation.'

He looked first then held her arm.

'I wish you'd reconsider. Jakub Hesseltolph is dangerous Helen and he likes hurting officials, women. I don't want you around where there's a risk that he could get to you.'

It was the first time in six months that he had touched her. She felt his energy shoot up her arm. She went closer.

'I thought you had stopped caring?'

'I would kiss you right here, right now and prove that I've never stop caring, but damn me if Mendes wouldn't walk around the corner if I did.'

His hand slipped away from her arm.

Chapter Twenty Nine

Mary Peterson stood on the veranda looking out at the beach and the water, it was a view that she had never grown weary of looking at and *Whispering Echoes* was full of happy memories, many around Abraham and their family, with only the occasional not so good. The worst of all when she had lost Abraham, when his heart had stopped beating.

Her holdall was all packed. It wasn't heavy although bulky it gave the impression that it was full. Mary had only taken what she considered essentials leaving the rest in chests, drawers and the wardrobes, believing that some memories were meant to remain with the house. Emily Lou sensed what was pending having seen Mary pack. She sat faithfully at Mary's side grateful of the affection that she was receiving, her instincts telling her that her best friend wasn't coming back.

In the past few hours a spiritual karma had settled over *Whispering Echoes* bringing with it an air of acceptance that had crept in between the shutters with the breeze. Mary believed the breeze was a sign and that it was time to leave. The Atlantic, she thought to herself was ringing in the changes and that with change would come new beginnings. In the last two hours Julianna and Emily Lou had been exceptionally quiet, keeping out of Mary's way. When Julianna came and stood inside the doorway of the bedroom Mary looked up.

'I really need to see my daughter and son,' she looked tired as though she hadn't slept at all the night before, 'and before you ask, I've made the necessary arrangements to fly rather than drive. You can keep the car, it runs perfectly well and will only require the odd wash to remove the sand grains.'

She rubbed her right knee and began stoking Emily Lou once again.

'The early morning sea mists have been playing havoc with my limbs this season and I've been falling behind this old girl more and more, even Abraham has noticed that I'm dragging my heels.'

Mary walked over hand hugged Julianna holding her tight gently patting her back.

'We talked about this remember. You coming here was an opportunity for us both Julianna. Since the last fall I knew, I felt that something or somebody was coming to make things different. You were, you are that change and Whispering Echoes has stopped groaning since you arrived. It approves. Abraham approves and so does Emily Lou. He knows too that I have been wanting to leave the house for some time now.'

'Why didn't you just sell up and move nearer your children?' Julianna asked, wiping the tear from her cheek.

'Emily Lou likes it here on the beach too much, I couldn't just take that away from her.'

'You said that there was a karma here, in what way?'

Mary smiled. 'You'll know when you feel it, just like I did.'

'And what about Abraham, will he go with you?'

Mary gave a shake of her head. 'No, he will still need to see the sunrise every morning down on the beach. We talked and he said that when it was my time, we could both stand and watch it rise together.'

'So you'll come back!'

'One day. Emily Lou will tell you that I've returned.'

Julianna grabbed Mary and held on like a young daughter would a mother. It has been a long time since anybody had shown her any love, any kindness. She was going to miss her brandy companion more than she could express or tell her.

'Thank you Mary, thank you for everything, and I promise that if you ever come calling, the chest under the table on the veranda will always be stocked and Emily Lou and me, we'll keep your chair dusted of sand.'

Mary hugged her dog and kissed the top of her head.

'I have never been one for long sentimental goodbyes, so please don't make my going difficult. She kissed Julianna on the cheek then picked up her holdall and walked to the waiting cab on the corner. She gave the driver her luggage, turned once to wave before she got in the back. It was the first time ever that Julianna had wanted to run after somebody and ask them not to leave. Emily Lou sensed her anguish, she clamped her mouth over the hem of the skirt and tugged hard. By the time that Julianna looked up again the cab and Mary was gone.

Fighting back the tears she knelt down and hugged the Labrador. 'Well girl... it's just you and me now. Do you fancy a breeze along the sand and later we'll watch the sunset together before we have supper.' Emily Lou ran to fetch her stick.

Later that night Julianna slipped out of her day clothes and took a long shower washing the grains of fine sand from her hair. She left her hair wet, slipping into a pair of shorts and a casual top. When she went out to the veranda Emily Lou was already asleep by Mary's chair. Pulling open the lid of the old wood chest she found an envelope which was addressed to her. Inside was a hand written letter.

Dear Julianna

If you're reading this note, then I have already left. Believe me, my heart is breaking as much leaving you and Emily Lou, but this is something that I knew that I had to do.

By the time that you settle down on the veranda with Emily Lou, I will be safely tucked up in bed at my daughter's house, no doubt with the grandchildren camping somewhere in the room as well, only we like to improvise and pretend that we're out in the wilderness for the night.

I did not forget to give you a forwarding address of either my son or my daughter, but I thought it best that they make contact with you when I am no longer around and it is time to join my beloved Abraham. Please don't feel that you are obligated to attend the funeral. It's not that I don't want you there, but I have never been one for funerals myself. I would rather you remember me when we went for our walks, sat on the veranda and sipped brandy into the small hours. Think of when we talked under the stars and enjoyed each other's company albeit only for a short while. Please Julianna only remember me like that and not as dead.

Remember that a house can heal, so let it. Emily Lou has grown very fond of you, so allow her the opportunity to show you what whispering

Echoes can do to help settle a restless soul. Not that I think you ever will, but in case you do ever feel tempted, I took the passport belonging to Melanie Anne Smith with me. Through a passage of resourceful means the passport will conveniently find its way into the laundry basket of a Las Vegas hotel, where it will be found by the staff and passed up the line to reception. It will give the police or FBI something to chew over and have them search the wrong state in their quest to find you. The distance between Florida and Nevada is over two thousand, five hundred miles so that should be more than adequate to keep you safe without you worrying about ever being found again. With a name change, a new hair style and colour, you could become literally anybody, even a nobody!

Whispering Echoes was a place always full of love, laughter and dreams Julianna. Let it be a place where you find yours. Our time together was short, but I'll never forget you.
Yours affectionately
With love
Mary

She held the note to her chest and wept, remembering a time when she had attended her parent's funeral vowing never to mourn at another, but Mary had been like a mother to her, albeit very briefly. When the tears were spent, she opened up the rum box and removed the bottle. Together she and Emily Lou sent their love, a ritual they would share every night. She replaced the letter in the envelope and put it back in the chest where it belonged, where it could be read whenever Julianna felt lonely.

'The world's a big place Emily Lou.' She stroked the back of the dog's head. 'I've a feeling that you and I will end our day's here!'

Universally people vanished daily and some never to be heard of, seen or found again. Jason had vanished and never been found so why couldn't she. The next morning she would visit the chemist buy some grey colouring and dye her hair. She would age and become a different woman. Over time she would make friends with select female groups and she integrate herself into the community and become part of the fabric. In time she hoped the authorities would stop looking.

To others who didn't know her she would be the woman who lived on the corner of Orchard Street kept herself to herself, never troubled anybody and occasionally waved at another walker on the beach. Julianna Hosseltolph would keep her promise to Mary, often wondering if she had met an angel. She never did look back and after time the nightmares too began to fade as did the memory of her brother.

Emily Lou suffered a touch of arthritis in her hip, but accepting that change was inevitable she would struggle through the pain enjoying her walks with Julianna. And in the evenings they would sit together on the veranda and become lost in their thoughts. Occasionally the Labrador would feel a presence, she would look up and wag her tail enthusiastically, her bright eyes filled with everlasting love.

'I know girl, I feel her too. One day Emily Lou, one day!'

Chapter Thirty

Surprisingly the drive back along the coastal road was without incident even when police cruisers went speeding by heading towards Bulow Creek. The car rented by Monica Jordan had been easily located, cordoned off and left for forensic examination as officers arriving first on the scene took a report of a stolen Hyundai belonging to the couple who had been walking the red trail. They reported seeing a man with two women, but they could give no additional details other than they had waved. Leaving the rented car at Daytona Beach Jakub took the bus back to Melbourne. It was time to look for Julianna, buy a change of clothes and visit Matt Baum.

Wearing a NFL peaked cap, sunglasses, a plain shirt and jeans Jakub stood at the four way junction opposite the campaign office. Each window was plastered with a large ostentatious poster of the senator and above the entrance hung the American flag. The pomp, the show made Jakub despise Matt Baum all the more. He stood in the shade watching the upstairs windows looking for signs that would tell him that Baum was in the office.

Despite the domineering presence that it was a campaign office the area was quite run down. It had been Ed Jackson's idea to keep everything low key and demonstrate that the senator's heart was with the people who would be his supporters, his voters. New posters, printed daily had a different message, todays read *'fighting for the right to live with our heads held high'*. Jakub scoffed, the only person who ever mattered was Matthias Baumgartner. He didn't have time for others without status, wealth or opportunity.

Jakub removed the sunglasses, wiped the perspiration from his forehead then put them back on. The day had been warm, but the afternoon seemingly hotter. It was no wonder that they called Florida the Sunshine State. Waiting for the traffic to clear he crossed the junction and walked in under the flag. A solitary guard, a powerfully built man in a suit that didn't quite fit watched him arrive. Jakub acknowledged the guard then took his place on the row of seats where he would be called. Already at the enquiry desk was a man and his wife, Latin Americans who had come to air their grievance with the senator about poor sanitation, poor housing and state benefits.

Behind the desk was a man and a young woman, both smartly dressed and using every ounce of diplomacy that they knew to keep heated situations under control. The guard was back-up where they failed. Jakub noticed that behind where the guard stood was a single glass door and beyond that a staircase, he guessed going up to Baum's first floor office. Next to where he was sat was a fire map for emergencies, but none of the upstairs offices had been detailed. Like the windows the walls were adorned with photographs of Baum, some shaking hands with voters at schools, soup kitchens, building sites and even at a children's playground. Propaganda images, but they looked convincing.

On the wall behind the reception desk there were two framed posters depicting places that should be visited locally, places of interest, one the zoo and the other the creek. It amused Jakub to think that he had seen both in the last twenty four hours. On the counter top was a small sign advising visitors that there was a zero policy tolerance on unacceptable behaviour. He wondered, would killing the senator be considered unacceptable or an act of kindness. The people of Florida knew nothing of the truth about their senator or his past.

Sited strategically were various security cameras, but keeping his head low only the tip of his nose and chin were visible. At one point the guard moved to the nearest monitor to check on the screen image, but having waxed his hair it had changed his appearance again from that of the zoo security images. Jakub had shaved too, but left a moustache, if anything he looked Hispanic. Satisfied the guard moved back to his post guarding the door. When the female receptionist smiled and called him forward he approached the desk.

Jakub returned the smile. 'Good afternoon. Is the senator in?'

'I'm afraid not this afternoon. The senator has a prior engagement, but if you would like to leave the nature of your enquiry we will endeavour to pass it along to his main office.'

'I thought this was his main office?' Jakub read the name printed on her lapel badge.

'No Sir, this is merely a campaign office where we attempt to deal with local resident issues.'

'Oh, I'm sorry it's my mistake Jessica. You see the senator and I go back a long way. We're old friends from Austria. I'm here on holiday and in the state. I thought I would call in and see if Matthias and Adelina were well.'

At that moment unseen by Jakub an image flash-up from the county sheriff's office. It was difficult to see the man's eyes under his blue tints and the only distinguishable feature was the same shape chin, even the mouth looked different part covered by a moustache. Where she had thought him Hispanic his voice was more German European. Running her finger down a diary on her desk to check on availability she used her free hand to activate a concealed button. The guard was busy talking to the Latin American couple who had been given a number of application forms to fill out. Twenty seconds later a suited man appeared having come down from the floor above. Jessica explained to colleague the nature of Jakub's enquiry.

'The gentleman here is passing through the state and is an old friend of the senator. He was wondering when Matt Baum is likely to be in next.'

The office manager offered a friendly hand which Jakub shook. 'Hi Teddy Gooch. We can certainly give the senator a call and have him call you back. I'm sure that he'd sure like to share a beer with you, although I will warn you he does have a tight schedule for the next few days.'

Diplomatic, friendly and always with a smile, officials were all the same, Jakub added his own. He wondered if Baum was upstairs watching a monitor. He took Monica Jordan's cell phone from his back pocket and gave Teddy Gooch the number.

'I'm only in town for another day then I'll be moving on. If Matt has time that would be great, otherwise I'll catch up with on the way back.'

Jessica handed Gooch a pad for him to write down the number. She took another look at the face on the screen, she wasn't sure. Without the glasses it could be, could be not. Jakub guessed what she was looking at.

He also surmised that the whole place was alarmed. Taking a printed card from his jacket pocket Gooch handed it to Jakub.

'That has my private office number at the bottom. If your plans change give me a call.'

Jakub thanked them for their co-operation then left nodding at the security guard on the way out. Standing on an alternative corner to the one that he had originally walked down he was in no hurry to get away. Cool, calm and unflustered could fool many a doubter.

'What do you think?' Jessica asked Gooch.

He looked at the screen behind the desk, rubbed his chin and zoomed in closer.

'It could be. The chin was the same, but the hair colour, it's darker and not as haphazard. The blue tints didn't help. He sounded German although it's next door. Give the police department a call and have them send down a unit. We better not take any chances.'

Jessica was still on the phone when Gooch took a call from Ed Jackson. When the call ended the colour from his face had drained. 'What did the police say?' he asked.

'They're sending over a couple of units to check the area.' Jessica noticed the change in his expression. 'Are you okay Teddy?'

'Yeah I'm fine. That was Ed Jackson himself to tell me that this serial killer, Jakub Hesseltolph kidnapped two woman this morning. He killed one of them, a public office employee over at Bulow Creek.'

Like a ghost Jakub vanished from sight moments before the first police cruiser arrived. Unseen and hidden behind some dumpsters in a service alley he noticed that the slats of a window blind in an upstairs office moved. From where he was stood it was impossible to say who was looking out. Other Dodge Chargers arrived followed by a car he recognised. This time the two agents from the hotel were accompanied by a woman. She was smartly dressed in a dark suit and had a side arm strapped to the belt of her trousers.

Hunter looked at the screen, made the comparisons and was convinced that it was Jakub Hesseltolph. Montgomery was astonished that the guard had not asked Hesseltolph to remove his cap. 'Where exactly is the senator?' she asked.

'At his official office down town. This is merely a call-in centre for local residents.'

'Does he have any immediate high-profile functions to attend this evening?'

Teddy Gooch didn't know. 'You would have to call Ed Jackson for his itinerary, but with the elections very soon it would be my guess that the senator is busy most days, evening and some nights.' Hunter wondered if it was the reason that Adelina Baum had gone back home.

The officers who had done a three sixty sweep of the area returned to say that there were sightings of the man who had visited the office. Montgomery thanked them asked that they stay vigilant. She then called Ed Jackson and introduced herself. She told him about the arrival of the US Marshall's. He was happy with the extra manpower. He said that the senator had the evening off and as spending it at his club. Ed Jackson told Helen Montgomery that if she needed any extra funds, he would find them somewhere to protect Matt Baum.

Mendes scoffed and gave a shake of his head. 'The price of power!'

From the balcony of a private residential apartment near to the four way junction, Jakub watched the agents stand outside the campaign office and talk for a few minutes longer before all three got back in the car and left. Snatching a bandana headscarf and clean tee-shirt from a nearby washing line heft twenty dollars under the wash basket. Using the earth from a flower pot he smudged his face. Minutes later he was different again. He checked himself in the reflection of a kitchen window. Making a minor adjustment to the headscarf he crouched back down and made himself comfortable.

An hour later the sign on the office front door was turned around and the door locked. Jakub watched as Jessica Kashaya appeared from a side door, walked across the junction holding onto a small clutch bag strapped over her shoulder. She appeared happy to be free of the office and back out in the sunshine. He waited patiently until she had gone past the apartment block before he stepped out and followed.

Baum might not have been inside the campaign office, but not all was lost and there were other ways to catch a rabbit.

Following not far that behind Jakub admired the way that she walked, wiggling her hips athletically, her leg were nice than Elise's, more shapely, longer. Going to the senator's campaign office had not been a complete waste of time.

Chapter Thirty One

Feminine intuition or indeed animal instinct it didn't matter which, Jessica Kashaya instinctively knew that somebody was following behind. Her heart rate had increased and her pace had quickened. She wanted to look behind, but she knew that to remain calm and prepared was her best defence.

Working on reception in the campaign office she'd had many admirers, offers of a date or a drink after work, but she had politely refused them all. She had changed her mind at the last minute that morning and opted for her clutch bag rather than her normal handbag that contained her mace spray. Karl, her older brother would be annoyed with her for making such a stupid mistake. Striding with more purpose she was only a block away from the garage where the mechanics were working on her car.

Breaking into a trot she crossed the tarmac forecourt heaving a sigh of relief. In the open entrance of the garage she looked back surprised to see that there was nobody there only the long shadows cast down by the late afternoon sun. Jessica frowned convinced that somebody had been following her. The garage owner, one Benny Vincenzi, a loud although loveable Italian American had seen her approach. He grabbed his rag and cleaned the grease from his hands.

'Hey princess, you been chased by a ghost. You look concerned!'

Jessica felt the relief drain down her body.

'Maybe Benny.'

He looked, but he saw nothing and the street was clear.

'Working for Baum, I'd be seeing things. That guys not as straight as he makes out Jessica.'

'He's okay Benny. He has a big agenda to step up the Whitehouse so he needs a big personality to match.'

Benny Vincenzi laughed out loud, his fatty jowls wobbling as he laughed.

'Well whatever, you'll always be my favourite customer.'

Taking a clean cloth from the workbench he gave the handle of her driver's door another quick polish in case one of the mechanic's had touched the car after he had finished working on it.

'I did the brakes myself only I can't trust these grease monkeys here with such a fine ride!'

The remark was answered with a series of whistles which bounced off the walls and down in the service pit, but Jessica knew every one of them. Since passing her test and buying the car from Benny she would never trust any other garage, other than Benny's. Making out that they were working they watched their boss flirt with Jessica. She didn't know it, but she was their favourite too.

'She could massage my aching back anytime...' muttered one of the younger tyre fitters.

'Keep that comment under your hat,' advised another, 'she works for the senator and Benny's cousin belongs to the same club as Matt Baum.'

The tyre fitter watched Benny and Jessica pass through the workshop to the office at the back where he kept the invoice book. Given the chance she could massage more than his back. When Benny tapped on the window of the office they went back to work. None of them noticed the lonely figure cross the forecourt to the service bay.

'Remember,' advised Benny, 'don't throttle the gas pedal too hard and then brake fast, new brakes are like a woman and need to be treated gently!'

She squeezed his arm and kissed his cheek, the highlight of his day. 'I'll be good Benny.'

Benny threw the car keys across to the mechanic nearest the door. 'Turn Miss Kashaya's car around please Enrique and make sure you don't leave any smudges on the seat or I'll smudge you!' He stamped the receipt and signed it. 'You get the usual ten percent discount.'

Jessica sighed. 'Oh Benny, thank you... but you know I like to pay the full price.'

Benny grinned. 'Working for Baum, you need to watch every penny!' He didn't elaborate.

Out front Enrique had turned around the car as was about to close the door when a dark shadow appeared from nowhere. He thought it was a seagull swooping low, until the metal bar connected with the back of his skull and everything went black. Jakub dragged the mechanic away and dumped him unceremoniously amongst the discarded tyres, covering his body with a tarpaulin nearby. He put the key in the ignition and climbed into the rear foot well. Waving at the mechanics in the pit Jessica was surprised to not see Enrique waiting beside the car. The young mechanic was always so attentive. She looked back inside, but Benny was already on the phone to another customer.

Putting the gear into reverse she drove slowly off the forecourt as Benny had advised. On the approach to the junction she tested the brakes feeling the pads and discs bite back. Jakub waited until they were clear of the junction before he sat upright behind Jessica. The first sign that she had company was when she noticed the blue tints in the rear view mirror and the blade of the knife below her jaw. Her captor issued his instructions calmly and clearly.

'Keep driving ahead Jessica, nice and even keeping up with the traffic adding no sudden moves and no harm will come to you!'

Removing the bandana she recognised the hair. Jessica Kashaya swallowed the saliva in her throat remembering what Teddy Gooch had told her about the two women being kidnapped earlier.

'Where are we going?' she asked, trying hard to keep her voice calm.

'For a drive. Somewhere quiet where we won't be disturbed.' She glanced at him in the mirror, her eyes full of apprehension. Jakub moved the knife to her side where it was close to her ribcage.

'I'm not the monster everybody thinks I am and it's not my intention to hurt you, not unless you do something stupid. I just need you to help me with a little problem.'

She continued driving for about a kilometre and a half to the outskirts of Melbourne where he gave her directions taking a left turn into a woodland glade. Switching off the engine and setting the brake she waited, expecting the assault to begin, only it didn't happen. Instead her captor relaxed his grip on the knife and climbed through to sit beside her. He asked for the car keys and to her relief placed the knife on the dashboard. He checked that her seat belt was tight across her chest and that it was locked in the safety ratchet.

'That is just a precaution for us both.'

'What do you want with me,' she asked, 'I don't have much cash on me?'

Jakub grinned. 'I'm not here to rob you. Tell me, was the senator upstairs when I came to the office earlier?'

'No. He would either be at the office downtown or out on the golf course. He's there most afternoons with some wealthy banker or rich entrepreneur. It's how he funds the campaign.' Jakub clenched his teeth together. He despised how the rich could abuse everything in life, including other's lives. Jessica continued without being asked, 'it's known as *the green office* where a handshake clinches a deal.'

'Do you know where the senator lives?'

She nodded.

'Yes. He and his wife have a big house on Mulberry Drive.' Jessica hesitated. 'Trust me, you'd never get anywhere near it or Matt Baum. He has a security detail with him twenty four seven unless he's sleeping. The gates are made of reinforced steel and locked by electro-magnet. The brick piers either side would crumble before the gates caved in.'

'You're very well informed, how come?' he asked.

'Before joining the campaign office I worked at City Hall in the engineers department. I saw the drawings for the extra security.'

He liked her she was smart just like Julianna and pretty too.

'How about in the evenings, when they're not spent at home?'

She looked puzzled. 'I don't follow you?'

'When I knew him, he was Matthias Baumgartner and he had a reputation amongst the ladies. As a young boy I remember my grandfather talking about the sins of the magistrate.'

'Oh that...' Jessica nodded, she too had heard the rumours.

'The senator owns a place called the Summer House. Some of the single guys go there for weekends, but they rarely mention what occupies their time there. I do know that Ed Jackson, the senator's aide politely refused a membership. Ed Jackson is happily married and with a family.' She stopped, the frown creasing her brow. 'You're not going to hurt Ed Jackson are you, I'd rather you rape or kill me than hurt the Jackson's.'

'No, I don't have a grievance with this man.'

'Thank you!'

'This Summer House that Baum owns do you know where it is...?'

'Yes. Its west of here near Sawgrass Lake. The estate and waters once belonged to a wealthy plantation owner. It came up for auction about two years back and Matt Baum made a killing on the price. As soon as he had the deeds a massive rebuild and renovation project turned the place around. He keeps membership very select.'

Jakub trusted her.

'Should I be caught, I'll make you a promise Jessica and that none of this information came from you!'

Jessica opened her mouth in astonishment. 'Why... why would you do that?'

'Because sometimes the underdogs have to win in this world.'

Intelligent and understanding his sentiment, she asked, 'has he hurt you in the past, you or your family?'

Jakub nodded. 'Both. His intervention killed my parents, had my sister run away from home and he put me somewhere where I never wanted to be. You senator controls people's lives using whatever means are available. He would destroy this country.'

'What will you so when you find him?' She guessed what, but needed to satisfy her curiosity.

'Talk with him. His future depends upon what answers he gives.'

Jessica Kashaya believed him.

Jakub looked around at the wooded area, he liked the trees, liked the energy that they gave out. He felt safe amongst them.

'You've answered my questions without hesitating, why?' he asked.

'Because I don't want to die.'

She was like Julianna.

'You won't.' He sensed however that there was something that she wasn't telling him. 'Has Baum ever made a pass at you, or hurt you?'

'No, not me, but he did with a friend of mine. The Summer House is more than what it seems. On paper it is no more than a gentleman's retreat, a place where they go to play golf, wine and dine, and have fun. Behind the façade it becomes more sinister.'

'Like what exactly?'

'The first floor is made up of bedrooms and bathrooms, nothing else and there are girls, lots of girls always available for the men.'

He detected anger and pain in her eyes.

'Go on...'

'A friend that I knew from college got a job there as a waitress. One night she texted me to tell me that she was in hospital and could I go see her. When I walked into her room she wasn't sick, she had been beaten and hurt bad. She refused to say how and made me promise never to say anything about going to the hospital. She was scared, terrified. She told me that if I ever told anybody about that night at the hospital she would disappear and things, bad things would happen to my family.'

At Ebenstatt Jakub had seen the bruises, scars on the other inmates. They too would never say how they got the injuries and the nursing staff would tell him that the injured had thrown themselves at the walls or cell doors. Jakub had known different. He had never suffered the indignity of being abused physically because Alexander Koskovsky and his staff had been too wary of his strength and how he could react if cornered. 'Baum runs a whore house.' Jessica Kashaya didn't reply she acknowledged with a solitary nod.

Jakub suddenly reached over, took her hand in his raising it to his lips, he kissed the back of her fingers then let go.

'You're smart and brave Miss Kashaya. I ask one more favour please. Drive me to this place that Baum owns and then you can go free, drive yourself home unharmed. And I promise you will never see or hear from me again.'

Jessica Kashaya turned the key in the ignition and started the engine. En-route he made small talk asking, wanting to know more about the Summer House.

'The young women that work at the Summer House, do you know where they come from?' He dropped the knife down into the foot well. Jessica heard it fall.

'Monique, my friend she told me that most are from Europe especially the eastern zones. They would arrive mainly in two's and three's, sometimes more. They underwent a medical examination at a private medical clinic where if they received a clean health check, they were put to work at the Summer House. Monique said many of the girls were virgins.'

'And Monique, did she go back to work after the stay in hospital?'

Jessica shook her head. 'No. She died as a result of her injuries a week later. I saw a copy of the death certificate. It said that she'd had an undetected heart condition. It was a lie. Monique was the fittest girl that I knew from college. It seems that even in death the lies never stop.'

'Baum made it happen.'

'Scandal is a candidate's worst enemy and Ed Jackson works very hard to keep the wolves working for the press away. I really don't envy him his job and Matt Baum acknowledges that he would be seriously lost without Ed.'

'Wealth and power is a dangerous combination Jessica. You would do well to put some distance between you and Matt Baum. He's a very dangerous man, I know!'

She continued driving hoping that they would not come across a police patrol. Circumstances would change dramatically if they did. Sensing that she wouldn't be harmed she told him more.

'Every now and then the body of a young woman would be washed up upon the beach a few miles down from Melbourne and their death would be recorded by the public office as suicide.' She looked at him. 'I know that they worked at the Summer House and that nobody ever came forward to claim their body. Soon even the press lost interest in the dead girls and so did the public. Life here can be extremely cheap sometimes.'

Jessica turned right down what looked like a dirt track.

'At least Monique died between clean sheets rather than on the rocks.'

She changed gear and took the road ahead very cautiously.

'What's wrong?' asked Jakub reaching down for the knife again.

'Nothing, I've never been here so I'm not entirely sure what lies ahead.'

She switched off the air conditioning.

'You do know that the FBI are hot on your heels.'

Jakub found the statement surprising considering her situation.

'I know. I've not much time left, but this is something that I have to do. If not for me, for my sister.'

Jessica nodded.

'Thank you.'

'What for…?'

'For not hurting me!'

Chapter Thirty Two

Matt Baum arrived late afternoon walking in and shaking hands, waving at members he recognised at the bar, generally pleased to have time to himself to relax as he wanted. His eyes keenly surveying everything he missed nothing. He sucked in the atmosphere sensing that the house had a good feel to it. The afternoon results were in and his election ratings were higher than expected. All in all life was good, even after he had watched his wife leave that morning vowing never to return.

Up and down the coast the hospitality trade went through peaks and toughs, seasonal differences analysts would say, but none of the other competitors could cater for their guests like that of the Summer House, and their bank balance was forever on the increase. It was the niche in the market that Matt Baum had successfully plugged. A shrewd businessman he had only one motto *'to succeed, win at all costs'*.

Crossing the carpeted room he was met by a large stocky Africa American woman, her most prominent features being her powerful forearms and mass of permed curly hair, copper tinted to match the colour of her favourite autumn tree. Grinning enthusiastically she was pleased to see the owner.

'If you could take your eyes of my bosom, you'd see that I'm wearing the earrings you gave me the other day.' To make sure that Baum noticed she jiggled her ample bosom making her earlobes follow suit.

Matt Baum laughed, he had felt comfortable with Philadelphia Brown the moment that she had arrived at the Summer House. She was good with the clientele, had a way with words that men and women respected and she kept house better than any drill sergeant. She also had an enormous bust and often or not most of it was on show.

'If I didn't know better Philadelphia I would say that you had been for one of those boob jobs and added the extra discount instead of taking it off the bill.' They both laughed as she hoisted up her bust before letting them fall to the amusement of the men sitting around having a drink. Some cheered. Philadelphia addressed the room.

'And if any of you is interested to see if they're real or not, get your arse upstairs and find out!' She winked at Matt Baum who was enjoying the moment. Enjoying how she made the punters happy.

'There you go fella's,' he added, 'the offers on the table and I guarantee you'll not be disappointed!' It was a ruse that they had used many times and it always worked a charm. He watched the first man step up. A young man, fit and lean. Philadelphia checked the room availability and told him to have a drink first only not to get drunk. She joined her boss tapping the bar top for the barman's attention, where she ordered his usual.

'How's business Philly?' Baum asked.

'On the up, even during the days. It's hot outside, too hot to be out walking around on the greens so the customers are coming inside where it's a lot cooler. I had to order more towels for the upstairs rooms.'

Towels were a drop in the ocean in the grand scheme of the business, but Baum watched his finances carefully. 'Why...?' he asked.

'The girls, they're working overtime helping burn off pent up energy that is left over from not walking down the fairways so they're taking more showers after. Often or not, not alone!'

Matt Baum smiled. In the bedroom set aside for his personal use he had an especially big bath that could easily accommodate three.

'As long as we keep our customers happy, that's all that counts.' He looked around coming close to Philly. *'Are they all behaving after the last unfortunate accident?'*

Philly sucked together her lips. 'After Zuzanna was found down on the rocks, they've decided that it's too risky complaining and realised what will happen if they do.'

Matt Baum was happy to have Philly at the helm helping to keep everything ticking along nicely. They'd had some unrest amongst the last batch of young women who had arrived only last month, but Philly had soon knocked them into shape, literally. What she was very good at was making sure that nothing ever came back that could damage the reputation of the Summer House or indeed the owner. In her usual deep southern drawl she asked if he was staying the night, telling his protection detail to cut away to the kitchen to avail themselves of a beef steak sandwich.

'Yes, I could with something to help me unwind, it's been a long week.'

Sipping at his wine Baum surveyed his empire. If he made it to 1600 Pennsylvania Avenue the Summer House would stay until his term was up. He needed a nest egg to come back too, somewhere where retirement would not be lonely or boring.

Dotted about the lounge were discreet booths, some occupied, others vacant although probably not for long as he spied a group of businessmen walking away from the eighteenth green. The restaurant was half full, but that too would fill as would the bar and sauna, along with the massage rooms. Between them he and Philly had designed and had built a good sized extension which included a pool and gymnasium. Beyond the restaurant was the games room with blackjack, snakes eyes and roulette tables, each a money spinner and draw for the rich who needed an adrenaline fix. There was no pleasure that could not be catered for and Philly made sure it was available.

'Sylvette...' instructed Philly, 'you please go tell the chef that Mr Baum is here and that we expect one of his finest steaks tonight.' She walked fast to the kitchen leaving another younger woman, her skin slightly darker than her own smiling at Matt Baum.

'And you Maisie girl, why don't you keep Mr Baum entertained until his steak arrives.' She winked his way, 'and if he tells me later that you made him very happy, you'll earn yourself a bonus, okay!'
Maisie Anouska smiled, a bonus was good and she knew that the senator always said that they were good and made him very happy.

Occupying the seat next to his Baum had accepted that the house at Mulberry Drive had already lost its appeal as a home. Adelina has sucked out the soul and packed it in her case. The gardens looked dreary and the young man who had tenderly cared for the hedgerows had left without giving a reason why. Rubbing Maisie Anouska's thigh he order another drink for her.

Later when he had finished his meal and disappeared to the mens room Philly took the opportunity to call Maisie over to where she was standing in the shadows, watching. 'You're doing just fine,' she said, 'now take one of the other girl's with you and show Mr Baum a real good time. Work that body like you've never done before only when I take him breakfast in the morning I want to see him smiling like never before!'

Philly liked Maisie and she saw a great potential in the Croatian as a right hand for when she needed to ease back, not give up the reins entirely, just ease back. Maisie promised Philly that she would see him smile at breakfast time.

Young and innocent, most certainly naïve and unknowing of men, Philadelphia Brown had found herself the wrong side of the tracks at seventeen, invited to cross the tracks by some of the older women her real education had begun. She soon learnt that exposing what the good lord gave her she could name her price. The more experienced women taught her how to deal with the rough ones, the aggressive types and even the perverts. Philly always kept handy a knife handy in her garter and she would use it if needed. Disposing of a dead body had never been a problem, not for someone like Philadelphia Brown.

At thirty eight, she was strong and street-wise, good with keeping house and had the respect of the man who could soon be the number one in the world. Philly watched Maisie and another of the girls latch onto Matt Baum's arm the moment that he reappeared. She smiled to herself knowing that she had done well. The trio were about to go upstirs when Baum caught sight of Harold coming out of the office. He told Maisie and her friend to go on ahead while he had a word with the bespectacled accountant.

'How are the books looking Harold?'

'Very healthy Mr Baum, real good. Do you want to see?' Matt Baum followed Harold to the office stating that he didn't have long. He smiled at Philly and gave her a knowing nod, which she took to mean that he was happy with her choice of company for the night.

Running his fingers up, down and across the page like a concert pianist Harold was enthusiastic about the monthly takings. 'We've been very busy since your campaign started.'

Baum walked over to the drinks cabinet and poured two generous brandies, one which he gave to Harold. 'A healthy cash flow is music to my ears, well done.' He screwed the top down on the bourbon putting it back. 'You know a good bourbon is like the after burn of the sun. It has a distinct fire all of its own, an energy like some of our girls.'

Baum laughed mocking the smaller man who'd hardly touched the glass with his lips. Baum was in a good mood. 'Having a deeply religious commitment is commendable Harold, but once in a while a man has to taste the other things in life that the good lord provided. Women, wine and bourbon. The stuff that puts hairs on your chest.' He slapped the accountant's back like a quarter back would a wide receiver.

'I've been on the wagon seven years now since I met my dear wife Mr Baum and I promised her that I wouldn't go back on the drink. If I did I could die.'

Matt Baum took the glass from Harold Lockhart and swallowed the measure in one. 'The devil already has my number Harold so I might as well enjoy life before I step into the lift and press 'down'.

Harold pushed his spectacles back up his nose. 'We're up by seventeen percent on this time last year.'

Matt Baum put the glass down on the desk which would be collected later and removed to the kitchen replaced by new ones. 'The figure would have been higher had it not been for those unfortunate accidents. Things are hard enough to make ends meet without trivial events upsetting the status quo. The girls arrive with nothing and we get them everything – free lodging, nice clothes to wear, a clean bed, decent money and food. Some people never know when they're better off.'

Harold Lockhart made no comment, he was just the accountant. His sole purpose was to keep the books and calculate the profits. Philadelphia dealt with everything else. He knew about the girls, didn't want to know really, but he had enough sense to keep his mouth shut and his eyes down on the ground. Philly and Matt Baum knew men who could deal with a problem and make it disappear, if Philadelphia could not.

'Will she have you back?' asked Baum licking his lips.

'I'm not entirely sure. Bethany is staying with her mother at the moment.' He looked across at the small framed photo that he kept proudly at the side of his desk. 'Bethany has still to forgive me my last indiscretion. Perhaps one day soon the good lord will see fit to intervene.'

Harold took off his spectacles, breathed on them rubbing them clean with his handkerchief. He replaced them and pushed them up onto the bridge of his nose, but they slipped down almost as soon as he had. Drink had not been the problem, a young pretty choir girl had, despite his insistence to his wife that nothing untoward had taken place. Baum nodded, not really interested.

'Me and the good lord, we have a deal going, he doesn't interfere in my life and I don't his.' He rubbed the sides of his mouth with his forefinger and thumb, tapped the ledger again telling Harold that next month the profit would be much higher. 'Philly's got it all under control again. Now I am needed elsewhere. I will catch you later Harold.'

He watched Matt Baum leave the office, there were times when he could plunge the letter opener into the man's back and watch as he lay dying on the floor.

Harold was envious of Baum's wealth, his big house and prospects, not that he wanted anything to do with the White House or running the country, keeping the ledgers accurate was enough. Opening the door of the drinks cabinet he put his hand around the neck of the bourbon, looking at the framed photograph of Bethany who was looking back. Would she ever forgive him he wondered, probably not. He poured himself an extra-large glass.

Chapter Thirty Three

The car engine stalled, the driver having hidden the vehicle under the trees ten metres shy of the edge of the drive, shielded by the long line of tall shrubs where the two occupants had a good view of club members arriving or leaving. Overhead the evening sky had turned from a turquoise blue to a canvas of fiery red, interspersed with streaks of yellow and orange as the sun started to drop below the tops of the mangroves west of the lake.

Knowing that they were safely concealed the two reporters had successfully managed to follow the senator's car from his downtown office to the Summer House following an anonymous tip-off that the leisure centre had more to offer than just gym and golf.

'I've never been here before,' said James Critcheon as he checked his equipment bag. Junior to his colleague Vanessa Bernstein shook her head.

'Me neither.'

'Do we go take or look or wait?'

Bernstein weighed up the options watching a group of golfers putting at the hole nearest where they were parked. 'My motto has always been let the prey come to you. It'll be interesting to see who turns up or leaves. Have you got your notepad ready?'

Critcheon waved it under her nose.

'Eventually,' she continued, 'a story always develops and presents itself, you just have to be patient.'

Having worked her way up the promotion ladder Vanessa Bernstein no longer ran despatches for senior reporters, proof-read cuts and editorials for the editor, instead she chased down serious leads and got to the story first ahead of her nearest rivals. A scoop on the state senator could earn her a mention in the annual awards. The anonymous call which had been brief had come direct to her desk phone, where it had been taped and played back several times until she was convinced that it was genuine. Telling Critcheon to grab and bring along his bag of tricks they had run to the car pool where he'd asked where they were heading. Vanessa Bernstein would only hint at the prize being monumental, a prize that would fire Critcheon's aspirations beyond the next moon.

Several cars went past slowly heading down the drive, serious rides and each highly polished, money cars. Although they didn't recognise most of the drivers or occupants, Critcheon recorded the details.

'So what do we know that's interesting about Baum?' he asked, having entered the registration number of the fourth car. As a junior reporter he had been out on several assignments with Vanessa Bernstein. She liked, admired his tenacity, but at times he was a little too impulsive and eager to please.

She saw a naked female walk across a first floor window space capturing the moment on her mobile as her colleague was too slow with the camera. The image helped corroborate the mysterious call that she had taken earlier. Bernstein answered the question.

'I'm not sure, but I think we're about to find out a lot more this evening.'

Critcheon who checked that the camera had enough battery life added his own interpretation. 'I'd read that he was native Austrian where he had been a magistrate. He tells everybody that he's a titled man, some sort of Earl, Lord or Baron.'

Bernstein was listening, although she kept her focus on the building lower down the long drive. 'We can't dispute that his political career hasn't been meteoric and not being home spun invites more interest.'

'He has business deals all over in Vegas, Chicago and Washington.'

Bernstein was surprised. 'How do you know that?'

'I have a cousin who works at the National Corporation Directory.'

Vanessa Bernstein put her hand over his mouth and pointed at the trees her side of the car.

'Over there,' she muttered, 'do you see him?'

Critcheon looked. He saw a man walking through the trees heading for the building below. He didn't seem interested in them. Bernstein suddenly grabbed Critcheon and pulled him in close to give the impression that they were lovers taking the opportunity of a quiet undisturbed moment in the trees.

'If you kiss me, I swear I'll kill you.' She warned.

Critcheon sniffed her perfume. 'You smell really nice.'

'Fuck off.'

When the mystery man carried on walking without looking back she pushed him away.

'He doesn't fit in and I get the impression that he's not an employee. Come on, I see a story developing.'

After a hot sunny day the evening clouds were darker than usual. They left the car in situ and began following, keeping a safe distance. Whoever the stranger was he moved fast, moved with stealth and the trees were good camouflage. They wondered if he was secret services. Seconds later he disappeared.

'Where'd he go?' asked Critcheon.

'I don't know. My instinct tells that he's down at the house.'

'Do we follow?'

Vanessa Bernstein stopped walking, she held onto Critcheon's arm and pointed. 'There he is by the door.'

Unusually like the dark clouds overhead Vanessa Bernstein experienced a flutter of doubt in her stomach.

'Something doesn't feel right here.'

Chapter Thirty Four

Jakub had seen the car, but the lovers were not of any interest to him. He has sensed somebody following, but he was so close to Baum that his only focus was getting into the house. Moving between the trees he had thought about Julianna wondering why they had not found one another. He had sensed that she was close when he had been on the beach with Elise, but since then nothing. Overhead a cloud seemed to be following.

Having left Jessica Kashaya's tied to the steering wheel instead of letting her drive away as he had earlier agreed, Jakub had explained that for the police forces to find her in the woods it would prevent any awkward questions later and it would remove any doubt in her story. Jessica agreed that it was in her best interests. Her instinct to survive didn't surprise Jakub, what did was when she told him to be careful.

Standing beside the kitchen door he called the sheriff's department to give them Jessica's location, then calculated that he had enough time to find and deal with Baum before they and the FBI arrived. By the time they did Matthias Baumgartner would not be talking to anybody.

When the kitchen door opened Jakub stepped back before following the kitchen assistant who went directly to the waste bins to discharge his bucket of used vegetables into the commercial bin. He wasn't aware of the man behind.

James Critcheon was keen to get much closer, but Vanessa Bernstein tightened her grip.

'No James, not yet.' She advised.

They watched the kitchen hand empty his waste and the mystery man step out from behind the kitchen door.

'Quick James, capture what happens next on camera.'

He changed the lens focus to manual, moving in on the scene below.

'Who did make that call?' he asked, leaning into a tree to help steady the shot.

'I don't know, but I got the impression that he's church goer. In the message he quoted from Colossians 3:5 – *'put to death, therefore whatever belongs to your earthly nature: sexual immorality, impurity, lust, evil desires and greed.'*

Having put the receiver down softly on the cradle Harold Lockhart finished his brandy. He was beyond caring about the consequences. He didn't care what Matt Baum thought if he found him drunk and he was past caring about what Bethany thought. If it came to it he would make a new start the choir girl. Sitting at the desk with his thumb rubbing around the rim of the glass it produced a high pitch squeal. It sounded like Bethany.

Before he lost complete consciousness Jakub caught the young man and dragged him to the grass bank behind the waste bins. He removed his catering work jacket and put it over his tee-shirt. Collecting the bucket where it had rolled away he casually entered the kitchen and walked over to the sink. Down by the lake the toads had started early with their evening ritual of calling one another. Looking through a handheld pan of angry flames the chef saw the assistant return, it was enough to know that he was back and prepared to deal with the dirty dishes at the sink.

Arranging, sorting pots and pans he looked at the door exiting into the restaurant beyond. When a waitress arrived with a tray of empties he took them and laid them down on the side.

'I only started today, where's the men's?'

She pointed at the door to the restaurant. 'You'll have to use the ones outside the staff facilities are being redecorated.' She picked up a tray of food from the servery the same time that Jakub picked up a carving knife.

Standing to the side of the restaurant he watched male customers with scantily dressed women on their arms playing roulette, turning over cards and rolling dice. Looking about he couldn't see Matthias Baumgartner, what he did see instead was an enormous black woman who was watching him. With a flick of her hand she ordered him back into the kitchen. Jakub ignored her looking at the time on the clock behind the bar. He reckoned on another ten minutes before he had to leave. Picking up a tray from the serving trolley he started collecting used crockery. Within seconds he had company.

'What are you doing out here,' Philly demanded her eyes blazing, her brow curved and meeting in the middle, *'your place is in the kitchen.'*

Sticking the kitchen knife in her side Jakub told her to move to the door marked private. She did as he asked, but she wasn't going quietly.

'You don't know who you're dealing with!' she warned, but Jakub didn't have the time to make small talk.

'Move you fat cow or I'll gut you here and now.' Coming back down the stairs was a man with his arm around a young woman. Both were smiling. Jakub noticed the man had a wedding ring on his left hand.

Philadelphia Brown looked towards the bar, but the senator's security were busy talking and munching through their steaks. Seeing her look Jakub pushed the point in a little closer.

'I'll leave you drowning in your own blood if you don't move!'

Philly had worked in enough saloons, dance halls and whore houses to know when a man meant business. Without the knife she would have let rip with a power driven fist and decked her assailant there and then, but his eyes were darker than her own. Standing at the door marked private she tapped in the four digit code. Once inside Jakub closed the door and delivered a rabbit punch for good measure into the woman's back. She immediately fell to the floor clutching her right kidney. Holding the knife across the back of her neck he looked at Harold Lockhart who holding a half full glass was rooted to his chair and sat next to an open safe. Harold who was looking down was pleased to see the disagreeable woman pinned to the floor and in pain.

'Have you come to rob us?' he asked, his voice slightly slurred.

'That wasn't my intention, but it's an idea.' Replied Jakub.

He told Harold to bring his chair over, place the legs either side of the woman and pin her down by sitting back on the chair. Harold happily obliged resting the soles of his feet on her ample backside.

'Make a sound. I'll cut your throat and then do hers, do you understand?'

Harold nodded that he did. 'Can I finish my drink?' he asked. Jakub gave him his glass. He wasn't worried about fingerprints, after dealing with Baum the police could have as many as they liked. On her front and unable to move Philly could only hear both men, not see them.

'Harold, do something you useless bastard. When Mister Baum finds out that you helped with this you're a dead man!'

Jakub kicked her thigh hard and told her to shut up. He looked at the weasel faced man who was smiling.

'Is the senator here?' he asked.

Harold stuck his finger upright into the air.

'Upstairs with a couple of the girls, room fifteen. The sins of his debauchery will be his undoing. The devil will come for him one day soon.'

Jakub grinned. He picked up the bottle and refilled Harold's glass. On the floor Philly was cussing and cursing. Chopping the back of her neck Jakub put her to sleep.

'I'd like to stay and chat Harold,' said Jakub, 'but if I was you, I'd take some of that money from the safe and hide it somewhere where it won't be found. If it helps tell the police it was me who took it.'

'Why?' asked Harold, his temples beginning to throb.

'Because I want to see Baum lose big time.'

The thought amused Harold. Despite his throbbing temples, he was still lucid enough to think about the girls upstairs.

'You won't hurt the girls, will you?'

'No, not the girls.' Jakub replied. 'I've come to save them!'

Harold smiled. 'That's good, thank you!'

It was the second time that Jakub had been thanked that evening. He left Harold to do whatever he wanted, climbing the stairs with a pair of clean glasses on a silver salver. Nobody would stop a kitchen hand delivering glasses to a client.

Once the door had been shut Harold stood up, stood to one side of the unconscious woman and kicked her hard. He kicked her several times. How dare she threaten him and drunk, but not so drunk that he didn't know what he was doing Harold took bundles of the money and stashed them behind a filing cabinet taping the bundles to the back panel. Whatever happened upstairs was not his concern.

Harold sat back down when it was done looking at the fat woman lying under his chair. To help the stranger get away he chopped the back of her neck with the heel of his shoe. It would be sometime before she regain consciousness. He kicked her again, perhaps she would need a visit to the hospital. She had put enough of the girls in the hospital so why not suffer as well.

Taking home each evening two bundles of the money hidden in his jacket until there was nothing left the money would help rebuild his life and with or without Bethany, whatever the future Harold would always have the church.

Chapter Thirty Five

Having witnessed the attack by the mystery man who had dumped the kitchen assistant around back of the waste containers and then watched him go inside the two reporters ran down through the trees.

'I hope you got all that?' cried Vanessa Bernstein as she dodged and jumped the fallen branches.

'What exactly is this place?' asked Critcheon following closely behind.

'I'm not exactly sure, but I've a funny feeling that we're going to find out what lies behind those doors tonight.'

Leaving Critcheon to check on the condition of the young man Bernstein poked her head inside the kitchen door. Throwing his arms up in the air and barking out orders the chef wanted to know why the dirty crocks weren't being cleared. Leaving the unconscious kitchen assistant where he was James Critcheon re-joined Vanessa Bernstein.

'I don't care what or who you photograph inside, just get as many photo's as you can.'

Passing through the kitchen to the amazement of all including the chef, they entered the restaurant where Critcheon wasted no time capturing everything that moved.

Moving fast from the bar the security detail approached the reporters. Bernstein pushed Critcheon through into the games room. A moment later they all heard a girl scream from the floor above and coming down the drive were a number of police units their blue and red lights illuminating the inside of the restaurant.

'Keep activating that record button,' ordered Bernstein and she tapped the video mode of her cell phone. Having heard the scream the security detail had diverted their focus on the staircase going up.

*****

Having walked past all the bedrooms there was only one to go. The corridor was lavishly furnished and behind the solid oak doors had come a variety of different sounds, some were gasps of passion, playful giggles and in one he heard a girl crying, but he didn't have time to stop and investigate. Standing before the door marked fifteen he detected the sounds of anguished moaning and groaning coming from inside. Knocking enthusiastically on the door panel, there was no answer so he knocked again only harder. This time it was answered angrily by a man's voice, a voice that Jakub recognised.

'What is it… we're busy!'

'Room service.'

'We haven't ordered anything, now fuck off.'

Jakub used the handle of the knife on the door. 'It's a special delivery from the lady of the house.'

Baum cursed and grabbed the door handle. Before the door was half open Jakub kicked it hard knocking Baum to the floor the other side. He was inside in a flash and had the door shut before the senator could call out. Naked, his face full of surprise Matt Baum looked up in horror. 'You crazy lunatic Hesseltolph. I'll send you away somewhere where not even the ghosts of the past will find you!'

Jakub kicked him hard several times not bothering where the blows landed. The naked girl on the bed could only watch completely mortified as she clamped a clenched hand to her mouth. While Baum lay writhing on the carpet Jakub went over to the bed tore away the top sheet and gave it to the girl to cover herself. 'I once had a young sister like you, only this monster tried to destroy her too. Pick up your clothes and leave now!'

Maisie Anouska ran to the door. She didn't look down at Matt Baum. Before she closed the door Jakub asked where the other girl was. Maisie told him that she was entertaining in another room. As soon as the door was closed Jakub engaged the lock. He turned to see senator getting to his feet. Slamming a clenched fist into the side of Baum's head the senator fell reeling onto the bed.

'You sanctimonious bastard, you once said that I wasn't fit to live amongst decent people. And yet here you are sexually abusing a young woman no older than your own daughter. You are the living manifestation of evil in this room Baumgartner.' He punched him again only this time breaking the senator's nose. 'Now put that on your campaign posters.' Jakub laughed. 'Show the people of this state just how much blood you are willing to give to be the president.'

Matt Baum tried to speak, but the blood rushing to his injured nose was clogging the back of his throat. He wondered why his security team had not arrived and kicked down the door.

'Sending me to Ebenstatt was a mistake, it left my sister alone and vulnerable. Of course, you knew that and your perverse plans to abuse her yourself backfired when she left Kurlor. How many lives of young women did you ruin Baumgartner?' Jakub sliced the knife across the senator's thigh. 'Too many I'd say.'

Matt Baum spat the additional blood from his mouth, clamping his free hand over his thigh.

'Your crimes deserved the punishment that I endorsed. And later that night you viciously murdered your poor unsuspecting parents. You are the son of the devil Jakub Hesseltolph. I had a duty to protect the public from your evil.'

Picking up the senator's sock he stuffed it in his mouth having heard enough. Using the sleeves of Baum's shirt he tied his hands behind his back then knelt between his legs. The bed sheet were already turning red, but as Jakub sliced, cut and patterned the senator's chest and abdomen the blood flowed freely seeping into the mattress below. Baumgartner could only watch in horror, his bulging as he tried to scream. When it was done, completed Jakub made sure that Matt Baum never passed sentence on any other young soul. He sliced the blade of the knife across the senator's throat and removed the sock.

'Now die you bastard. Join Albrecht Hartmann where the two of you can discuss your sins. Because of you, I will have to keep running and hiding for the rest of my life. You made me who I am Matthias Baumgartner.'

Somewhere along the corridor a girl screamed. He had no idea why, but the blue and red lights bouncing off the bedroom walls were a good indication that the sheriff's had arrived.

Knowing that death was only moments away Jakub removed the bond freeing Baum's hands. He wanted the man from Kurlor to feel his life slipping away as he tried to clamp his throat together. Staring up at the ceiling Matthias Baumgartner saw a clouded vision appear of Adelina, their son and daughter, to his dismay all three were smiling. Holding up bundles of money, his money they would survive and enjoy life to the full.

Chasing the security detail up the stairs Hunter and Mendes had their side arms drawn. Standing at the top of the landing Maisie Anouska stood to one side as she pointed. 'Last door on the left,' she said, 'and the intruder has a knife.'

Putting the empty glass in the drinks cabinet along with the near empty bottle Harold Lockhart waited for the door to open. Picking up the paperweight he smacked it hard against his cheek then laid down beside Philadelphia Brown kicking the chair away from where it had held her pinned to the office floor.

Helen Montgomery made sure that somebody looked after Maisie before she went upstairs. She was running down the corridor when she heard Hunter call out *'FBI open the door'* moments before Mendes kick open the bedroom door. At the same time they heard a window shatter inside.

They found Matt Baum dead on the bed still clutching his throat. Somebody behind Hunter and Mendes uttered loudly *'fuck...'* then it went quiet. Mendes went to the shattered window and shouted out a warning to the figure of the man clambering over the rooftops above the kitchen.

'Stop or I'll shoot Hesseltolph!'

Jakub kept on running. Mendes climbed through the open space followed by David Hunter. Mendes repeated the warning then fired at the figure across the lawn heading for the boat jetty. Hunter and Mendes saw Jakub fall, roll and then get up dragging his left leg.

'You hit him,' said Hunter as they began descending the drain pipe beside the rear kitchen door.

Turning the ignition key of a pleasure cruiser Jakub gunned the throttle lever forward. A minute later Mendes and Hunter had their own boat and were giving chase. Helen Montgomery could only watch from the bedroom window as uniformed officers ran across the lawn to occupy the boats left behind.

'Hurry,' she cried, *'they'll need all the help they can get!'*

Overhead the helicopter had its searchlight trained on the boat leading the chase. Arriving at the jetty Helen Montgomery saw the blood stains. She hoped that it didn't belong to David Hunter. Sensing that somebody was walking towards her from behind she turned recognising the face of the taller woman, but she didn't know the man accompanying her.

'It's been a while Helen.' Announced Vanessa Bernstein. 'Is that Jakub Hesseltolph they're chasing?'

Helen Montgomery told her it was. Bernstein told Critcheon not to photograph the Section Head from BSU. Helen thanked her.

'If he gets to the glades they'll have a real job of finding him,' Critcheon added, checking the light sensor on his camera.

Helen Montgomery saw the ambulance attendants putting Philadelphia Brown in the back of the ambulance, she was handcuffed to the cradle side of the stretcher and accompanied by a female deputy. In his office Harold Lockhart was drinking a mug of strong black coffee and happy to give his version of events by way of a statement. He would be arrested after, but the next day released no charge and his evidence would secure the prosecution making sure that Philadelphia Brown went to prison for the murder of several Jane Doe's found down at the breakwater. In less than a week all the money from behind the cabinet had found it way home to Harold's house where it would be hidden beneath the floor boards.

That evening the late night news on CNN and other televised agencies would have a breaking story about the horrific death of the Senator Matt Baum. News teams and reporters from miles around would be putting together their own version of events and set about delving deep into why he had been attacked and had his throat cut. The more experienced reporter would also want to know about the Summer House, owned by one of Baum's many companies. Come the morning the newsstands would be unable to cope with the demand for papers.

Much later Ed Jackson would call Adelina in Austria and tell her about her husband's demise. None would shed any tears and Adelina would not attend the funeral. When their studies were over with only the son would remain in America, but returning to using Baumgartner nobody would know that Matt Baum had been his father.

Attending the Summer House for the first time Ed Jackson had asked Helen Montgomery if he could see the body of the dead senator. Standing beside the bed with only them in the room Ed Jackson spoke first.

'A long time back when we started working together, I always suspected that he had a shady past, but he would clam up tight whenever I mentioned Kurlor and Austria.'

Helen Montgomery looked at the corpse lying naked on the bed. 'The past finally caught up with him.'

'And Jessica Kashaya, is she okay?' he asked.

'She's fine. Astonishingly Jakub Hesseltolph didn't harm her in any way, shape or form.'

Ed Jackson was pleased to hear it. In the morning, he would make it his priority to go see her and make sure for himself.

Chapter Thirty Six

Jakub Hesseltolph manoeuvred the boat carefully between the banks guided only by the light of the moon overhead. Having turned sharply from Lake Sawgrass he was now in a narrow channel unaware that following the natural water course would take him down river southwest of the county and to the much larger St John River. Minutes earlier he had seen the emergency lights of an ambulance heading for the private house. He grinned knowing that it wouldn't be for Matthias Baumgartner. He would have liked longer with the senator and made him suffer longer, but time was always his enemy, that and the police.

Jakub cut back the throttle revolutions, drifting for a few moments to get his bearings knowing that not far behind were the FBI agents. He took the opportunity of stopping to take the belt from his waist and strap it tight around the upper part of his right leg where the bullet had gone clean through the muscle. Cursing the agent who had shot him, he vowed that one day he would pay the man a visit much like he had Hartmann and Baumgartner. Revenge could be so satisfying.

Pushing the throttle lever forward once again he cut through the water making his approach towards a very dark patch that looked like the mouth of a monstrous black slug. He passed a white painted sign with stark red lettering that told him he was entering the Jane Green Creek, but should be aware of crocodiles. Taking another cutaway channel the helicopter lost sight of him in the thick undergrowth.

Either side of the boat, overhead and scrapping the underside of the hull long twisted and tangled roots from the base of mangrove trees spread wide disappearing beneath the brackish murky waters seeking out a place in which to hide in the mud. Every so often Jakub had to use the boat pole to push himself clear where they had become too entangled.

Jakub cursed the swamp, hated it and it was nothing like the clear waters of the river in Kurlor. There on the banks the wolves would howl, a familiar echo, but here everything seemed to either slither, crawl or watch as he drifted on by and fireflies dancing on the riverbank performed an eerie sequence as though lighting the way head into an unknown abyss. Pulling up the pole once again the mud was getting thicker.

From somewhere behind he heard men talking, although he could not make out what they were saying. He was surprised when the helicopter suddenly veered right and left.

On and on he went blindly bumping into the entangled roots as small creatures, river rats, lizards and large toads foraged on the banksides looking for something smaller to eat. With the engine cut he was still drifting when the bow suddenly hit something large and immoveable bringing the boat to a halt. Jakub checked forward thinking that it had become jammed on a log, but he jumped back, startled when the log opened its jaws wide and snapped back at him, the sudden commotion in the darkness causing nearby birds resting in the trees to shriek and animals to cry.

'It came from over there...' Mendes pointed as Hunter adjusted the angle of the wheel. 'It has to be Hesseltolph, only crocs and game birds get agitated when they're disturbed.'

'How would you know that?' Hunter asked.

'Because as a young teenager I would come here during the autumn semester with my father. We would hunt panther in the everglades only not to kill, but as part of his conservation work. You'd be surprised how many there are roaming around here amongst these trees. Many are abandoned as young cats by unscrupulous owners with unregistered private collections.'

David Hunter wiped the moisture from his wanting to keep them clear. He didn't like big cats, large snakes or crocodiles of any size.

'Nothing much to worry about then,' he said. He sent a text message to Montgomery to inform her that they had entered the mangroves. Alvarez checked the clip in his gun, then held on tight keeping it close to his side. Behind them the helicopter had returned.

'I wonder where he's been,'

Hunter looked up, he had a good idea where. With the powerful beam sweeping left and right they had much better vision than before. Everywhere seemed to be eyes looking back.

'Is it always this friendly?' he asked Mendes. Hunter cut the engine when they hit the back of the other boat.

Dragging his injured leg over the uneven undergrowth Jakub heard the boat crash into the one that he had taken. The agents were much closer than what he had though they were. He forged ahead as fast as his injured leg would allow, but losing blood and painful it was slowing his progress. Adding another notch he made the tourniquet tighter hoping that it would help. He was about to move when a river rat run across his path running from something following behind. Jakub stood perfectly still as a small two metre long python gave chase. Watching its tail vanish he kept on moving not wishing to see any other variety. Deadly accurate and as fast as greased lightning their bite and venom would easily bring his escape to a sudden halt.

Stepping onto the bank Helen Montgomery watched from above. She sent Hunter a text to tell him to be careful as she and the helicopter pilot had seen a shadow move a short way away head from where they were standing.

Mendes loosened his tie. 'I guessed she'd want to be part of the action.'

Hunter had rather that she not be there at all.

'At least she has our back.'

Sitting alongside the pilot she had made some conscious decisions with regards to her future. Having called the helicopter back to collect her she wanted to know that they were both safe. Other boats began arriving with deputies and park rangers on board, some with high powered rifles and flash lights. Pushing aside the large leaves of a nipa tree the bullfrogs nearby began chattering amongst themselves, sending out a warning of his presence. Jakub rubbed his thigh, his leg was beginning to go numb and the inside of his right shoe felt moist. He was leant against the broken bough when the moon suddenly reappeared from behind a large dark cloud casting the ground below in a ghostly blanket of white light. Not more than thirty metres away he saw Hunter and Mendes looking over at him.

'Give it up Jakub,' called Hunter, 'very soon this whole mangrove will be crawling with deputies and rangers. You've nowhere to run or hid and we know that you took a hit. Very soon it will slow you down.'

Jakub stood still his arm outstretch holding onto the kitchen knife, it was all he had against their guns. His head weighed heavy, very heavy on his shoulders and he felt tired, more tired than he had for ages. He thought about Julianna and hoped that she was somewhere safe.

'I would rather die here than go back to any prison!'

Unstrapping the belt from his leg which had started to go annoyingly numb Jakub realised that he would struggle to go any further. He heard a sudden movement like the oozing of mud being sucked up through a straw and turned to look. Coming out of the water and up onto the mud bank was a huge crocodile, which was joined by another, then another. Looking left and right, behind and ahead he was surrounded. Hovering overhead the circular beam from the helicopter lit up the scene below. Having emerged from the water the semiaquatic reptiles stopped moving momentarily. The largest had its mouth open wide baring its teeth.

Jakub went to move, but his good foot had sunk into the soft mud and it was already over his shoe. When he looked down so had the other although he hadn't realised. He tried to lift them, but the mud was not prepared to let go. He looked at the two agents as they approached.

'Stay where you are,' he yelled, **'the place is alive with crocs!'**

They stopped walking and raised their guns sweeping the ground. Overhead Helen Montgomery frantically reached forward for the loud speaker.

'Hunter – Mendes, GET OUT OF THERE NOW – there are crocs everywhere… RUN!'

Throwing the knife at the closest crocodile it bounced off the thick scaly coating landing insignificantly in the mud, where without any warning the reptiles all charged coming at him fast from all sides. Jakub Hesseltolph refused to scream not even when they tore him limb from limb, but the voices in his head did.

Death was instantaneous and a happy release from the years of torment. Hunter and Mendes kept on firing until they had no bullets left hitting some of the smaller reptiles who died, but a lot didn't. They added a fresh clip to their Glock, but each realised that their quarry was no more and like a ghost Jakub Hesseltolph had disappeared. Some of the crocodiles slid from sight back into the water as others watched as the two agents turned and ran back in the direction from where they had come. Finding a clearing between the trees Helen Montgomery dropped a rescue line down where Mendes tied two loops as foot holds and seconds later the helicopter hauled them clear of the mangroves.

She called the sheriff leading the hunt in the other feeder channels telling him that the chase was over. On the safety of the grass bank clear of the mangroves the helicopter landed so that the agents to climb aboard. Relieved that they were both safe Helen Montgomery turned as David Hunter closed the door.

'You two will be the death of me!'

Hunter smiled and Mendes nodded. He was still holding his Glock. Two minutes later they were back safely on the lawn where the chase had started. When the helicopter took off the three of them stood alone beside where they had left the car. It was all over and Jakub Hesseltolph was no longer, the case was closed. Although not quite as there was still the matter of Julianna.

'You did a great job here,' said Montgomery, 'I suggest we head back inside and make sure that they're tying up all the loose ends before we go find ourselves somewhere quiet where we can have something to eat and a cool drink.'

'What about the sister,' asked Mendes, 'are we staying to continue the search?'

'No. I've a hunch that Jakub Hesseltolph was working alone in order to get to Matt Baum. My guess is that she's already elsewhere. Quite possibly on her way to somewhere quite remote in Canada or Alaska.'

Neither Hunter nor Mendes made any further comment believing that however gruesome the end had been, it was a fitting finale for a monster who had terrorised the minds, the bodies and souls of so many victims, and in the last moments of his life only he would know how just how justified had been his retribution that had brought about the end of his destiny.

Somewhere in the deepest darkest void of the equidistant a place none of us has ever seen, not unless we're dead, Thomas and Gabriele greeted the soul of their wayward son. Their meeting together would be very brief and tinged with sorrow as they said their final farewells. Jakub was doomed to wander the dark void, the abyss and to never be reborn.

His biggest regret was that he never did get to see his sister again. The rest he could accept and the peace would be welcome, even the voices had disappeared.

*****

Sitting on the veranda with Emily Lou peacefully at her side Julianna felt the sudden change in the breeze as it swept across the road. They had not long returned from their late evening walk. She knew that something significant had taken place during the evening which she instinctively recognised involved her brother. Wiping away the single tear that had run down the side of her cheek she closed her eyes and whispered *goodbye*.

Filling Emily Lou's bowl with brandy Julianna held Mary's letter in her hand. She had taken to reading it every night, found it comforting and helped dispel her nightmares.

It was almost midnight and the beach was calm, and the tide was on the way out. They were content and happy, just sitting there together watching the stars come out and the moon dance between the clouds. When Emily Lou suddenly raised her head producing a knowing whine which was barely audible, but enough for Julianna to understand she continued to stroke the head of her best friend.

'I know girl, I know,' she said reassuringly, 'one day soon Mary will come back home again.'

Other Books by Jeffrey Brett

A Moment in Time

ISBN – 979 - 8642194461

Barking Up the Wrong Tree

ISBN – 978 - 1073495290

Beyond the First Page

ISBN – 978 - 1980681991

Leave No Loose Ends

ISBN – 978 – 1549552984

Looking for Rosie

ISBN – 978 - 1980369400

The Little Red Café

ISBN – 978 - 1980912583

Rabbits Beside the Track

ISBN – 979 - 8635555187

The Road is Never Long Enough

ISBN – 978 - 1794541948

The Moon, Balloon and Stars

ISBN – 979 - 8634519852

©

About the Author

Jeffrey Brett

I was born in London during the middle of the last century, when the days were long and sunny, and most of our time as children was spent outside whatever the weather, waking in winter to ice on the inside of the bedroom windows.

Those times could be best described as our legacy, a time of fun and wonder, technological promise and even a man landing on the moon. An era of creativity which inspired me to become a writer and artist.

We each have a niche in life that makes us happy, writing and painting are mine. I cannot begin to measure the satisfaction that I get from seeing a book published, knowing that one day somebody else will I hope derive the same amount of pleasure from reading it that I had writing the story. I have no particular genre writing short stories, psychological thrillers and humour.

I live with my wife in Norfolk, where the skies are big and blue and the field's always green. After working for so many year in the public service sector I have finally put my feet up, only to find that I work harder than ever writing, but you won't ever find me complaining. Wishing you many hours of happy reading and if you have any comments regarding any of my books please email me and let me know.

Magic79.jb@outlook.com

www.Jbartinmotion.co.uk

Printed in Great Britain
by Amazon